"I know where to find you,"

Slade said, giving the words a faintly ominous sound. Or maybe it was Tory's worried state of mind that made them seem so.

"One more thing before you go," he said, donning a phony, quizzical expression. "Do you have a nickname, or do people call you Victoria?"

She gave him a withering look. "My friends call me Tory," she said, "but you can call me—"

"Ms. Clayton," they said in unison.

"I'm so glad we understand each other," she said.

"Oh, I still don't understand you completely." His mouth twisted into a suggestive smile. "But I fully intend to."

Before Tory could react, Slade reached over and grazed her cheek with the pad of his thumb. A tingling current surged through her.

"Smudge of soot," he said.

How long she stood there, staring up at him like some moony-eyed teenager, Tory couldn't estimate. Probably only a few seconds, though it se
an eternity....

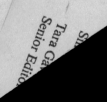

Tara Ga
Senior Editor

Dear Reader,

Welcome to Silhouette **Special Edition** . . . welcome to romance. Each month, Silhouette **Special Edition** publishes six novels with you in mind—stories of love and life, tales that you can identify with—romance with that little ''something special'' added in.

November brings plenty to be joyful and thankful for—at least for Andy and Meg in *Baby, It's You* by Celeste Hamilton. For with the birth of their child, they discover the rebirth of their love . . . for all time. Don't miss this compelling tale!

Rounding out November are more dynamite stories by some of your favorite authors: Bevlyn Marshall (fun follows when an abominable snowman is on the loose!), Andrea Edwards, Kayla Daniels, Marie Ferrarella and Lorraine Carroll (with her second book!). A good time will be had by all this holiday month!

In each Silhouette **Special Edition** novel, we're dedicated to bringing you the romances that you dream about—the type of stories that delight as well as bring a tear to the eye. And that's what Silhouette **Special Edition** is all about—special books by special authors for special readers!

I hope you enjoy this book and all of the stories to come.

Sincerely,

vin

KAYLA DANIELS
Rebel to the Rescue

Silhouette Special Edition
Published by Silhouette Books New York
America's Publisher of Contemporary Romance

To my pal and favorite slave driver, Crystal Johnson.

SILHOUETTE BOOKS
300 East 42nd St., New York, N.Y. 10017

REBEL TO THE RESCUE

ISBN: 0-373-09707-7

First Silhouette Books printing November 1991

All the characters in this book have no existence
outside the imagination of the author and have
no relation whatsoever to anyone bearing the same
name or names. They are not even distantly
inspired by any individual known or unknown
to the author, and all incidents are pure invention.

®: Trademark used under license and
registered in the United States Patent and
Trademark Office and in other countries.

Printed in the U.S.A.

Books by Kayla Daniels

Silhouette Special Edition

Spitting Image #474
Father Knows Best #578
Hot Prospect #654
Rebel to the Rescue #707

KAYLA DANIELS

has three great passions: travel, ballroom dancing and
Norwegian cuisine. She is currently working her way
from Afghanistan to Zimbabwe by reading one book
about every country in the world. She takes breaks
from writing to play baritone horn with the local college band and to study piano.

THE FRENCH QUARTER

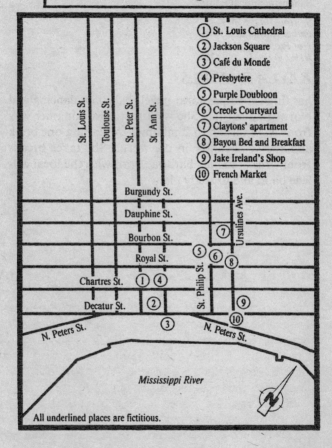

1. St. Louis Cathedral
2. Jackson Square
3. Café du Monde
4. Presbytère
5. Purple Doubloon
6. Creole Courtyard
7. Claytons' apartment
8. Bayou Bed and Breakfast
9. Jake Ireland's Shop
10. French Market

St. Louis St.
Toulouse St.
St. Peter St.
St. Ann St.
St. Philip St.
Ursulines Ave.

Burgundy St.
Dauphine St.
Bourbon St.
Royal St.
Chartres St.
Decatur St.
N. Peters St.
N. Peters St.

Mississippi River

All underlined places are fictitious.

Chapter One

All of Tory Clayton's dreams went up in smoke one hot, humid New Orleans night.

That's what it felt like the next morning, anyway, as she picked her way through the smoldering ruins of the Creole Courtyard guest house. She'd hoped to find *something* to salvage from the disaster—clothing, family photos, some of Nana's jewelry, perhaps. Despair swept over her as she scanned the ruins of what she *thought* used to be the dining room. Ridiculous to have hoped even for a moment that the exquisite antique china her grandfather had brought home from one of his trips to the Orient could have survived this holocaust.

Tory's eyes misted over, but not from the acrid, overpowering stench of burned wood and melted plastic that wafted from the ashes like noxious swamp gas. She wiped the tears impatiently away. Time enough for tears later. She had other matters to deal with first—like figuring out where she and Robby and Nana were going to live from now on. And how she was going to be able to support all of them in the future. And where she was going to come up with the money to pay for—*oh, never mind,* she told herself wearily. Before last night she'd thought nothing more could possibly go wrong with her life. Ha!

"It just goes to show, things can always get worse," she muttered. "Kind of makes you wonder what's in store next. Terminal illness? World War Three?" She wrestled with the uncharacteristic bout of self-pity for a few seconds before her natural optimism reasserted itself. After all, things really *could* have been worse. Thank God no one had been hurt last night. It was incredible luck, actually, that the fire had started at a time when the normally crowded guest house was empty.

Maybe a little *too* lucky. A speck of doubt buzzed through her mind, but Tory pushed it away as she stepped into what had once been a cool, leafy, brick-walled courtyard.

The swaying banana trees and glorious azaleas were nothing but blackened memories. The stone cherub that had tickled Tory's fancy ever since childhood still perched in the center of the brick fountain, but now it looked like a lone sentry standing guard over the ruins. Suddenly she couldn't endure being here one second longer, and she whirled quickly to make her way out of the awful wreckage that had once been her home.

The centuries-old brick of which the guest house was constructed had emerged basically intact. It was the cypress balconies overlooking the courtyard, the wooden doors and window frames and floors and support beams that had turned to ash, leaving the scorched brick walls to form an eerie framework. Even as she cautiously picked her way over chunks of still-smoking debris, Tory was wondering if the place couldn't be restored somehow, the antique furnishings replaced, the skeletal staircases rebuilt....

Then reality came crashing down like the flaming roof had last night. All those extensive repairs would require money, persistence and determination. Tory had plenty of the latter two items, but without the first, any dream of rebuilding would remain exactly that: a dream.

Money, unfortunately, was in short supply for her these days.

Tory wiped a sheen of sweat from her brow. It wasn't even seven in the morning yet, but New Orleans in July rarely cooled off, even at night. She gathered her long black hair into a ponytail and tied it into a loose knot at the nape of her neck. The sweltering humidity, combined with the heat still rising from the rubble, was like a sauna. And it would be even steamier later in the morning, when the tourists and French Quarter residents began venturing outside, pausing to gawk at the charred hulk of the guest house, gathering in excited little clusters on the bumpy stone sidewalk that bordered this block of St. Philip Street.

Oh, no—it was starting already! As she groped her way past the remains of the lobby area, Tory spied a tall silhouette near the end of the arched passageway to the street. A man with a camera hung around his neck was aiming it at a twisted tangle of wrought iron.

Lousy reporters, she thought, as she hurried toward him. *They're no better than vultures, just waiting to swoop down on other people's misfortunes.* Or maybe the man was a tourist after some gruesome shots for his vacation album. Either way, Tory wasn't about to let this ghoul trespass on her private sorrow. Coming on top of everything else, this intrusion was simply too much to bear. Something inside Tory snapped.

"You there!" she shouted. "Get out of here!"

The man ignored her, continuing to focus the camera to his apparent satisfaction. A bulb flashed right before Tory reached him, blinding her. She stumbled forward, and he shot out a hand to steady her.

Tory yanked her elbow from his grasp. Blinking, she strained to make out the face of her tormentor in the shadowed passageway. Then her eyes adjusted to the dim light, and for a moment she felt as if someone had knocked the wind out of her.

The man wasn't movie-star handsome in the conventional sense; his rugged features were too asymmetrical for that. His wheat-brown hair was swept back as if he'd raked it off his forehead upon arising that morning and hadn't given it a second thought since. Judging from the shadow of stubble, he hadn't bothered to shave recently, either. Tory placed his age at somewhere in his mid-thirties.

From beneath sandy eyebrows his sea-green eyes studied her calmly, with a glint of humor that unsettled her even further. His nose was just slightly out of alignment, making her suspect it had been broken at least once. He didn't look like the kind of man who would run away from a fight. His confident, almost cocky air was underlined by the bold slant of his jaw and the rakish cleft bisecting his chin.

An unusual face... and a strangely attractive one. Tory was so entranced by his appearance that she nearly forgot about chasing him off her property. Then the bitter smell of ashes permeated her senses and reminded her of all she had lost.

"What do you think you're doing here?" she demanded, cross with herself for letting this intruder distract her.

He quirked one eyebrow and regarded Tory with an unruffled amusement that only increased her indignation. "I could ask you the same question," he replied in a lazy, not-quite-arrogant drawl. "Didn't you see those bright yellow ribbons strung around the property? The ones that say Police Line—Do Not Cross?"

"Obviously *you* didn't see them," Tory snapped. "Now, are you going to leave peaceably, or do I have to call the cops?"

He removed the dangling camera from around his neck, revealing a broad, well-muscled chest under his half-unbuttoned shirt. Tory's gaze flickered over the thick dusting of dark hair exposed in the V below his collarbone. She swallowed, quickly averting her eyes.

"Do you have any idea how dangerous this place is?" he asked. "The slightest little tremor, and things start shifting around. Ceilings cave in, floors collapse..." He brandished a scolding finger at her. "You shouldn't be in here, you know."

"*I* shouldn't? Look, you morbid, fire-truck-chasing snoop, I'll give you exactly ten seconds to get off my property before I—"

"*Your* property? Let's see, that would make you—" he consulted a clipboard he had whipped out of nowhere "—either Gideon Fontaine or Victoria Clayton." He slid his glance from the clipboard to scan Tory slowly from head to toe in a manner she found infuriating. "Using every scrap of my investigator's training and ability, I'd deduce that you must be Victoria Clayton. Am I right?"

"Very good, Sherlock," she retorted. "Maybe you can get a job as a police detective. You can talk to them about it as soon as they arrive to haul you off to jail." She tried to sidestep around him, but the man was too quick for her. Effortlessly he blocked her path without seeming to move at all. For the first time Tory felt a flutter of apprehension, although she wasn't about to let this obnoxious creep see it. "Listen, mister, if you don't get out of my way—"

"Are you always so full of threats this early in the morning?" he asked. In the dim passageway Tory couldn't be certain, but she thought she detected a twinkle in his eye.

"Only when I've just seen my home, my livelihood and my life's savings go up in smoke," she replied angrily, forgetting her anxiety.

The man's face altered instantly. A blend of sympathy and regret smoothed the rough edges from his chiseled features. But he still didn't apologize for tormenting her.

Instead, he cleared his throat and riffled through the sheaf of papers clamped to his clipboard. "As a matter of fact, that's what I'm here about," he said, suddenly all business. "You *are* Victoria Clayton, co-owner of the Creole Courtyard guest house?"

"Yes, but—"

"My name is Slade Marshall." He grinned and stuck out his hand. "Investigator for Coliseum Insurance."

Automatically Tory extended her hand. "Coliseum In—" She snatched back her hand. "You're from the insurance company?"

He nodded. "Actually I'm a freelance investigator. Coliseum hired me to help them catch up with their backlog of cases."

Nervously Tory pushed a damp lock of hair off her forehead. "Why didn't you say who you were in the first place? Why did you let me go on and on—"

"Because you never gave me a chance, what with all your threats and name-calling. I couldn't get a word in edgewise."

Tory had a few more choice names she'd like to hurl at Slade Marshall, but she couldn't afford to antagonize someone who could jeopardize the insurance settlement. She needed that money desperately for Nana, Robby and herself to live on.

Besides, it was too darn hot to let her temperature rise any further.

"I'm so sorry for the misunderstanding, Mr. Marshall," she said sweetly, nearly gagging on the words. "I assumed you were a newspaper reporter or a curiosity-seeker or something. You'll have to forgive me—I've been through a lot in the past twelve hours." She swept her arm around the devastated building to indicate the scope of her ordeal.

Slade Marshall's mouth twitched as if he were smothering a smile. No doubt he could see right through Tory's sudden change in attitude and was aware how much this conciliatory tone was costing her. His knowing expression made her struggle to keep her temper even more difficult.

"Don't worry about it," he said with a magnanimous flip of his hand. "Let's let bygones be bygones, shall we?" Without waiting for Tory's reply, he tugged a pen from his shirt pocket and clicked the end of it with his thumb. "I need to ask you some questions for this witness report. Let's see, your name . . . I have that. Current address?"

She shrugged unhappily. "We're staying at the Bayou Bed and Breakfast around the corner on Royal Street. Temporarily, at least. Until I can find some other place for us to live."

"Us?" He asked the question without looking up from his clipboard.

"I live with my grandmother and younger brother," she said. What did her living arrangements have to do with finding the cause of the fire?

"What about this Gideon Fontaine? Your partner, I believe." He stressed the word "partner."

Tory muffled a groan as a fresh surge of exasperation and betrayal welled up inside her. "I don't know Gideon's current address," she said evenly. "He...left town recently."

Slade Marshall glanced up at that. "Left town? Permanently?"

Tory studied her close-cropped fingernails. "I'm not sure. It's possible."

"He *is* your business partner, isn't he?"

"Well...yes."

Slade Marshall frowned. "Seems kind of odd that he wouldn't let you know where he's gone or how to get in touch with him."

She turned up her palms in a helpless gesture. "Maybe so, but that's the way it is."

"Hmm." He chewed on the end of his pen and regarded her thoughtfully. "Fontaine doesn't live with *you,* then."

So that's where this line of questioning was leading! This professional busybody was simply probing around in her love life. "We weren't lovers, if that's what you're fishing for," Tory said, intending to cut off *this* line of investigation before it went any further.

He arched his eyebrows, indicating surprise. "I had no intention of suggesting any such thing," he said. "I'm just trying to determine the facts for my investigation."

Tory didn't believe him for a minute. She could still see a sly grin lurking beneath his phony innocent expression. Then once again the weight of all her troubles came crashing down on her like an avalanche. "Could we get on with this?" she asked wearily.

"Sure. But I'll have to speak to the other co-owner before I can complete my report."

Alarm spurted inside her. "But Gideon wasn't even in town last night! How could he know anything about the fire?"

"You just told me you don't know where he is. How do you know he wasn't in New Orleans last night setting a torch to this place?"

"That's ridiculous! Why would Gideon burn down his own property?"

Slade Marshall handed Tory a disbelieving look. "Do I really need to spell it out for you?"

She stared back at him as dismayed comprehension dawned. "You're not just any old investigator, are you?" she asked slowly. "You're an *arson* investigator."

He gave a noncommittal shrug. "I'm here to find out how the fire started, that's all. Regardless of whether or not somebody set it."

"But the idea's crazy! Believe me, Gideon would never—"

"What makes you think I suspect your partner?" He leaned forward until his face was mere inches from hers and said, "After all, I could just as easily suspect *you* of torching the place."

Tory recoiled with a gasp. She couldn't tell which unsettled her more: being accused of arson, or the way a certain rough, untamed quality about Slade Marshall sent peculiar sensations swooping through her stomach when he moved close to her. "You can't be serious," she said, startled by the breathless note in her own voice. "This was my *home,* for God's sake."

"You'd be surprised—people do it all the time," he said, looking as if not much surprised him anymore.

"I'm sure when you complete your investigation, you'll determine the fire started because of faulty wiring or something."

He scribbled a note on his clipboard. "Are you saying the wiring for the guest house wasn't up to code?"

"No, of course not," she said hastily. "But the building was *old,* for heaven's sake. Even though we passed the last city inspection, that doesn't prevent rotting wire or a frayed lamp cord or an overloaded circuit from—"

Slade Marshall was writing furiously. When Tory broke off, he glanced up and remarked, "Doesn't sound to me like you were any too careful with your electrical system."

"No! That isn't true, I *was* careful, we were *all* careful, but accidents happen, after all, and my point is that you can't simply assume that someone *set* the fire, when there are a million other ways it could have happened. . . ." Her voice trailed off as he propped his chin on his fist, pretending to be totally absorbed by her discourse. "Why don't you hurry up and get on with your investigation?" she said, tossing her wandering hair back over her shoulder.

"Exactly my intention," he said. "If you've finished your statement, that is."

"That wasn't my statement. I was only pointing out several ways the fire could have started by accident. I didn't know you were going to write everything down."

"Oh, but your comments were so informative. So many different ways a fire can start." He scratched his unshaven chin and shook his head. "Who'd have thought?"

"Okay, so you don't need me to tell you your job," Tory grumbled. "Why don't you get back to it, then?"

"What I also don't need is your making my job any more difficult."

"What are you talking about? I've answered all your questions, I'm prepared to cooperate completely—"

"Hmm, well, that's certainly reassuring...." He gave Tory another one of those infuriating once-overs, making her suddenly conscious of how she must look in her rumpled shorts and T-shirt. "But that's not what I mean," he continued. "I'm referring to the way I found you prowling around the fire scene, disturbing clues, wiping out evidence—"

"I was not *prowling*—"

"—Not to mention the fact that you might have been hurt. This brick might *look* stable, but as you yourself pointed out, the building is very old and the fire undoubtedly weakened it in spots."

"Thank you so much for your concern, but—"

"It's not your safety I'm thinking of. The rescue squad has better things to do than dig you out from under a pile of rubble because you had to go pawing around for your shoe box full of old love letters or the emerald bracelet your Aunt Minnie gave you when you graduated from high school."

"I do not have a shoe box full of old love letters, and if I did, what business is it of yours? This is still my property, and if I want to paw through it for yesterday's crossword puzzle, you can't stop me." Tory's chest was heaving with indignation by the time she'd finished. Honestly, she'd never before met anyone who could shuttle her back and forth between worry and anger so quickly!

And she'd never before met a man who attracted her so strongly against her will.

Slade Marshall stuck his face close to hers. His eyes glowed with triumph. "Oh, yes, I *can* stop you," he said. "Until the fire department relinquishes control of the scene, I don't need your permission to explore the premises. And I'm not about to let you mess up the evidence any more than you have already." He peered past Tory into the building's interior. "Who let you in here, anyway?"

"No one let me in. I told you, this is my guest house— *was* my guest house," she corrected with a catch in her throat, "and I don't need permission to be here."

"Wasn't anyone from the fire department here when you showed up?"

Tory shook her head. "They left someone here last night to watch for flare-ups, but he was gone when I came back this morning."

"Damn." He slapped the clipboard against his thigh. "They weren't supposed to leave the scene until I got here." A roguish grin erased the lines of frustration from his face. "What do you know? Looks like I have no legal right to be here, after all."

"In that case, you have exactly ten seconds to—"

"Of course, if you won't allow me to examine your property, I can't very well complete my report, can I? And without a complete report, Coliseum Insurance can hardly send you a check, can they?"

Tory gnashed her teeth. The man had her cornered, and worst of all, he knew it. Obviously no insurance company would pay off on a policy without determining the cause of the fire. She had no choice but to let Slade Marshall poke through the wreckage of her life.

A bead of perspiration trickled between her breasts. What if he concluded that someone had deliberately set the fire? Even after their short, unpleasant acquaintance Tory could tell that Slade Marshall wouldn't quit until he'd tracked down the culprit. And she had no doubt that your basic, run-of-the-mill arsonist was no match for this man. Especially an amateur arsonist.

Despite the heat, Tory suppressed a shiver—of dread. But it wasn't herself she was afraid for.

"All right," she said in what she hoped was an indifferent voice, "you can look around if you want to."

His jade eyes glittered. "I knew you'd see it my way." He winked. "Especially after you promised your complete cooperation." Tory was sorely tempted to kick him off her property and into the street and to hell with the insurance check.

But she had more than her own welfare to consider.

"Do you need me for anything else?" she asked, wanting to bite her tongue as soon as the words were out of her mouth.

"We can discuss that later," he replied, slicking the tip of his tongue across his lower lip and sending Tory a look that would have melted most women into a puddle at his feet. "For now, my first priority is examining the fire scene. Then I'll be talking to other witnesses—the neighbors, your brother and grandmother, guests—"

"My grandmother is in the hospital. She won't be able to help you."

"I'll need to talk to her, anyway."

"But—"

"Don't worry, I won't tire her out." He made a note on the form in front of him. "I'm not *completely* insensitive, you know."

"Could have fooled me," she muttered under her breath.

He kept on writing as if he hadn't heard her, but one edge of his mouth curved up. "Where did your guests stay after they were evacuated?"

Tory hesitated before replying. "We didn't have any guests last night."

He pounced on that. "All your guest rooms were vacant? Isn't that a bit unusual?"

She tried to seem offhand. "Most of them were booked this week by a group in town for a family reunion. Then they started arguing over who should get the silverware when Cousin Matilda croaks and they all packed up and left in a huff without speaking to each other."

Slade shook his head, chuckling. "You didn't rent out any of those rooms later?"

"Not with temperatures in the nineties and humidity to match. Summer's the slow tourist season in New Orleans."

"What about the other guest rooms?"

"One couple canceled their reservation after that hurricane warning three days ago that never materialized. The other room was scheduled for plumbing repairs." Well, that was *one* bill she wouldn't have to worry about, anyway. Small consolation.

"Your brother's staying at this bed-and-breakfast place with you?"

Careful, now, Tory cautioned herself. "He's actually my *kid* brother. Really only a child," she said. "I doubt he'd be able to tell you anything useful."

"Oh? How old is he?"

"Let's see now—his birthday was back in March, and he's fifteen years younger than I am, so I guess that'd make him about, oh . . . seventeen."

Slade's eyebrows drew together. "Hardly a child, if you ask me."

Tory forced a laugh. "I guess it's hard for me to realize he's almost grown up. You see, I raised him after our parents died ten years ago, and I still think of him as my baby brother."

"So he's staying with you at the place on Royal Street?"

Tory paused, sifting quickly through all possible answers. "He's staying with some friends."

"What's the address?" Slade asked, pen poised above the form.

"I—I'm not sure of the address."

"Phone number?"

"I don't have that, either."

Slade narrowed his eyes. "You don't keep very close tabs on your baby brother's whereabouts, do you?"

Tory raised her hands, palms up. "In all the commotion last night I forgot to ask him which friend he was going to stay with."

"I see." Slade scratched the back of his head with the pen. "As soon as you hear from him, find out, will you? I want to talk to him."

"Sure. The minute I hear from him." Tory exhaled a breath of relief as soon as Slade went back to his note-taking.

"Okay, that's all the information I need from you now," he said. "I'll talk to you again after I interview all the other witnesses."

She frowned, puzzled. "Why wait until then?"

"Standard procedure in cases of suspicious fire."

"Why? And what do you mean, 'suspicious' fire?"

"Any fire is considered suspicious until its cause is determined." Slade gave Tory a look she was already coming to recognize—a look that warned her he was about to antagonize her, and relished the prospect. "I want to question you last because the property owner usually has the most to gain from setting a fire. By talking to all the other witnesses first, I can figure out the right questions to ask when I interrogate the chief suspect."

"Chief suspect?" she squeaked.

"The arsonist," he said. "In most cases, anyway."

"Well, not in *this* case."

"That remains to be seen."

Tory checked her watch. "I really must be on my way," she said. Originally she'd planned to stick around and keep an eye on Slade Marshall while he poked and prodded through the charred ruins, but by now the thought of spending any more time in his presence was too much to bear. What she wouldn't give to be a million miles away from him! "I have to go break the news about the fire to my grandmother before you show up to grill her."

"I promise to leave my rubber hoses at home," he said. Then something with an amazing resemblance to concern flickered across his face. "Your grandmother...uh, she's not deathly ill or anything, is she?"

"My grandmother is eighty-three years old and in failing health. She had a fainting spell several days ago, and her doctor admitted her to the hospital for some tests." Tory smiled for the first time that day. "But she's got plenty of years left, believe me. I think she's too stubborn to die." Her smile faded. "Don't worry, she'll survive long enough for you to finish interrogating her."

Slade flinched slightly, as if Tory had slapped him. "That wasn't why I asked."

Immediately Tory regretted her words. The man was only trying to be nice for once, and she'd practically flung his concern back in his face. Words of apology rose in her throat, but before she could speak, his normal cynical expression had dropped back into place.

Maybe it was better this way. If she apologized, Slade might be tempted to do something nice again. And Tory had a feeling that if Slade Marshall ever started actually being nice to her, she was in deep, deep trouble.

"Let me know when you hear from your brother," he said, tapping his pen against the clipboard. "And I'll have to track down Gideon Fontaine before finishing my report, so I'd advise you to contact him."

"I told you, I haven't the faintest idea where he is," Tory protested.

"Yeah, that *is* what you told me." He clicked the end of his pen. "Let's hope he returns from this mysterious trip of his sometime in the near future. I'd hate to see you waiting too long for that insurance check."

Tory nearly moaned aloud. How had things gotten so complicated so fast? Maybe she ought to go ahead and tell Slade Marshall the whole story right now.

No. He wanted to question her last, didn't he? Well, Tory would certainly cooperate then. Besides, maybe by the time he got around to questioning her, he would already have determined the cause of the fire.

After all, the blaze had undoubtedly started because of a faulty electrical connection or something. There had to be some perfectly logical, perfectly innocent, explanation.

Otherwise, Tory could think of only one person with both a motive and the opportunity to set that fire.

And she refused to consider that possibility for even a moment.

"I'll let you know if I hear from Gideon," she said. "And when you need to talk to me again—"

"I know where to find you," he said, giving the words a faintly ominous sound. Or maybe it was Tory's worried state of mind that made them seem so.

"One more thing before you go," Slade said as she turned to leave.

"Yes?"

He donned that phony, quizzical expression again. "Do you have a nickname, or do people call you Victoria?"

She gave him a withering look. "My friends call me Tory," she said, "but you can call me—"

"Ms. Clayton," they said in unison.

"I'm so glad we understand each other," she said.

"Oh, I still don't understand you completely." His mouth twisted into a suggestive smile. "But I fully intend to."

Before she could react, Slade reached over and grazed her cheek with the pad of his thumb. A tingling current surged through Tory, shocking her, leaving her paralyzed.

"Smudge of soot," he said.

How long she stood there, stunned, staring up at him like some moony-eyed teenager, Tory couldn't estimate. Probably only a few seconds, though it seemed an eternity.

At last she broke free of his mesmerizing spell and stumbled off down the bumpy sidewalk, leaving Slade alone to probe for the secret of the fire's origin. But the memory of his touch lingered long after her escape, along with a nagging twinge of anxiety.

She wondered what other secrets Slade might discover by the time his investigation was through.

Chapter Two

Slade Marshall strode into the dark, malty interior of a rather seedy Bourbon Street bar. He ordered a mug of draft and slid onto the cracked black vinyl of the rear booth. Quaffing beer before noon wasn't his usual style, but the late-morning heat and humidity had turned the ruins of the Creole Courtyard into a broiler, making his job even more unpleasant than usual. Besides, he'd been up for nearly thirty hours now, having spent all last night at the scene of a fire over in the Garden District, so in a way it was still evening, wasn't it?

Nice rationalization, anyway, he decided. He rubbed his hand over his unshaven jaw and wondered when he'd have a chance to use a razor again.

The bartender slopped a little beer on the table as he clunked down a mug in front of Slade. "Gonna be another hot one," he said with a yawn.

Slade took a long, icy swallow before replying. "It'd stay cooler in here if you kept that front door shut."

"Nah, the owner figures if people walk by and feel that cool air coming out the door, they might come inside for some more."

"And buy a drink or two or three while they're sitting around cooling off."

The bartender nodded. "You got it." He shuffled off to mop halfheartedly at a puddle on the floor in front of the bar.

Slade pried a wad of napkins from the dispenser on the table and mopped his brow. The paper came away with a black film of soot . . . a little souvenir from the remains of Tory Clayton's guest house.

Slade grinned at the thought of her, then pushed the image aside along with the pile of sweat-soaked napkins. This bar would also be a lot cooler if the owner got that ancient air conditioner fixed. Despite its energetic clattering, Slade suspected the contraption was accomplishing little more than pushing the warm air around. It must be eighty degrees in here.

Still, eighty degrees felt remarkably comfortable when the temperature outside was climbing through the nineties. Otherwise, this bar had little to recommend it besides its convenient location around the corner from the Creole Courtyard. Slade leaned back and draped his arm across the back of the booth. The place was definitely a dive—the kind of joint tourists wandered into curiously before beating a hasty retreat.

Beyond the rim of his mug he watched the motley collection of high-school kids huddled over the bank of video games in the back room. He was willing to bet not one of those kids was twenty-one, and equally willing to bet no one had checked their identification at the door, either.

Well, never mind. It was none of his business. His job was catching arsonists, not harassing teenagers with too much time on their hands, or busting bar owners who let them hang around all day.

He dragged his thoughts back to his latest investigation.

After exploring the remains of the Creole Courtyard guest house for three hours, Slade had a pretty good idea how the fire had started. Luckily Tory hadn't disturbed any significant evidence during her early-morning explorations.

Slade drummed his fingers on the table, annoyed as always when other people got sloppy and ignored procedure. The fireman on duty last night shouldn't have left the scene unguarded. Granted, Slade hadn't arrived to take over until early this morning, but the Garden District fire had turned into a real fiasco, and wrapping up the preliminaries had taken longer than he'd expected.

He was only doing his job; why couldn't the fire department do theirs?

Slade plowed his fingers through his uncombed hair. Aw, hell, who could blame the poor guy for wanting to go home and get some shut-eye? No one knew better than Slade how exhausting firefighting could be. Maybe it was his own fault for taking on too many investigations at once. Maybe he was pushing too hard.

Pushing . . . always pushing . . . driven by the memory of that other fire thirteen years ago in a decaying tenement on Chicago's South Side. In a flash he felt the searing heat, smelled the acrid, eye-watering smoke, heard the crackle of flames and the terrified, heart-wrenching cries for help.

Shuddering, Slade closed his eyes and tossed down a huge gulp of beer. He wiped his sweaty palms on his thighs, then forced himself back to the present as he ticked off points in his mind.

The first fact he'd established about the Creole Court- yard fire was its point of origin. Or *points* of origin, to be exact. By examining the burning patterns, he'd deter- mined that the fire had originated in not one, but four places, revealed by the areas of deepest charring. A sure sign of arson.

His second clue was the small wax deposit he'd scraped off the floor at one of the points of origin. Candle wax, to be precise. Someone had no doubt followed the example of countless other arsonists and left a lit candle in a card- board box, surrounded by stuffed newspaper or some other kindling.

His third clue was the faint but unmistakable scent of lighter fluid lingering in one of the downstairs rooms. Anyone who'd ever been to an outdoor barbecue would recognize the smell of the accelerant the arsonist had used to speed up and spread the blaze.

Slade was almost disappointed by how easy it had been to figure out how and where the fire had started. But he had one challenge left: discovering *who* had started it.

As he absently took another pull from his mug, a vision of Tory Clayton danced before his eyes like the bubbles in his beer.

Slade didn't seriously suspect her at this point. There was something so damn angelic about her appearance, even when she was scowling at him. Maybe it was those enormous eyes peering at him from beneath those thick black lashes. Or maybe it was the delicious contrast be- tween her lustrous black hair and her flawless, magnolia- white skin.

Maybe it was the petal-soft feel of her cheek when he'd brushed off that smudge of soot.

Still, arsonists came in all shapes and sizes, and sometimes the most unlikely suspects turned out to be guilty. Often people who wouldn't think of committing other crimes were able to rationalize arson.

And Tory Clayton was definitely hiding something from him. Those crystal-clear, baby-blue eyes were useless for concealing the truth, and Slade could have read the guilt written on her lovely face a mile away. An accomplished liar she wasn't. Bitter experience had taught him to recognize one of *those* when he met one.

But Tory Clayton was feeling guilty, all right. The question was ... guilty of what?

Maybe whatever she was hiding had something to do with Gideon Fontaine. Now there was someone Slade was definitely interested in talking to. Did his disappearance have some connection with the fire? Slade knew of countless cases where a professional torch had been hired to set a building on fire while the owner was conveniently out of town.

Was it possible Tory was in cahoots with this Fontaine guy? And what exactly was the nature of their relationship, anyway?

Too many questions and not enough answers. Time to start interviewing witnesses, starting with Tory Clayton's neighbors. *Former* neighbors, rather.

Slade felt an unaccustomed pang of sympathy for her. In this job either you learned not to let tragedy and destruction get to you, or else you didn't sleep at night. But Tory had looked so sad and forlorn, standing there amid the ruins of her business. And she'd lived on the premises as well, hadn't she? So the poor kid had lost everything.

Knock it off, he told himself, tossing a couple of crumpled dollar bills onto the bar on his way out the door. An arson investigator couldn't afford to feel sorry for fire victims—no matter how gorgeous—or he'd lose his objectivity. That was the quickest, surest way to blow an investigation. And Slade had struggled too long and too hard to jeopardize his career over a pair of big blue eyes and a nice set of curves.

Besides, the last thing he needed was some destitute, helpless female insinuating herself into his life. Well, that wasn't really fair. Tory Clayton might be destitute at the moment, but Slade had a feeling she was far from helpless. He chuckled at the memory of the determined outrage on her face when she'd first spotted him that morning and tried to throw him off her property, like Scarlett O'Hara defending Tara or something. Even when she was angry, her voice had a languid, musical lilt that caressed his northern ears like whispering peach blossoms.

Damn it, he was wasting far too much time thinking about Tory Clayton and not enough time concentrating on more important matters. Like chasing up some lunch, for example.

As he stepped outside into the oppressive heat, Slade glanced up at the sign dangling over the sidewalk from rusted chains. The Purple Doubloon. He made a mental note to avoid the place in the future. It was too depressing a reminder of what his life might have been like if he hadn't managed to escape his misspent youth.

On his way back to the guest house he bought a Lucky Dog from one of the vendors whose giant hot-dog-shaped carts seemed to be stationed at nearly every street corner in the French Quarter. Wolfing it down in half a dozen bites, Slade redirected his attention to his investigation, mentally composing a list of witnesses he wanted to question by the end of the day.

He consulted the clipboard hanging from his belt and, lost in concentration, nearly collided with a tour group as he rounded the corner of St. Philip.

He was about to ring the doorbell of the Queen Anne-style cottage opposite the guest house when he glimpsed a flash of yellow across the street.

Slade's eyes lit up when he recognized Tory at the far end of the arched entrance passage. She was standing in the former courtyard, gazing upward, hands pressed to her cheeks in a gesture of unconscious horror. So wrapped up was she in her private, unhappy thoughts that she failed to hear Slade's approach until he stepped out of the passageway and into the blackened patio.

She dropped her hands to her sides. "Oh, it's you." She seemed none too pleased to see him. "I thought you were finished here."

"And I thought I told you that poking around in here is dangerous."

"I was *not* poking around—" She made a visible effort to control her temper. "I was waiting for someone."

"Who, Gideon Fontaine?"

She winced at the name. "No, I told you—I don't know where he is. I was waiting for LuAnne."

"LuAnne?"

"LuAnne Thatcher. She works—*worked* for us part-time as a maid, or sometimes she covered the front desk if I had to leave."

"Really? Why didn't you mention her this morning?"

"Because I forgot, okay? I had a few other things on my mind, in case you didn't notice. Why do you have to take everything I say and twist it around to make it sound as if I'm some kind of criminal or something?"

"Okay, okay, simmer down. I'm just trying to get the facts." He made a note on his clipboard, using the opportunity to study Tory obliquely.

He'd never believed that old line about a woman being beautiful when she was angry—until now. He found the cobalt sparks sizzling in her eyes almost as intriguing as the pink flush spreading down her face and neck and over the creamy white shoulders exposed by the sleeveless sundress she was wearing. Either she'd gone shopping at some trendy boutique this morning, or she'd managed to borrow a dress from someone—someone with extremely provocative taste in clothing.

Not that she hadn't looked damn sexy even in the wrinkled shorts and T-shirt she'd worn earlier. But the short yellow sundress revealed certain curves and slopes her previous garb had concealed. And the way the thin fabric clung to her shapely thighs was rather enticing, to say the least.

For an instant Slade imagined the silken feel and whispery sound that dress would make if he slipped it from Tory's shoulders and let it slide down her long, slender legs to pool at her feet.

He slammed his mind shut against the image, but his mouth was suddenly dry and he wished he had another beer.

He cleared his throat. "Why is this LuAnne meeting you here?"

"She's not, exactly." Tory fiddled with a lock of her long, coal-black hair. "I meant to call her this morning and tell her about the fire—"

"She wasn't working last night?"

"I gave her the evening off, since we didn't have any guests."

"Okay, go on."

"But I haven't been able to get hold of her today. She has morning classes at Tulane." Tory shrugged one smooth, bare shoulder. "I guess I could have called the university and had them deliver a message to her, but then I couldn't be sure she'd gotten it before coming to work. I'd hate for her to show up and find the place like this without anyone here to explain what happened."

"So you came back here to intercept her."

Tory nodded. "It seemed the logical thing to do."

Slade jerked his thumb over his shoulder. "Well, you can intercept her out on the sidewalk. I don't want you hanging around in here."

He enjoyed the way Tory's dress stretched taut across her breasts when she clamped her hands on her hips. "Haven't we been over this before? Or maybe I didn't make myself clear." Slade watched, fascinated, as a tiny pearl of sweat trickled down her temple, mingling with a few loose wisps of her hair. "I'll stay here as long as I want to. This building may be burned to a crisp, but it's still mine—do you hear me?"

Now she was starting to get under his skin. "Look, I'm only thinking of your safety—"

"I'm a big girl. I can take care of myself."

Slade propped his hands on his waist, imitating Tory's stubborn stance. "Do you have any idea how many needless injuries I've seen in my line of work? People take stupid risks, like running back into burning houses to rescue their golf clubs or mink coats. Sightseers get hit by falling debris when they sneak closer to get a better look at the flames. And some idiots think a building's safe just because the fire's out."

"You wouldn't understand, you heartless clod! I can't simply shrug my shoulders, turn my back and walk away from this place. I grew up here, for God's sake! It's more than my home and my livelihood—everything I am, everything I remember, is all wrapped up in this place. Memories of my childhood, my parents, my grandfather..." She turned away, but not before Slade saw the tears brimming in her eyes, threatening to spill down her cheeks.

He cursed under his breath. He was used to being called a heel, but not used to feeling sorry for acting like one. He ran his hand over his face, the stubble making a rasping sound. Tory stood with her back to him, shoulders trembling slightly, as if she were fighting to hold back sobs.

He lifted his hand to give her a comforting pat. The sundress swooped halfway down her back, and right before Slade's fingers made contact with her skin, he paused, then pulled back his hand. He had a feeling that touching Tory Clayton's bare skin might be as electrifying—and dangerous—as getting struck by lightning.

"I'm sorry that... you lost everything," he muttered. "It was a tough break, but at least you and your family weren't hurt. And maybe, once you get the insurance check, you can even rebuild. The basic structure still looks pretty sound to me...." Slade knew he shouldn't be raising her hopes. Actually the building looked like a total loss and if Tory—or more likely, her partner Fontaine—had had anything to do with the fire, there wouldn't *be* any insurance check.

But she looked so damn upset, and for some reason that made Slade desperate enough to snatch at any straw of comfort.

To his relief, something he said must have worked, for she turned around at last, lowering her head and wiping her eyes before giving him a wobbly smile. "You're right," she said. "I didn't mean to start feeling sorry for myself. When I think what could have happened if this place hadn't been empty last night—'' She shuddered, and once again Slade had to resist the urge to slip a reassuring arm around her. "I'm so grateful that Nana and Robby are safe. I—I guess I lost sight of how lucky I really am." She pushed a strand of hair from her face. "Thank you."

Slade blinked. "Thank you? For what?"

"For putting things in perspective. I still have everything that's truly important to me—my grandmother...Robby...all my memories. The fire didn't hurt any of them."

Slade scratched his head. Was she for real? All he'd done was mouth a few automatic words of comfort, and suddenly happy days were here again. He couldn't figure her out, and that made him uneasy. What kind of game was she playing, anyway?

She was still smiling shyly at him in a way that clutched at something inside Slade's chest. It also made him nervous as hell. He grabbed his clipboard and yanked the pen from his pocket. "Speaking of your brother, have you heard from him?"

A worried frown chased the smile from Tory's lips. She averted her gaze. "No, I haven't."

She had to be the world's worst liar. But strangely enough, her attempt at deception was almost a relief. Now Slade was back on familiar territory at least. "Isn't that kind of odd?" he asked in his most skeptical, witness-intimidating voice. "That your brother hasn't called or come by to see how you are?"

Tory uttered a short laugh. "You know how teenage boys are. He probably went with his friends to some video arcade and got caught up in a rousing game of Space Invaders or something." She stepped to the door of the nearest guest room and peeked inside, as if captivated by the sight of twisted metal and charred furnishings.

Slade probed his cheek with his tongue. "Seems kind of irresponsible to me."

"Oh, no, Robby's a good kid," Tory said quickly. "It's just that sometimes he—"

"Look out!" Slade shouted, springing forward.

Tory's eyes flashed with the startled expression of a deer trapped in a car's headlights. As the creaking sound overhead registered, she glanced up. Then Slade tackled her.

The momentum of his body carried them both to the ground. With his arms wrapped tightly around Tory they rolled over several times before coming to rest beside the brick fountain.

The second-floor balcony collapsed right where Tory had been standing, peppering Slade's head and shoulders with falling debris. Tory, her five-foot-seven-inch frame completely sheltered by more than six feet of lean, hard male, was conscious only of a deafening crash that seemed to go on forever.

But as silence filled the courtyard she became aware of other sensations. Like the protective pressure of Slade's body on top of hers. Like the coarse whiskers bristling against her cheek. Like the piny scent of soap she smelled on his neck.

His breath came in warm puffs against her ear. "Are you all right?" he panted.

"I—" She drew in a long, quavering breath. "I think so." She managed a dry swallow. "How about you?"

"Still in one piece, as far as I can tell." He made no move to get off her.

"Did—did the balcony collapse?"

"Uh-huh."

"Oh." She wondered when he was going to move, and wondered why she didn't care if he took his time about it. "Guess I owe you another thank you," she said.

"Uh-huh."

"Is that all you can say?"

"What would you like me to say?" He lifted his head. "I know—how about, 'I told you so?'"

He was grinding his teeth, but whether from disgust or pain, Tory couldn't tell.

"I guess I deserve that," she said. This close up, she could see his green eyes had little gold flecks in them.

"That's not all you deserve," he growled. "Damn it, Tory, you could have been killed!"

"*Me?* What about you? If anything had happened to you because of me, I'd—I'd . . . never forgive myself." He had the sexiest little crinkles at the corners of his eyes, especially when he was grimacing. Like now.

"Is something wrong? Are you in pain?" Tory asked.

"No . . . well, maybe a little." He emitted a groan that sounded a teeny bit counterfeit. "If I can rest here without moving for a few more minutes, I'm sure I'll be all right."

Tory smelled beer and mustard on his breath, but her strange, sharp hunger had nothing to do with food. She licked her lips. "Where does it hurt?"

Slade groaned again, and this time she realized it was only for her benefit. "Um . . . not in any one particular spot, exactly . . ."

"In that case, I think I can help you."

"Oh, really? How?"

"Why, I'd be glad to make it hurt in one particular spot," she said. "Now get off me, you big lug, before I start screaming for the cops."

Slade shook his head sadly. "Tory, Tory," he said, "is that any way to treat the person who just saved your life?"

"I told you to call me Ms. Clayton," she said, wedging her hands between them and pushing as hard as she could against his solid chest.

Slade didn't budge. "Some people might call your attitude pretty ungrateful," he remarked.

"Some people don't know what a scheming, under-handed cad you are," she retorted, clenching her jaws with effort.

"Cad?" he echoed with delight. "I must say, Ms. Clayton, I've been called a lot of things in my life—"

"I'm not surprised."

"—But I don't believe anyone has ever actually called me a cad before."

"High time, then."

"If you'll stop struggling for one second, I'll be more than happy to let you stand up."

"Gee, thanks."

He wagged a finger in front of her nose. "You know, sarcasm doesn't really become you."

"The only thing I want to become is as far away from you as possible." Tory's heart was thumping wildly, whether from anger or from her recent scare or from something else, she couldn't tell. "Now get the hell off me."

Slade went so far as to prop himself on his elbows, but his lower body still pinned her to the ground. "Well, if you're sure that's what you want . . ."

"I'm going to report you to Coliseum Insurance, to the state insurance commission, to the—" Then she noticed the torn sleeve of his shirt and the smear of red on his upper arm. She gasped. "Slade, you're hurt!"

"Why, Ms. Clayton, I'm touched by your concern! Does this mean we're on a first-name basis now?"

"You're lying here bleeding, and all you can think about is flirting with me?"

He roared with laughter. "*Flirting?* Ms. Clayton, Slade Marshall does not flirt. He makes passes, he seduces, he sweeps women off their feet—"

"Okay, okay, I get the picture." Tory couldn't take her eyes off his arm. "Maybe you should go to the emergency room."

Slade casually rotated his head to inspect the injury. "It's nothing, just a flesh wound."

"Are you sure?"

He nodded. "I've survived much worse, believe me." He moved his hand to stroke her hair. "It's nice to know you care, though."

Tory swallowed. "I—I don't want you suing me or anything."

He lowered his face closer to hers. "Is that all it is?"

"Yes. No! I mean—" The smoldering gleam in his eyes was definitely unnerving. "Why shouldn't I be concerned about you?"

Slade drew his forefinger down the line of Tory's jaw and stroked the underside of her chin. "Oh, I don't know...I was under the impression that you didn't like me very much."

"I like you—" Good heavens, what was she saying? "I mean, we only met this morning, I don't really know you...."

"We can correct that easily enough," he said, slowly outlining her mouth with the tip of his little finger.

Tory could hardly breathe, but told herself it was because Slade's weight was crushing all the air out of her lungs.

Her attention drifted to the cleft in his chin, but she sensed his eyes focused on her, commanding her to meet his gaze. As if a relentless heat melted her will to resist, Tory slowly raised her eyes.

Slade lowered his head, so gradually she wondered if she were imagining it. But then she felt his breath on her face and saw his lips part with anticipation. Her own mouth trembled with instinctive response.

My God, he's going to kiss me! cried an inner voice.

My God, I'm going to let him, answered another.

Slade angled his head slightly and tilted up Tory's chin with one finger. His hot breath mingled with hers. Her eyelashes fluttered closed as she slowly inhaled.

Then someone screamed.

Chapter Three

It was a high-pitched, horrified scream that came from the street, and it snapped Tory and Slade apart quicker than a catapult.

Slade sprang to his feet and took off down the passageway, ungallantly leaving Tory to struggle upright by herself. She flew after him and emerged onto the sidewalk to find LuAnne Thatcher staring openmouthed at Slade.

Tory could hardly blame the girl. Poor LuAnne had shown up for work not only to find her place of employment reduced to a pile of cinders, but also to find a soot-streaked, blood-spattered stranger bursting out of the ruins like a wild-eyed maniac. She looked almost ready to scream again when Tory stepped forward. "It's okay, LuAnne."

"Okay?" She mouthed the word incredulously, but no sound came out. Then she found her voice. "Tory, what in heaven's name happened? The guest house—what—

when—?'' She looked Tory up and down. "And you . . . what on earth happened to *you?*''

Tory glanced down at herself and realized she did indeed look a little worse for the wear, especially in contrast with the fussy, frilly concoction LuAnne was wearing. The skimpy dress Tory had borrowed was even more revealing with a jagged tear up the side, and an observer might suspect she'd recently been sweeping chimneys in it. Her arms and legs weren't in much better shape, and she could only imagine what her face looked like.

Like a coal miner's, if LuAnne's expression was any indication. "I'm fine," Tory assured her. "We, uh, had a little accident a minute ago, but we're okay."

Behind her red, wide-framed glasses, LuAnne's huge brown eyes darted back and forth between the two disheveled figures. "You're bleeding, sir," she informed Slade. Then she inched closer to Tory. "Who's he?" she whispered from the side of her mouth.

"The arson investigator," Tory said dryly, noting that despite LuAnne's long-standing infatuation with Gideon, she wasn't blind to some of Slade's finer qualities beneath the blood and grime.

LuAnne primped her cloud of strawberry-blond curls. Then Tory's answer finally penetrated. "Arson? But doesn't that mean—" She pointed a pink lacquered fingernail at the building. "Are y'all saying someone burned down the Creole Courtyard? Someone set it on fire? But that's crazy! Who would do such an awful thing?"

"That's exactly what I intend to find out," Slade said, flicking a speck of soot from his shirt collar. A useless gesture, Tory thought. The shirt wasn't even good enough for the rag pile anymore.

"You don't know whether *anyone* set the fire yet," she pointed out.

Slade aimed a contented smile at her. "Oh, yes, I do."

Tory's head jerked back. "What are you saying?"

"That I found obvious evidence of arson during my inspection of the fire scene this morning." He glanced up from the sliver he was trying to extract from the palm of his hand. "That fire was deliberately set, ladies." With a flourish he pulled out the sliver. "And I intend to find out who set it."

A swirl of black dots sprinkled Tory's vision like confetti. As she swayed forward, Slade leaped to her side and grabbed her arm. "Sit down on the curb here. Are you all right?" He knelt beside her and cupped her chin while he studied her face closely. "LuAnne, run to the corner market and get her a cold soft drink, will you?"

When the unsteady click-click of LuAnne's high heels had faded away down the sidewalk, Slade gently brushed Tory's hair off her forehead. "What happened?" he asked.

She drew in a ragged breath, wishing her stomach would stop doing flip-flops. And Slade wasn't helping matters any, not with that uncharacteristic frown of concern creasing his brow and his hand resting on her bare shoulder.

"I—I'm not sure," she replied in a shaky voice. "It's terribly hot out here . . . then it was such a shock when you announced someone really *did* set the fire. . . ." She blinked, trying to clear her vision. "I think maybe I banged my head when we hit the ground earlier."

Slade grasped her elbow. "I'm taking you to a doctor."

"No!" She tugged away from his grip. "I don't need a doctor. I'll be fine, as soon as LuAnne brings me that drink."

Slade crossed his arms. "You look like a war casualty."

"You look pretty battle-scarred yourself," she said. "You ought to have a doctor look at that gash on your arm."

"Aren't you going to insist on bandaging my wounds yourself?" he asked. "It's the least you could do, since you're the one responsible for them."

"Who do I look like, Florence Nightingale?"

"More like Joan of Arc. *After* she'd been—"

"All right, all right. Let me see your arm."

What was wrong with her, anyway? Maybe it was the trauma of losing the guest house, but ever since meeting Slade Marshall, Tory hadn't been acting like her usual self at all. Years of placating creditors and dealing with recalcitrant guests had taught her the value of maintaining a pleasant, even-tempered, reasonable facade. Honey caught more flies than vinegar and all that.

So why did she keep flying off the handle today, flinging threats at people and calling them names? Well, not *people,* actually. One person. A person who had an uncanny knack for pushing exactly the right buttons to send her temper skyrocketing.

And now she'd allowed him to goad her into playing nurse. Immediately Tory regretted it. The sight of blood never failed to make her woozy, even when she wasn't feeling a bit light-headed already. Years ago, at the only horror movie she'd ever taken Robby to see, she'd had to drag him out of the theater before the opening credits finished rolling. And the one time she'd donated blood, it had taken two quarts of orange juice and half a package of cookies to revive her.

She tried to push those memories aside as she gingerly touched his sleeve. Beneath the cotton fabric Slade's upper arm was solid and muscular. As he flexed his forearm the tendons rippled under her fingers, sending an echoing ripple down Tory's spine.

Holding her breath, she forced herself to examine his injury. Neither his wound nor her own reaction to seeing it were as bad as she'd thought they'd be. "Doesn't look like a very deep cut," she said. "Does it hurt much?"

"Not anymore," he said in a sly, suggestive drawl.

She whipped her hand away. "I hope you get gangrene."

"Not a very nice attitude for an angel of mercy to take, is it?" He craned his neck to see the injury for himself. "I told you it wasn't serious. You were the one who insisted on checking me over."

"I did no such—"

"And don't think I don't appreciate your concern. But now I really have to go get washed up before I start interviewing your neighbors. In my present filthy state they'll probably barricade their doors when they see me coming."

"What a good idea," Tory mumbled.

"And if you don't mind my saying so, you could use a little cleaning up yourself." He winked at her. "Care to share a shower with me? I'll scrub your back if you'll scrub mine."

Tory chose not to dignify his outrageous suggestion with an answer. But she couldn't help imagining, just for a second, what it might be like....

"Tory, are you feeling any better? Here's your drink. I know you like root beer, but he didn't have any in the cooler and I didn't want to buy a big bag of ice for one li'l old drink, and besides, then I would have had to buy a whole package of cups, too, so I bought you a cola. Is that okay?"

Tory watched annoyance flicker over Slade's face at LuAnne's reappearance, and felt a tiny prick of satisfaction. Deciding to take advantage of the interruption to make her escape, she took the can of soda from LuAnne and handed it to Slade. "Here, I think you need this more than I do." She climbed to her feet. "Come on, LuAnne. Don Gerard is putting me up temporarily at his place on Royal Street. You can walk me over there while I fill you in on what's happened."

LuAnne made no attempt to hide her reluctance to bid farewell to the handsome arson investigator. Her painted, Cupid's-bow lips formed an adorable pout, but before she could utter a peep of protest Tory was propelling her down the sidewalk by the elbow, lobbing Slade a farewell over her shoulder.

"'Bye, Mr. Marshall," LuAnne echoed.

Shaking his head, Slade watched the two women walk off down the street. It had been a long time since he'd met a woman who could hold her own with him, and he had to give Tory Clayton credit. She gave back as good as she got.

He chuckled to himself as his gaze followed them down the block. Despite all of LuAnne's feminine frills, in Slade's expert opinion Tory was by far the sexier of the two, hands down. Even with scraped knees, a dusting of soot and a torn dress. LuAnne's carefully applied makeup was no match for the cute smudge on the tip of Tory's nose.

So what was it about Tory Clayton that drove Slade to bait her so relentlessly? She definitely brought out the worst in him. And he suspected Tory herself was perfectly sweet and good-natured whenever he wasn't around.

He shifted the soda can and pressed his cold hand to the back of his neck, savoring the fleeting chill as moisture dripped onto his shirt collar. Tory Clayton was something else, all right. Running a guest house, raising her younger brother, looking after her ailing grandmother. And on top of all that she had looks, personality and class. She was almost too good to be true.

Maybe that was it. She was *too* classy, *too* good, *too* perfect, tempting Slade to rattle her cage, to tweak her dignity, to muss up that Pollyanna image of hers.

And resisting temptation had never been Slade's strong suit.

She was so different from Kathleen. He could already tell that Tory placed great value on her family, on loyalty and integrity. Whereas his ex-wife...

Slade scowled, gripping the can so hard his knuckles turned white. One thing Tory did have in common with Kathleen: she was concealing something important from him. And Slade intended to find out what it was.

Maybe he antagonized Tory for another reason: to keep his emotional distance from her. Any personal involvement between them would spell nothing but trouble. She might be an arsonist, for Pete's sake! Any hint of impropriety, the slightest suggestion that Slade's investigation was less than objective, could cast a blot on his entire career. And he'd worked too hard to risk his career for any woman—even a woman as tempting as Tory Clayton.

Yet for some reason he was unable to treat her with the same detached interest other women roused in him. And that annoyed him.

He pressed the icy soda can to his forehead and felt the cool rivulets slide down the side of his face.

Was Tory Clayton really as perfect as she seemed? Or had something pushed her over the edge one hot New Orleans night?

He wondered why she was so afraid of him.

She was a mystery, all right. And Slade *loved* mysteries.

* * *

"Ninety-eight, ninety-nine, one hundred. There! All finished." Tory set the silver-backed brush on the table next to the hospital bed where her grandmother lay propped up with pillows. She leaned back in her chair and inspected the results. "Your hair looks beautiful, Nana."

Marie Clayton's snow-white hair cascaded over her shoulders. If she had stood up—a feat she found increasingly difficult and painful these days—her hair would have fallen nearly to her waist.

"When I was a little girl, my mother taught me to brush my hair one hundred strokes before I went to bed. And that's what I've done every single night of my life without fail." She lifted one gnarled, trembling hand. "You inherited your hair from me, Victoria. And it would look just as beautiful as mine used to if you followed that same advice." She gestured at Tory's hastily combed mane with disapproval.

Tory patted her grandmother's hand. "Now, Nana, where would I find the time to brush my hair a hundred strokes every day?"

"A lady of breeding *makes* the time. If she cares about her appearance, that is."

"I've got more important things to worry about than my looks."

"Is that so? I don't seem to recall any young gentlemen calling on you lately."

"Nana..." Tory warned.

"You're thirty-two years old, Victoria. Although one would never know it from the way you're dressed this evening. What do they call that ridiculous getup, anyway?"

"A miniskirt. I told you, Nana, I had to borrow it from Jenny Gerard."

"Who?"

"Don Gerard's teenage daughter. At the Bayou Bed and Breakfast, remember? Jenny's almost the same size as I am, and she was generous enough to lend me some clothes until I get a chance to go shopping."

"Humph. Child needs a new wardrobe, if you ask me. Couldn't you find anything a bit more...dignified?"

Tory sighed. "Believe it or not, this is the most conservative outfit she owns." At least, after her yellow sundress perished during Tory's latest encounter with Slade Marshall.

Marie sniffed. "Well, at any rate...where was I, now? Oh, yes. You're thirty-two years old, Victoria—"

"You said that already."

"—And it's high time to think about starting a family. How do you expect to find a husband when you spend every waking moment running that guest house?" Marie plucked at the bow on the neck of her lacy bathrobe. "Perhaps this terrible fire was a blessing in disguise."

"Nana, how can you say such a thing?" Tory exclaimed.

Telling her grandmother that the guest house she and her late husband had started over sixty years ago had gone up in flames had been one of the hardest things Tory had ever forced herself to do. If it had been up to her, she would have kept the devastating news from Nana until she was feeling stronger, maybe until she checked out of the hospital.

But that obstinate Slade Marshall was dead set on questioning Nana as soon as possible, leaving Tory no choice but to break the news immediately.

Her grandmother had reacted amazingly well to the destruction of the family business that had been a major part of her life for over half a century. Her resigned acceptance had worried Tory at first, so she was relieved to discover that Nana still had plenty of energy to nag her about her flyaway hair, her unsuitable clothing and her lack of a husband. Business was back to normal.

"I know this is hard for you to hear, Victoria. It's hard for me to say. But the Creole Courtyard has become too much of a burden in recent years. And my greatest regret is that most of the burden has fallen on your shoulders."

"But I love running the Creole Courtyard! I've never considered it a burden."

"Nevertheless, that's what it's been, and we both know it. It's cost you any kind of normal social life—"

"Nana, there's nothing wrong with my social life."

"Because you don't *have* one, child! You don't even have time to see your old school friends, much less meet any suitable young men." She shook her head sadly. "I should have sold the place when your parents died."

"Nana, please don't talk like that!" Tory gulped down a lump in her throat.

"The Creole Courtyard has been nothing but a white elephant for years. Tourists want fancy modern hotels these days, places with swimming pools and room service and valet parking lots. We couldn't possibly charge the rates needed to keep up with expenses."

"If only we could have kept it going a little while longer—"

"Oh, nonsense, child! The place needed all new plumbing and wiring, not to mention redecorating. We'd have needed an enormous sum of money to fix it up properly." She crooked a scolding finger at Tory. "And look what happened with the last investor you found."

Tory sighed. The room was silent for a moment, until her grandmother said in a disdainful voice, "I don't suppose you've heard a peep from that scoundrel."

"No." Tory sighed again. "If Gideon doesn't want to be found, he won't be. He knows his way around those bayous like he knows his way around a gambling casino. And he's got all those Cajun relatives more than happy to hide him."

"I still think you should call the police."

"Gideon hasn't done anything illegal, Nana." Tory threw up her hands in a helpless gesture. "What could I tell the police, anyway? That I was dumb enough to trust someone who'd abscond with all the money in our business bank account? Unfortunately Gideon had as much right as I had to draw out funds."

"But only to pay Creole Courtyard expenses!"

"Ethically that's true, Nana. But Gideon and I didn't have a written agreement saying so." Another stupid move on her part. "Legally he could have cleared out the account and donated the money to a traveling circus if he'd wanted to."

"No doubt his reasons for stealing us blind were equally noble," Marie said with a sniff.

"I've got a couple ideas about those reasons myself. But don't forget, that money *was* originally Gideon's. If he hadn't agreed to invest in the guest house a year ago, we'd have been out of business by this time."

"I'd like to know what we are now," Marie grumbled. "I warned you not to get involved with that lazy, no-good, smooth-talking scoundrel! That boy was altogether too charming and handsome for his own good."

"Ladies? I hope I'm not interrupting anything."

Tory spun around, startled. Instead of Gideon Fontaine, she found Slade Marshall lounging in the doorway. Another handsome scoundrel, but one who definitely could have used a big dose of charm. How long had he been standing there, anyway? And how much had he overheard?

She jerked the short denim skirt down over her thighs as far as it would go. Not nearly far enough, unfortunately. Slade noticed, of course. His eyes narrowed in frank admiration, and one corner of his mouth tugged upward in a suggestive half grin. Why was it that no matter what time of day Tory had the misfortune to run into him, he always looked as if he'd just tumbled out of bed with a woman? He seemed to have a permanently lazy, satisfied, slightly rumpled appearance, as if he'd thrown on his clothes in a hurry.

And likely as not leaped out of a window to escape an irate husband.

"Nana," she said, "this is Slade Marshall, the arson investigator I told you about." Her lips pinched together in a tight line when she turned to Slade. "This is my grandmother, Marie Clayton."

"Marie *Delacroix* Clayton," amended the older woman, extending her hand in a royal gesture.

Slade crossed to her bedside, bowing low as he carefully clasped Marie's fragile fingers in his. "A pleasure, ma'am." For a second Tory thought he was actually going to kiss her hand.

"Why, Victoria, you didn't mention your arson investigator was so handsome."

Tory blushed. Since when had he become *her* arson investigator? She kept her mouth firmly shut, even when Slade flashed her a wicked grin.

"Marshall...Marshall...let me see..." Marie tapped her chin thoughtfully. "Are you by any chance one of the Marshalls from Baton Rouge?"

Slade folded his hands politely in front of him. "No, ma'am, afraid not. I'm originally from Chicago."

"Chicago? Oh, my, you're a Yankee then. I can tell by your accent." Marie's eyes glowed with interest. "The Delacroix, as you may know, are one of the oldest, most respected Creole families in New Orleans." She wagged her finger. "Believe you me, it caused quite a scandal when I rebelled against my father's wishes and married a Yankee. Of course, Randolph's family had lived in New Orleans since before the Civil War, but when I was a young girl, Creole society still looked upon the Americans as newcomers and ruffians who were only interested in making money." The harsh creases etched in her face softened as she drifted into some fond, distant reminiscence. Then she blinked and fixed her appraising scrutiny on Slade. "I suppose if a Yankee was good enough for me, a Yankee is good enough for my granddaughter."

"Nana, really!" Tory busied herself fluffing the pillows behind her grandmother's back. Bending over, she whispered, "Behave yourself!" in Marie's ear.

"Speak up, child, I can't hear you," her grandmother retorted.

Tory pursed her lips. Other parts of Marie Clayton's body might not work as well as they used to, but her hearing was still sharp as an owl's. Tory clicked her tongue in exasperation.

"Mr. Marshall, do be kind enough to pull up a chair, won't you?" Marie patted the edge of the mattress. "Victoria, dear, you can pin up my hair while Mr. Marshall asks me his questions."

Tory gathered up a handful of bobby pins and sat down on the edge of the bed, doing her best to ignore Slade.

He folded himself into a chair on the opposite side of the bed and crossed one long, lean leg over the other. "The only question that concerns me at the moment is that of your health, Mrs. Clayton." He leaned forward and pasted an earnest expression on his face. "If it's not too forward, may I ask what the doctors say about your condition?"

"They can't find anything wrong," Tory mumbled around a mouthful of bobby pins. "None of their tests showed anything."

"The young man asked *me* the question," Marie said in a haughty voice. "I may be old, but I'm still capable of speaking for myself, thank you."

"Sorry," Tory muttered. "I thought maybe you couldn't hear him."

"I've been poked and prodded for three days now," Marie continued, jabbing the air as if to demonstrate, "and the doctors still can't come up with a reason for my little swooning spell the other day."

"Nana, you passed out cold."

"I've told them and told them it was simply one more side effect of getting old, and there's no cure for that particular ailment yet, as far as I know. But Victoria insisted on dragging me to the emergency room, and then once those doctors get their hands on you they never want to let go. Such a waste." She shook her head with scorn, loosening the hair Tory was trying to pin up. "All this money wasted on doctors and tests and hospital rooms—why, do you know what they charge for an aspirin in this place? Two dollars! That's for one single aspirin, mind you. Have you ever heard anything so outlandish in your life?"

"Your health insurance covers most of it," Tory pointed out quickly.

"Not nearly enough of it. As if we didn't have plenty of money problems already without having to pay some over-educated, wet-behind-the-ears doctor to—"

"That's enough, Nana," Tory blurted out, dropping several bobby pins on the floor. "I'm sure Mr. Marshall isn't interested in our personal finances."

But from the way he perked up his ears, she could tell Slade was *extremely* interested in the subject.

"You can't pinch pennies when it comes to your health," he said in a soothing tone. "I'm sure your granddaughter is only concerned that you have the best care possible—no matter what the cost."

"It's foolish to waste money on an old woman like me. Victoria's been a godsend ever since we lost her parents, but the fact is that I've been too much of a burden lately."

"Nana, that's just plain silly."

"Soon I'll be too much for even Victoria to handle. And when that day comes, I intend to pack myself off to a nursing home."

Tory clamped her jaw in a stubborn line. "You'll never go into a nursing home as long as I have anything to say about it."

"We have to be realistic, child. The time is soon coming when you won't be able to take care of me anymore—not while you have to earn a living and look out for Robert as well." She frowned. "By the way, where *is* your brother? He hasn't stopped by to see me once since I've been in the hospital."

Tory avoided Slade's eyes. "I'll make sure he drops in to visit soon."

"Never mind. You've got better things to do than browbeat your brother into visiting his old grandma." She sighed. "I've said it before and I'll say it again, even if you don't want to hear it, Victoria. That fire last night might have been the best thing that could have happened."

"Nana!" Tory exclaimed in a panic.

Her grandmother continued blithely on. "Now we don't have to argue about my entering a nursing home. That decision's been made for us. After all, the home where I've spent the last sixty-two years is gone. What better time to move myself into a more suitable place to live out my remaining months?"

"For heaven's sake, you've got years left to live. I won't listen to such nonsense for one more minute." Tory was desperate to change the subject. If only Slade would get down to work and ask his damn questions!

Judging from his look of fascination, however, Slade was perfectly content with the way the conversation was proceeding. "The fire was a terrible shock, naturally, and a great loss to all of you," he said, adjusting his face to convey sympathy. "But I can understand how you might also consider it a blessing in disguise."

"My sentiments exactly." Marie beamed in triumph. "Weren't those my very words, Victoria?"

Tory groaned.

"And with the insurance money, Victoria can make a new start, set herself up in a more profitable business, perhaps. One that would leave her time for... other interests." She slid her glance to Tory, then sent Slade a meaningful smile.

"Other interests?" Slade cocked an eyebrow at Tory.

"Never mind. Don't you have some questions you'd like to ask my grandmother?"

"Actually I think I've got all the information I need from her right now." He retrieved Marie's hand from the blanket and covered it with his. "Thank you very much for your time, Mrs. Clayton. I'm so sorry I had to intrude during your time of sorrow." He switched his attention to Tory's anxious face as he continued, "You've been more than helpful, I assure you."

Marie patted the bun at the nape of her neck. "The pleasure was all mine, Mr. Marshall. If either Victoria or I can be of any further assistance to your investigation, please don't hesitate to call." She threw a sly look in Tory's direction.

"Sorry, y'all, but visiting hours are over," a nurse sang through the door. "Time to say goodbye."

Slade gently replaced Marie's hand on the blanket. "What perfect timing," he said. "Now I can walk you to your car, Ms. Clayton."

"That won't be necessary. I mean, I have to stop in the hospital gift shop for something."

"The gift shop is closed, Victoria." Her grandmother shot her a stern look. "And you know how unsafe parking lots can be at night." Her glare vanished. "How kind of you to offer, Mr. Marshall. Victoria, I'll see you tomorrow. *Tomorrow,*" she said firmly when Tory opened her mouth to protest.

Resigned to the inevitable, Tory tugged down her skirt and preceded Slade into the hallway. She could just imagine him licking his chops as he ogled her backside.

"I notice your suave routine isn't reserved strictly for younger women," she said as they walked down the hallway.

"Whatever do you mean?" He pressed the elevator's down button.

"You know what I'm talking about, you big fake. All that phony charm you were oozing back there to con my grandmother into thinking you were so concerned about her."

"What makes you think I'm not?" Slade asked. They stepped into the elevator. "You know, you've got a pretty cynical attitude."

"*I've* got a—" Tory bit off her words, mindful of the other elevator passengers.

When the doors slid open and they emerged into the reception area, she continued, "You've got a lot of nerve, trying to pump an old lady for information by pretending to be some kind of Mr. Nice Guy. All that bowing and scraping, all that hand-kissing—"

"I did not kiss her hand."

"You know what I mean. I've never seen such a self-serving, nauseating display of—"

"What are you so worried about?" Slade pushed open the exit door.

"Nothing." She edged past him into the parking lot. Even this late in the day it was like stepping into an oven. "I'm worried about my grandmother, that's all."

"The doctors seem to think she's fine."

"Only because they don't want to admit they can't figure out what's wrong with her."

"I take it you haven't told her that someone deliberately set the fire."

"Of course not. She's had enough shocks already." Tory rooted through her purse for her car keys. "I don't intend to upset her any more than I have to."

"Your granddaughterly devotion is commendable, but I'd be willing to bet your grandmother's a lot tougher than you think."

"I'm not taking any chances." Now where was her... there! Tory spotted her tan Honda in the next row, and once again blessed the shortage of French Quarter street parking, which had forced her to rent garage space two blocks from the guest house. At least her trusty Honda had escaped the fire.

She strode rapidly across the parking lot, hoping to outdistance Slade before he could ask her any more questions. But he was still hot on her heels when she reached her car.

"That's funny," she muttered to herself. "I could have sworn I left it locked." She opened the door. "And I can't believe I left the windows rolled down." The events of the past twenty-four hours must have dazed her more than she realized.

Then her hand flew to her mouth and she leaped back with a cry at the sight of the figure lying in the back seat.

In a flash Slade had pushed Tory aside and dragged the intruder out of the car. "What the hell were you doing in there, pal?" he snarled, seizing the kid by the front of his shirt and slamming him against the side of the car.

The boy's scruffy T-shirt and torn jeans were streaked with grime. His jet-black hair stood up in spiky disarray, and dark circles rimmed his bloodshot eyes, which darted wildly back and forth between Tory and Slade. All the color had drained from his face, leaving his skin sickly pale.

Tory gasped. "Robby!"

Chapter Four

Tory's brother?

Surprised, Slade loosened his grip on the front of the kid's shirt. The boy jerked free and stood with his feet planted apart in a defiant stance, fists clenched at his sides, glaring bullets at Slade.

Now Slade could see the Clayton family resemblance. He'd certainly seen that expression on Tory often enough. But features that were strong and determined in Tory's face turned stubborn and sulky when transferred to her younger brother.

This sullen, defiant teen was hardly what Slade had expected after meeting his older sister. In his shabby T-shirt and jeans—universal symbols of rebellious youth—he reminded Slade of someone else instead.

Himself.

But that was a thousand years ago, in another lifetime. Slade's concern was with the present, like figuring out why

Tory looked so worried. "Didn't you recognize your own brother?" he asked.

"I—all I saw was someone lying in the back seat." She knelt to pick up the keys she'd dropped on the ground, then turned to Robby. "What are you—how did you get in the car, anyway?"

Robby raised one shoulder, then dropped it. "Hey, it's no big deal breaking into a car."

"You sound like you've had lots of practice," Slade said.

Robby scowled at him.

Hastily Tory said, "Mr. Marshall is an arson investigator. He's trying to figure out what started the fire at the guest house last night."

Slade got the distinct impression she was trying to convey some secret message to her brother. A warning, perhaps?

Robby scratched his head, making his hair even spikier than before. "Yeah, I wanted to talk to you about that. Geez, Tor, what hap—"

"Mr. Marshall. Slade." Tory turned to Slade with the most dazzling smile he'd seen from her yet. Not that she'd shown him that many so far. "I know you want to ask Robby a couple of questions, but we're in kind of a hurry right now, so I wonder if—"

Slade tapped his pen against his clipboard. "I need to talk to him *now*, Ms. Clayton. Tory." He returned her smile.

"But—"

"This won't take long."

"But—"

"Hey, Tory, what the hell—"

"Watch your language, Robby."

"Hey, how many times I gotta tell ya, don't call me that anymore. My name's Gator."

"If you think I'm going to call you by that ridiculous—"

"People, people!" Slade inserted two fingers into his mouth and emitted an earsplitting whistle. Instantly the other two fell silent. He smiled. "Thank you. Now, if I might make a suggestion, why don't we adjourn to that nice air-conditioned coffee shop across the street? It's awfully warm standing out here in this parking lot, and I think we're all getting a little hot under the collar."

"I'm sorry, but we really don't have time—"

"Or..." Slade held up a warning finger. "Or we could do this down at the police station."

Tory's jaw fell open. Her eyes narrowed. "You're bluffing! You're not a police officer—you can't just arrest people and haul them off in handcuffs!"

Slade moved his face so they were nose-to-nose. "Wanna find out whether I can or not?"

"Hey, Tory, it's cool, okay? No reason I can't answer the guy's questions."

Tory glanced at her brother in surprise. Robby licked his lips nervously, then studied his grimy fingernails.

Slade wrapped his arms around the clipboard and tapped his foot. "Well? Any more objections?"

At least she was a good sport about losing. As they crossed St. Charles Avenue on the way to the coffee shop, one of the historic green streetcars rumbled by. Slade half expected Tory to push him onto the tracks in front of it.

In the coffee shop, Slade stepped aside to let Tory slide into the circular booth. Then he quickly slipped in next to her so that she and Robby couldn't sit side by side. Tory arched her dark eyebrows. "Are you afraid I'll tap out answers in Morse code on his knee?"

"No point in taking the chance, is there?" Slade patted her knee. She jerked it aside and slid as far away from him as possible, which wasn't nearly far enough. Robby slouched into the booth and watched them both with suspicious eyes.

"I'll have a root beer," Slade cheerfully told the waitress. "Tory? Robby—I mean, Gator?"

Tory rolled her eyes, while Robby straightened up a little and actually looked almost pleased. "Me, too," he muttered.

"I'm not thirsty," Tory grumbled.

"Oh, come on, it's on me. Three root beers, please." Slade held up the appropriate number of fingers. "Now, let's get down to business, shall we?" He folded back some sheets on his clipboard.

"What's that?" Robby asked, not looking at Slade.

"What, this? Witness questionnaires."

"But I didn't see nothin'."

"Anything." Tory leaned forward, but fell back when Slade and Robby each gave her a withering look.

Slade clicked the end of his pen. "You might not have witnessed the fire itself, but you might have seen something before or afterward that would give me a clue about who set it."

Robby stared first at Slade, then at Tory. "Someone *set* the fire?"

Tory scanned his face intently, searching desperately for a sign that Robby's surprise was genuine. Not that she actually believed her own brother was guilty of setting the Creole Courtyard ablaze. Sure, he'd fallen in with a rather unsavory crowd lately...maybe he *had* come home with the faint whiff of alcohol on his breath last week...and he *had* been cutting his summer school classes. But those transgressions certainly didn't mean he was capable of a

monstrous act like arson. It was disloyal of Tory to allow
that remote possibility even to enter her mind.

Still...

Also in Tory's mind was the ugly scene two days ago,
right before she discovered Gideon had swiped all the
money from their account. Robby had come home from
wherever he was hanging out these days while he was supposed to be in summer school, breathless with an excitement Tory hadn't seen in him for a long time. She'd been
delighted...at first.

"Tory, I got a favor to ask." He was sliding one hand
casually up and down the railing of the courtyard staircase, but Tory could sense tension running through him
like an electric current.

"Sure, Robby. What is it?"

"Well, I got a chance, see, to buy this car."

"A car?"

He looked up eagerly. "It's not a *new* car or anything,
but it's really cool, and I know I could fix it up...."

"Robby, you don't know anything about fixing cars."
She propped her chin on the handle of the broom she'd
been using to sweep the courtyard. "Besides, where would
you get the money to buy a car?"

"Well, see..." He shifted uneasily from one foot to the
other. "That's the favor."

"Oh." Tory sighed and brushed back her tangled hair
with her wrist. She couldn't help wondering for an instant
how much more trouble her brother could get into with a
set of wheels. "Robby, we've talked about this before. I
wish I could afford to pay you to do some of the work
around here. Heaven knows, I could certainly use the extra help, but—"

"Naw, that ain't what I'm talkin' about." His jaw
worked back and forth with annoyance.

Tory's forehead creased in confusion. "What do you mean, then?"

"I don't want a job, I just want the money!"

The brazenness of his request made her want to laugh at first, but then she grew irritated. Resuming her sweeping, she said, "That's out of the question. Even if I could afford to give you the money, which I can't, I'd expect you to work a little harder for it than just holding out your hand. I'm kind of disappointed in you, Robby."

"So what else is new?" he mumbled.

"And since the subject has come up, you're going to have to pitch in more around here, anyway. LuAnne and I can't do it all ourselves."

"When do you think you might have the money to buy me a car?"

Tory grabbed the broomstick with one hand. "Are you listening to me? I told you, I can't afford to buy you a car. I can barely afford to keep this place going—" She swept her arm around the courtyard, then lowered her voice, mindful of the guests who might hear her words echoing off the brick walls.

"If you want a car," she continued, trying to stay calm, "you can get a part-time job and earn the money yourself. But I'm still going to expect you to help out more around here."

"I don't get it! Where does all the money go around this place, anyway?"

"Shush! Will you keep your voice down, please?"

"I mean, you charge enough for people to stay in this dump."

"Robby!"

"How come we can never afford stuff like a decent TV or a new car or even a damn vacation once in a while?"

"Quit swearing! You know perfectly well all our income goes back into keeping this place afloat."

"What about Gideon's money? I thought that was supposed to fix everything."

"Going into partnership with Gideon was a last-ditch effort to keep us from going bankrupt. I used most of his investment to pay off bills and for that repair work to bring the building up to code."

"There's still money left in the bank."

Tory's eyes narrowed. "Oh? And just how do you know that? Have you been snooping through my desk again? Never mind." She started sweeping again, flailing the broom back and forth with exasperation. "We need that money for emergencies."

"Like what?"

"Like plumbing repairs. Or fixing the car if it breaks down. Or for Nana. It's getting harder and harder for her to look after herself. Once she's home from the hospital, I'll probably have to hire someone to take care of her eventually."

"Why can't *you* take care of her?"

"Because *I* have to run the guest house!" Tory shouted, forgetting to keep her voice down.

"I *hate* the damn guest house!" Robby shouted back. "It's nothing but work, work, work, with nothing to show for it." He stormed down the passageway to the street. Just before he clanged the wrought-iron gate shut behind him, he hurled one final statement over his shoulder. "I wish the damn place would burn to the ground!"

Those words, which Tory had shrugged off at the time, had come back to haunt her from the moment she'd turned the corner of St. Philip Street and seen flames leaping through the Creole Courtyard's shuttered windows. She'd been returning from an appointment to meet Robby...an appointment he hadn't kept.

So even though the idea was crazy...impossible...Tory couldn't help wondering what Robby had been up to while she was waiting in vain for him to show up at that awful dive where he'd reluctantly agreed to meet her.

Now as Slade questioned Robby, Tory hung on her brother's every word, desperate to know the truth...yet afraid to know the truth. Afraid for Robby.

"First off, why don't you give me the address and phone number of these friends you're staying with."

Robby's dark brows jumped together. "Friends? Huh?"

Tory interceded quickly. "Robby's going to be staying with me from now on, at the Bayou Bed and Breakfast."

Both Slade and Robby eyed her curiously, but Slade jotted down a note without comment.

He waited until the waitress had set down their root beers and departed before continuing. "Where were you yesterday?" he asked Robby.

"Huh? You mean like, all day?"

"Yeah. Like all day."

"Oh." He sent Tory a furtive look. "Well, summer school, of course." He tore off the end of his straw wrapper and appeared to be concentrating hard on extricating the straw.

Tory knew for a fact he was lying.

"What time did you get out of school?" Slade asked.

"Uh, let's see. Two o'clock."

"Where did you go then?"

"Oh, around. You know." He sucked up root beer as if he were dying of thirst.

"No, I don't know. If I did, I wouldn't be asking." Slade's tone was perfectly friendly, but something in his voice made Robby sit up straighter.

"Well, gee, uh, I just hung out. Around the Quarter. With some friends." He was busily occupied tearing his straw wrapper into little bits.

"Until what time?"

"Uh, let's see. It was dark out," he said helpfully.

"What time did you return to the guest house?"

Tory held her breath.

"Oh. Well . . . actually, I uh, stayed out all night." His straw made a loud slurping noise as he vacuumed up his root beer.

"Let me get this straight." Slade tapped his pen on the rim of his glass. "After you left for school yesterday morning, you never went home the rest of the day?"

Robby paused, as if sensing a trick. "Yeah, that's right," he said slowly.

"Then when did you find out about the fire?"

Tory shaded her eyes with her hand.

"Well, like, this afternoon. Just a little while ago, you know, when I finally went home. There was nothing there, nobody around. So I came over to the hospital to see if my grandmother knew what was going on. Then I saw Tory's car and decided to wait for her instead."

Slade very deliberately rotated his head to study Tory. Tory, meanwhile, studied the ice cubes floating in her soda.

"Gator," he said slowly, "your sister and I need to talk privately for a moment."

Robby shot to his feet as if propelled by gunpowder. "Hey, sure, man—no problem. I gotta take off, anyway."

"Robby, where are you—"

"Catch you later, Tor."

"I'll see you back at Don's place later, all right?" she called after him anxiously.

His only response was an absent flip of his hand.

"Hey, Gator," Slade called.

Robby turned around and reluctantly shuffled back to the booth. Slade reached into his pocket. "Here's some change for streetcar fare back to the Quarter. And while you're at it—" he dug into his pocket again and handed Robby a fistful of coins "—buy yourself another root beer to go. It's hot outside."

Robby examined the change as if it were exotic foreign currency. "Uh, sure. Whatever you say." He actually mustered half a smile that for a second transformed his expression into that handsome, boyish face Tory loved so well and so rarely saw. Her heart performed a painful backflip. "Thanks," Robby told Slade.

"So, you'll meet your sister back at this bed-and-breakfast place tonight, right?"

"Yeah, right." He jingled the change before shoving it into his jeans pocket. "Thanks again, man. See you in a while, Tory."

She watched, astonished, as he sauntered out of the coffee shop. Before she could collect her wits, Slade launched his attack. "You lied to me," he said as calmly as if he were discussing the weather.

Tory took a swallow of root beer before replying. "I didn't lie to you," she said. "I just didn't tell you everything, that's all."

"Why not?"

She stirred her drink with the straw. "Look," she sighed, "as you can see, Robby has kind of a chip on his shoulder these days. I guess you could call it an attitude problem. He's going through a phase where he resents all authority, and I just thought I could avoid a lot of unpleasantness by keeping him out of this."

"You didn't think I'd be mildly interested in the fact that your brother's whereabouts last night are unknown? That he was out roaming around somewhere when the fire started?''

Tory set down her glass with a loud *thunk!* ''Surely you don't think *Robby* had anything to do with starting the fire?''

Slade took a long drag of root beer. ''Not really. But I guess that's what *you* think, huh?''

''I most certainly do not—'' She blinked. ''Did you say you *don't* suspect Robby?''

Slade shrugged. ''Not seriously. He doesn't seem to have much of a motive from what I've seen. Even if this gang of friends he hangs out with decided to torch the place as a lark, I can't see Robby going along with it. He might have some problems, but I'll bet he's basically a good kid underneath.''

Tory sank back with relief at Slade's understanding. ''You wouldn't believe the awful riffraff he's been hanging out with lately. They prowl along Bourbon Street, wearing leather jackets even when it's ninety degrees out, calling themselves names like Snake and Scorpion—''

''—And Gator,'' Slade finished.

''Uh, right.'' Suddenly realizing she might be making Robby seem more of a likely suspect after all, Tory halted her flow of complaints about the hoodlums he'd fallen in with. ''So, you don't believe Robby was involved,'' she repeated for emphasis.

Slade shook his head. ''I'm looking for someone with a strong motive,'' he said. ''For example . . .'' He sucked on an ice cube between his back teeth. ''Where were *you* last night when the fire started?''

Tory choked on a mouthful of root beer. ''Me? Are you going to start *that* ridiculous line of questioning again?''

''Humor me,'' he replied. ''Just satisfy my insatiable curiosity and answer the question.''

But she couldn't answer the question. Not truthfully. Not without casting suspicion back on her brother.

Because last night, while some sinister figure was skulking through the Creole Courtyard preparing to burn down the only home Tory had ever known, she'd been waiting for Robby in a sleazy Bourbon Street bar called the Purple Doubloon.

Not the kind of place Tory would normally frequent for an after-dinner sherry. Not the kind of place she would normally have been caught *dead* in, if Robby hadn't insisted on meeting her there.

Yesterday morning the high school principal had phoned Tory, informing her that Robby had shown up for summer school only two days out of the last two weeks, warning that he was in danger of flunking again, the way he'd flunked half his classes last semester. With only a year of high school left, chances were Robby would never make up the missing units in time to graduate next spring. Which probably meant he would never graduate at all.

Now on top of her money problems and poor Nana in the hospital, Tory had to worry about Robby dropping out of school. By the time he finally drifted into the guest house around four o'clock yesterday afternoon, Tory was at the end of her rope.

"Robby—"

"Who's Robby? I don't see anyone by that name around here."

Gritting her teeth and refusing to address him by that stupid nickname, Tory continued, "This isn't a joke. We need to have a serious discussion about school, or else—"

"No time for that now, Tor. The guys are waitin' for me." He pulled on a wrinkled T-shirt that didn't look any cleaner than the one he'd just stripped off.

"Well, the *guys* will just have to wait." Tory grasped her brother's elbow, only to have him angrily jerk his arm away and glare at her with dark, glowering eyes.

She drew back, startled, and for the first time was fully aware that Robby wasn't her *little* brother anymore. Soon, when he turned eighteen, she would lose her few remaining shreds of control over him.

"Either we talk about this," she stated in a deadly still voice, "or I wash my hands of you for good. You can find food to eat and a place to sleep with those so-called friends of yours."

Inside Tory was quaking, but the determination in her eyes must have convinced Robby she was serious. A shadow of concern flickered through those stubborn eyes that were so like her own.

"Look, I really do have to go right now," he said in a semiplacating tone. "But I'll meet you tonight, okay? We'll talk about this stuff then."

"Robby, I mean it, you—"

He was halfway out the door. "The Purple Doubloon on Bourbon Street," he called over his shoulder. "Meet you there at nine."

"Robby, I have no intention of holding this discussion in a *bar,* for Pete's sake!"

But he was already gone. Sighing, Tory decided to give her brother one last chance. After all, he *had* agreed to talk to her about school, so she didn't have to follow through with her threat to kick him out ... did she?

And that was how Tory found herself reluctantly sipping cheap white wine out of a suspiciously smudged water glass in the booth nearest the door of the Purple Doubloon—at the same time someone was setting a match to her guest house.

Robby never showed up, though Tory waited for him until nearly eleven o'clock. Her relief at finally escaping that disreputable dive mingled with despair about how she was going to handle Robby. Her heart and mind engaged in fierce debate until the moment she turned the corner of St. Philip Street and found the Creole Courtyard in flames.

Tory was positive the bartender at the Purple Doubloon would remember her. For one thing, white wine was undoubtedly a rather eyebrow-raising request in that establishment. And judging by the suggestive remark the bartender had made under his breath when he handed Tory her drink, she'd made quite a lasting impression on him.

So she had an alibi for the time period in question. The only problem was, she would have to explain to Slade why she'd been in a sleaze pit like the Purple Doubloon. And that would lead to the fact that Robby had never shown up. Which would make it look as if he'd deliberately lured Tory away from the Creole Courtyard so the place would be empty when it burned down.

But that was nonsense . . . wasn't it? The reason Robby hadn't kept their appointment was nothing more than his usual irresponsible behavior. He'd been somewhere having a good time with his pals, that was all. Or else he just hadn't felt like getting another lecture from Tory.

Even Slade didn't seriously consider Robby a suspect.

But Slade didn't know how much Robby resented the guest house, or that only two days ago he'd expressed a very explicit desire to see it burn to the ground.

Providing Slade with her alibi for last night would only incriminate Robby.

Yet if he really *had* set the fire, didn't he deserve to be punished? Wasn't it about time Robby learned to suffer the consequences of his actions, instead of letting Tory bail him out as usual?

Part of her brain assured Tory that this would be the correct, fair course of action. But the guilt that never lay far from the surface nagged at her conscience.

If only I'd done a better job of raising Robby after Mom and Daddy died... if only I'd spent more time with him, or shown him more affection, or bought him that bicycle he wanted so much when he was nine years old...

If only... if only... if only...

Robby was right: the Creole Courtyard *did* take up too much of Tory's time; it *was* too big a drain on the family finances. Hadn't Nana said pretty much the same thing this evening?

If only Tory had been a more competent guardian, Robby wouldn't have started hanging out with the wrong crowd. He wouldn't have started skipping school and staying out all night and... getting into trouble.

The familiar guilty refrain echoing through her head convinced Tory once again that she owed it to Robby to protect him. Her guilt, combined with her inherent sense of family loyalty, made any other choice impossible.

She could no more betray her brother than she could burn down the Creole Courtyard.

"My whereabouts last night are none of your business," she told Slade.

He scooted closer to her. "I beg to differ," he replied amicably, "your whereabouts are *exactly* my business."

Well, she couldn't really argue with him there. Tilting her chin up, she said, "I don't remember where I was."

"Oh, really?" He cocked one sandy eyebrow. "You don't recall coming home and finding your guest house going up in smoke?"

"Of *course* I remember that," she said impatiently. "I mean, I don't remember exactly where I was all evening."

"Must have been quite a memorable date," Slade said. "If I were you, I'd cross that guy off my dance card."

"It wasn't a date." Honestly, the man had a real knack for sending her temper soaring! "I . . . went for a walk. By myself."

"All evening?"

"It was a long walk."

"I see." He kept his eyes riveted on her face in a fascinated way Tory found distinctly uncomfortable. "Where?"

"I beg your pardon?" She wished he wouldn't sit quite so close to her. She could feel his knee brush against hers.

"Where did you go on this long walk of yours?"

"Oh . . . you know. Around the Quarter. Down by the river."

Slade groaned. "What is it with you Claytons? You seem to possess some kind of genetic tendency to wander around the French Quarter paying absolutely no attention to where you are."

Tory smiled weakly and shrugged.

"I don't suppose you ran into anyone you know during this walk."

She pretended to think for a moment. "No, I don't believe I did."

He pounced on that, bringing his face mere inches from hers. The startling movement made her pulse race. Either that, or the fact that he was now close enough for Tory to see the sexy crinkles at the corners of his eyes and smell his pleasant, faintly woodsy scent.

"You're telling me," he said, "that a local businesswoman, someone who's lived here all her life, could take a *long* walk through the Quarter on a hot summer evening and not run into *anyone* who knew her?" His breath was warm against her lips.

She gazed at him in dreamy distraction. "Amazing, isn't it?"

He drew back and fixed her with a skeptical stare, drumming his fingers against the table. "Unbelievable is more like it."

His irritated tone broke the strange spell his closeness seemed to cast over Tory. She *had* to remember that this man, no matter how attractive in his rugged, slightly disheveled way, posed a threat to her family. "Guess you'll just have to take my word for it," she told him, her mouth suddenly dry despite her cool drink.

"Not a chance," he said. "You've lied to me once before that I *know* of. I'm not about to take your word about what planet we're on, much less something this important."

"You don't have to be so rude about it," she muttered.

"Hey, I'm from Chicago, remember?" he said with a cocky grin. "I'm not one of those gallant southern gentlemen who wouldn't dream of questioning a lady's word—even if the lady in question is a proven liar."

"You're right about one thing—you're certainly no gentleman," Tory said icily as she slid out of the booth. Slade's words stung. She hated hearing herself labeled a liar, even if there *was* a grain of truth to his accusation.

And for some reason, it hurt that he should hold such a low opinion of her.

He spread his arms across the back of the booth. "Sit down and cool your jets," he said mildly, infuriating her with his supreme confidence. "I'm not finished asking questions yet."

"Well, I'm through answering them," she announced over her shoulder as she made her way to the door.

He caught up with her just as she prepared to step off the curb into St. Charles Avenue. In the distance she could see the glittering beacon of an approaching streetcar.

Slade grasped her gently yet firmly by the wrist, drawing Tory back from the edge of the street. She wrestled futilely within his grip. Slade nodded his head and smiled reassuringly at a concerned passerby. He levered Tory's arm between them as if they were merely holding hands— albeit rather forcefully. "Quit wriggling around," he ordered. "I'll be more than happy to let go, once I have your assurance that you're not about to dart in front of a passing truck or something."

"Fine," she said through clenched teeth. "I give you my word. Not that that counts for much, I realize."

With a chuckle, Slade released her. "See what a trusting soul I can be?"

Tory rubbed her wrist and glared at him, prevented from escaping by a continuous flow of cross traffic. "Let me ask *you* a question for a change," she said.

Slade was fiddling with the clipboard hanging from his belt. "Shoot."

"I'd love to," she muttered beneath the steady whoosh of cars. Unfortunately Slade glanced up in time to read her lips. A particularly maddening grin spread across his unshaven face. Maddening...yet somehow incredibly sexy. Tory sucked in a quick breath and checked for a break in the traffic.

Realizing she was stuck on this curb for at least another thirty seconds, she figured she might as well take advantage of Slade's enforced presence and check out something that had been bothering her. "Earlier in the hospital parking lot, you threatened to haul Robby down to the police station if he didn't cooperate."

"Actually the threat was intended to obtain *your* cooperation."

"Whatever." She peeked at him curiously. "Do you really have the authority to do that? Haul people off in handcuffs? Or were you bluffing?"

"Do you play poker?" he asked. "'Cause I'd love to get you in a game sometime."

"Then you *were* bluffing?"

He shrugged modestly. "Of course."

So he'd put one over on her again! Anger and humiliation churned through Tory's bloodstream, making her reckless. She dove into the traffic, dimly aware of Slade's warning shout. Reaching the neutral ground, the grassy median where the streetcar ran down the center of the avenue, she plunged headlong across the tracks. She barely had time to register the warning blast of the oncoming streetcar before a deafening clatter filled her ears, a gust of hot air swirled up her skirt and the electric smell of ozone lay thick in the air.

Then she was across the avenue, half running, half stumbling, across the hospital parking lot. Slade caught up with her before the hum of the streetcar had faded in the distance.

"You crazy fool," he said roughly, seizing her shoulders and spinning her around to face him. "You could have been killed. You could have gotten us *both* killed."

"It might almost have been worth the price," she retorted. "Now let go of me, will you?"

Instead, he gripped her shoulders tighter, yanked her against him and kissed her. Hard.

For the briefest span of time Tory was aware only of the hot, dizzy pressure of Slade's mouth on hers and the heavenly feel of his strong arms wrapped tightly around her as if he would never let her go.

Then it was over.

She tripped backward a step, heart slamming frantically in her chest, as Slade suddenly released her. He appeared nearly as stunned as Tory felt, but he recovered more quickly. "Whoops," he said. "Guess when your life passes before your eyes, you want to grab for all the gusto you can get."

His flippant remark wounded Tory, but she bounced back nicely. "You're despicable," she announced. Then she pivoted on her heel and strode toward her car with as much dignity as she could muster.

She half expected to hear the thud of feet and the slap of clipboard against thigh as Slade followed her.

But what followed instead were his words, floating after Tory as ominous and persistent as a school of piranha.

"Since you won't tell me where you were last night, maybe you'll answer a different question."

Tory's gait faltered ever so slightly.

"Why did your partner Fontaine empty out your bank account last week?"

This time he stopped her dead in her tracks.

Chapter Five

Slade knew his shot in the dark had hit home when Tory slowly turned and he saw her face.

On it were painted surprise... exasperation... resignation. She raked her fingers back through her long hair and sighed. "How did you know?"

"I checked your bank records, of course."

Tory's eyes dilated with shock as she sputtered, "But those records are supposed to be private! Even the government has to get some kind of court order to examine them."

She never ceased to amaze Slade with her naïveté, the way she expected everyone else to play by the rules just because she did. Didn't she realize there was a way around everything if you knew the right palms to grease? "I have contacts," he said. "Now, are you going to answer my question?"

She lifted her head with one final show of defiance. "Gideon had nothing to do with the fire. And I'm not about to discuss our private finances with you, not when you've already snooped through them by obviously illegal means."

Slade shifted his weight to one foot and folded his arms. "When are you going to stop protecting people who don't deserve your loyalty? First you try to cover up for your kid brother, who causes you nothing but trouble. Then you try to protect this Fontaine character, who repays you by cleaning out your bank account and skipping town."

Another lucky shot. Tory turned pale, and her shoulders slumped in defeat. Slade almost felt sorry for her, sorry for badgering her. But he couldn't afford that luxury.

"All right," she said. "I'll tell you about Gideon." Her eyes focused beyond Slade, as if she were searching for a place to begin her story. "I met him a year ago—"

"Hold it, hold it." Slade raised his palm in a motion to stop.

Tory frowned. "What's the matter? I finally agree to tell you everything, and now you won't let me."

"I'm all ears, I assure you, but I have no desire to hear your confession in the middle of a parking lot. Are you hungry?"

"I'm not *confessing* anything, because I haven't— what?"

She was pretty damn adorable when she got confused. Those cute little crinkles bunched between her eyebrows, one corner of her mouth quirked up...

Slade cleared his throat. Patiently he repeated, "I asked if you were hungry. It's going on nine o'clock, and I haven't had dinner yet. Bet you haven't, either."

She had a neat trick of arching only one eyebrow at him. "You've got to be kidding."

"You mean you've eaten already?"

"You honestly expect me to have dinner with you, after everything—"

"Hey, whoa there!" He waved his arms as if flagging down a runaway freight train. "You're making it sound like a date or something. This is business. We need to discuss some important matters, and we can't do that effectively if we're both starving."

Tory looked halfway convinced. Or at least, less doubtful.

"Come on, I'll let you pay for my dinner if that'll make you feel better."

She snorted, but in a very ladylike fashion. "We'll go dutch," she said. "*And* we'll go in separate cars and meet at the restaurant."

"It's a deal." Slade stuck out his hand. Tory eyed it as if it were a submerged crocodile, then quickly shook it. He resisted the urge to hang on a little longer. "I know a great little seafood place on Chartres Street," he said. "Just opened last month."

"I know the place you're talking about. I'll meet you there."

Slade watched her disappear into the lengthening evening shadows. She teetered unsteadily on what had to be borrowed shoes, as if she weren't used to wearing high heels too often. Her backside swayed alluringly, but from the way she moved, Slade could tell she was totally unconscious of the sexy effect of her miniskirt clinging to her shapely thighs.

What a waste. If only his job didn't prevent him from making some very serious moves on the lovely Victoria Clayton.

As Slade strode back to his car, whistling, he had a sharp flashback to that delicious, spontaneous kiss they'd shared. He stopped whistling. That kiss had been something totally new in his experience, but he couldn't quite put his finger on what made it so different, so—he might as well face it—so special.

All he knew was that in one brief moment Tory's lips had somehow branded him, and he had a sneaking, disturbing suspicion that kissing women would never be the same again.

Other women, that is. As he relived the sensation of Tory's soft lips melding with his, Slade was rocked by a powerful desire to taste those lips again, to feel her arms slide around his neck and her lush breasts press against him.

"Damn," he muttered, realizing he'd stopped walking. He kicked himself into motion again. This nonsense had to stop. Right now. His little fantasies about Tory were at the very least distracting him from his job. And at worst, if he allowed himself to carry a few of them out, they could jeopardize his entire career.

As the engine of his Corvette roared into life, a small voice inside Slade's head taunted him. *Isn't there something you're even more afraid of than risking your career? Like falling in love, perhaps?*

He punched the car stereo up full blast to drown out the voice and accelerated down St. Charles Avenue, tires screeching.

What kind of lunacy had possessed her to agree to meet Slade for dinner?

At least she hadn't had to worry about what to wear...one advantage of having your entire wardrobe reduced to cinders, Tory decided. She had enough to worry about this evening. Like keeping Slade at a distance and her own emotions at bay.

As she sat in the restaurant opposite Slade, it occurred to her that she'd only known him since this morning, and at least ninety percent of that time they'd been fighting. Yet he intrigued her, excited her, in a way no man had for a long time. Maybe not ever.

Against a backdrop of weathered-brick walls, with candlelight flickering over the hollows of his unshaven cheeks, Slade reminded Tory of a buccaneer. He could have passed for a modern-day Jean Lafitte, New Orleans's famous pirate, who smuggled whiskey and slaves through the murky Louisiana swamps, then went on to help Andrew Jackson win the Battle of New Orleans in 1815.

Tory shivered.

Slade peered over the top of his menu. "Cold?" he asked.

"I wish places wouldn't crank up their air-conditioning so much during the summer," she said, rubbing her hands up and down her bare arms. "Outside it's hot, inside it's cold. It's a good way to catch pneumonia." The room temperature had nothing to do with Tory's shivering, but she had no intention of letting Slade know that.

"What can I get you folks this evening?"

Tory glanced up at the waiter, then back at her menu. She'd been so absorbed in her silly swashbuckling fantasies that she'd completely forgotten about food. "You order first," she told Slade. "I haven't decided yet."

He scanned the menu. "I'll have seafood gumbo and the crawfish—what's the name of that stew?"

"*Etouffée*," Tory and the waiter answered in unison.

Automatically she smiled at Slade. Something intimate in his eyes flared in response, and for a second Tory felt oddly connected to him. She wasn't sure whether she enjoyed the breathtaking sensation or not.

He closed his menu, still keeping his eyes on Tory. "Crawfish *étouffée,*" he told the waiter. "And bring me another bourbon on the rocks, please."

Tory ducked behind her menu. "I'll have the jambalaya."

"Would you like something to drink with that?"

"No—yes!" She rubbed her damp palms on her skirt. "I'll have a glass of white zinfandel, please."

Slade leaned forward and propped his elbows on the bare oak table. "I bring you to the best seafood joint in the Quarter, and you order jambalaya?"

"For one thing, you did not *bring* me here, we came separately." She handed the waiter her menu. "And for another, I don't care for seafood."

A lock of hair slanted across Slade's forehead as he shook his head in disbelief. "You were born and raised in one of the best seafood regions in the country, and you're telling me you don't like fish?"

She squirmed defensively. "Just tuna."

Slade exchanged a look of profound disgust with the waiter, who shrugged as he left their table. "Oh, and bring me a dozen oysters on the half shell, would you?" Slade called after him.

He raised his glass of bourbon. "You know what they say about oysters," he said in a sly voice.

"From what I've seen, you don't require much help in that department," she retorted.

Laughter made him choke on his whiskey. "Why, Tory, you've never seen me in action. How would you know? And are you interested in finding out?"

"Are you this obnoxious with all the women you meet? Or only the ones who pose some kind of emotional threat to you?"

Pleased, Tory saw she'd struck home with that last jab. Maybe the sublimely confident Slade Marshall wasn't invulnerable after all. For once he had no quick comeback.

He studied her over the rim of his glass. "You're a very perceptive woman, Tory Clayton," he said finally. "And I apologize for being obnoxious."

He looked so ill at ease, so trapped by his own admission, that Tory felt sorry for him. Her natural impulse with anyone else would have been to reach out to him, to cover his hand with hers and assure him all was forgiven.

But Slade wasn't anyone else. And Tory knew she'd better learn to curb her natural impulses around him.

To smooth over the awkward impasse, she brought up a subject that had her wondering what other sensitivities might lurk behind Slade's arrogant facade. "You surprised me before," she said, thanking the waiter as he set her wine in front of her.

"You mean when I kissed you?"

Heat flooded her face, leaving her cheeks the same color as the brick walls. "No... I wasn't talking about that. I mean, that *was* a surprise, but..." She took a gulp of wine. "I meant the way you handled Robby."

"Gator?" Slade winked at her. Tory rolled her eyes. "No problem."

"I wish I could say the same." Tory frowned unhappily. "He was never an easy kid... I don't think he ever really got over the trauma of our parents' death when he was seven. But ever since he started high school..." She twirled the stem of her glass. "Lately I've almost given up on him. He's so moody and uncooperative all the time, and those *hoodlums* he hangs out with..."

"Careful," Slade warned. "You'll break that glass if you clutch it any tighter."

A smile danced across her lips, quickly vanishing. "I don't know how to handle him anymore. I feel like it's all my fault, that if only I'd spent more time with him, or been stricter, or more lenient, or...oh, I don't know."

Slade enclosed Tory's hand in his, catching her off guard and making her jump. His lightly callused fingertips stroked her wrist. She knew she ought to pull away. But Slade was being so nice for a change, and it was such a relief to unburden herself to someone else for once, and...oh, hell. She *loved* the way her hand felt in his.

"Believe me," he said, "Robby's problems aren't the result of anything you have or haven't done."

"Oh?" She watched the shadows from the ceiling fan glide slowly over his face, around and around again. "And how do you know so much about it?"

Anticipating another argument, Slade withdrew his hand from Tory's. But instead of the expected challenge in her voice, he heard only curiosity. His usual reticence to bring up his past began to dissolve under the genuine interest glimmering in her eyes.

He took a sip of his fresh bourbon, and with his thumbnail began to trace the delicate bones forming the back of Tory's hand. "Let's just say I understand where Robby's coming from."

"And why's that?" Her voice sounded dreamy and faraway, as silky and smooth as Puerto Rican rum.

"Because I came from the same place myself once." He cradled his glass in both hands and stared into the foggy depths of his drink. "I—had some problems myself when I was his age."

"You?" Tory blinked in surprise.

Slade chuckled at the amazement on her face. "Don't look so shocked."

"It's just that you seem so...so sure of yourself, so in control of your life."

His mouth curled into a wry grimace. "Thanks. But I wasn't always so sure of what I wanted to do with my life. Believe me, I got into more than my share of trouble when I was a teenager."

Tory skimmed one delicate fingertip along the rim of her glass, arousing a sharp and totally unexpected quickening in Slade's loins. "You're full of surprises tonight," she said.

He licked his lips. To his immense relief, the waiter arrived at that moment with their meal. Slade wasn't sure how to deal with the peculiar, tender sensations constricting his chest. He could handle Tory's icy hostility with no problem. But this unanticipated thaw in their relationship threw him for a loop.

After they'd had a chance to sample their food, she picked up where Slade had tried to leave off. "So what kind of trouble did you get into?"

He swallowed a savory morsel of crawfish. "Oh, the usual stuff. Joyriding, malicious mischief—that sort of thing."

"You seem to have turned out all right." She held a forkful of rice poised at her lips. "Maybe I shouldn't worry so much about Robby."

Slade scooped up the last spoonful of gumbo and swiped his napkin across his mouth. "Worrying won't help. Everyone's got to choose for himself what he's going to make out of his life. Some kids straighten out and others, well..." He shrugged. "With other kids, not all the worrying in the world makes any difference."

He was conscious of a harsh, uncompromising note creeping into his voice. Apparently Tory noticed it, too, for she fell silent and concentrated on eating. After a few minutes it was obvious their newfound camaraderie was cooling off faster than the food on their plates. They might as well have been sitting at separate tables.

Funny. A little while ago Slade had been anxious to keep Tory at an emotional arm's distance, but now he longed for that growing closeness, that spark of budding friendship that had ignited so unexpectedly.

He set down his glass harder than he'd intended to. "I didn't mean to sound callous," he said, not sure whether he was trying to apologize or not. "But believe me, I've been there. I've seen in my own family how some people seem destined for trouble, and how others manage to escape the most . . . disadvantaged circumstances."

"Is that what you did?"

Slade watched her slender fingers curl around the bowl of her wineglass, as if all that really interested her was exploring its shape, its texture. He could tell she was reluctant to pry, yet perversely, that knowledge made him want to tell her everything.

"I was third in a family of four brothers," he said. "The other three are either in jail or on parole."

Tory dropped her fork with a clatter. "Oh, Slade," she said in a low voice. "I don't know what to say."

"What's to say?" He finished chewing a mouthful of *étouffée* before continuing. "We grew up in a rundown part of Chicago that slid even further downhill as the years passed. I'd say the percentage of jailbirds in my family is a pretty accurate reflection of the neighborhood as a whole."

"Slade, you don't have to—"

"My father worked for the railroad, though he never rose very high on the job ladder because he kept showing up for work drunk. My mother worked in a factory—that is, when she wasn't busy drinking or dodging my father's fists."

"Dear God." Tory's hand trembled as she set down her butter knife.

"We never had much money since my parents drank most of it up. I guess that's why my brothers started stealing as soon as they were big enough to outrun the victims." He made a conscious effort to unclench his fists. "God only knows why I didn't do the same," he muttered.

"But you didn't."

The anxiety on Tory's face made Slade want to smile. "I confined my youthful hijinks to the occasional act of vandalism. Once in a while I'd borrow a car without the owner's permission." He shook his forefinger. "But I always returned it with a full tank of gas."

"Too bad all car thieves aren't so considerate."

"I guess I had a conscience even back then. I had my occasional scrapes with the law, but even at that age I could see there weren't any shortcuts to a better life." He pushed a chunk of French bread around his bowl. "I knew the only way I was going to escape my miserable background was to finish school and get a decent job."

Slade paused to quench his thirst. What the hell had possessed him to tell Tory all this stuff, anyway? He hadn't spoken of his childhood to anyone in years. Yet somehow the words kept tumbling out, as if the dam holding them back had finally collapsed under the strain. Or maybe it was Tory's concern, her sympathy and understanding that had made the dam disintegrate.

"That's why I can relate to Robby," he said, toying with his knife. "He reminds me of myself at that age."

"I only hope Robby turns out as well as you did." Tory blushed furiously as soon as the words were out of her mouth. "I mean, at least you're not a criminal or anything."

"Please, such praise! You'll embarrass me."

The heat subsided from Tory's cheeks, only to flame up again as she watched Slade's tanned fingers squeeze a lemon wedge over the last oyster. His eyes twinkled at her as he slid the slippery morsel into his mouth and smacked his lips. Well, now she knew at least *one* reason oysters were considered an aphrodisiac.

Her mouth went dry. "So what did you do after high school?" she asked, reaching for her water glass.

"Joined the fire department." He crossed his forearms on the table.

Tory nearly swallowed an ice cube. "*You* were a fireman?"

"No, they hired me as a dalmatian." He paused, then grinned at her. "Yes, I was a firefighter."

She didn't know why that should surprise her. Maybe because firefighters always seemed so...so selfless, so altruistic. Somehow she couldn't picture Slade coaxing a scared kitten out of a tree or giving fire safety lectures to schoolchildren.

On the other hand, it was easy to imagine him battering down a door with an ax or scrambling up a ladder to the fifth floor of a burning building. He had a reckless air about him, as if constantly eager to spring into action and barely capable of restraining himself.

Tory began to revise her original opinion of him. Maybe Slade was more than a shallow, self-centered, arrogant womanizer, after all. This evening, Slade had shown previously unsuspected facets of his character, like pieces of a jigsaw puzzle falling into place to reveal glimpses of the final unexpected picture.

Tantalizing glimpses. Glimpses that made Tory yearn to explore further this complex, intriguing man with the shadowy past.

This compelling desire to learn more about Slade overcame Tory's normal aversion to snooping. "Your parents must have been proud of you when you became a fireman."

Ooops! She'd gone too far. A curtain dropped across Slade's face as if signaling the end of his personal revelations. But he answered, inching the pad of his thumb along the blade of his knife, not looking at Tory.

"My father was slouched in front of the TV when I told him I'd been accepted by the fire department. He said, great, now that I had a job I could run down to the corner liquor store and buy him some booze. And before I left I could get him another beer out of the fridge."

The food in Tory's mouth suddenly tasted like sawdust.

"I guess I didn't move fast enough to suit him," he continued in a matter-of-fact monotone, "because he took a swing at me for some reason. I grabbed him by the wrist while his fist was still in midair." Slade raised his glass to his lips. "Except for the times I tried to defend my mother from him, that was the first time in my life I ever stood up to my father." He polished off the bourbon. "It was also the last time I ever saw him."

Tory gasped. "Oh, Slade."

"I left home for good that afternoon. My dad was killed a few weeks later in an accident down at the railroad yard. A couple of years later Mom finally drank herself to death."

Tory's eyes brimmed with tears. "Slade, I'm so sorry...."

"Yeah, well." He started to signal the waiter for another bourbon, then thought better of it. "I didn't mean to make my parents sound like complete monsters. They weren't." He laced his fingers together on the table. "They were just...weak. Weak and unhappy and beaten down by life. I guess they coped with it the only way they knew how."

"But to hit your mother, your brothers and you..."

The blows still hurt Slade. Maybe they always would. But he'd learned to cope with the pain. "You have to consider the times. Today child abuse horrifies us, but back then the old spare-the-rod-spoil-the-child philosophy made physical punishment a lot more acceptable." He reached for the check. "And in the neighborhood where I grew up, there was still an unspoken consensus that slapping the old lady around somehow made you more of a man."

"But still, I can't imagine what it must have been like—hey, wait a second!" Tory snatched at the check. "We're going dutch, remember?"

Slade extracted a bill from his wallet and covered the check with it. "Keep your money. You're going to need it until you get the insurance check."

Unspoken was the caution, "*If* you get the insurance check."

Reality was like a cold bucket of water dashed in Tory's face. Here she was, enjoying a wonderful meal and practically swooning under Slade's spell, while her whole life lay in ruins. How could she have forgotten the very real possibility that—thanks to Slade—there might *be* no insurance check?

And how could she have wasted money on a sumptuous dinner while Nana and Robby were counting on her to provide for them?

But pride took precedence over poverty. Tory shoved a handful of bills at Slade. "I only agreed to have dinner with you if we each paid our own way."

He pushed the money back. "Consider this dinner payment for suffering through my melodramatic life story."

"I didn't suffer, I'm glad you confided in me." She nudged the money back in his direction. "Besides, we had a deal."

"Come on, Tory." He moved the money back to her side of the table. "I promise I won't expect you to sleep with me or anything." He gave her a lascivious wink. "At least not tonight."

She scraped back her chair so hard it nearly tipped over. "You're insufferable, do you know that?" She flung the bills at him one last time. "Just when I start to think there might be a decent human being beneath that obnoxious facade, you say something like that." She grabbed her purse from the table. "I don't know why it surprises me anymore."

With that, she fled from the restaurant with as much outraged dignity as she could muster. It was hard to be outraged when Slade's nasty remark had cut her to the quick, and hard to be dignified while dodging waiters and maneuvering around crowded tables.

Outside on Chartres Street she took a quick left, figuring Slade would expect her to turn right, toward the bed-and-breakfast where she was staying. She scooted nimbly past a group of out-of-town conventioneers gawking at the sights, and was soon in Jackson Square. On her right loomed the enormous white expanse of the St. Louis Cathedral, ghostly in the moonlight. Even at this hour tourists were clustered in front of it, surrounding a group of street musicians who poured forth a raucous rendition of "When the Saints Go Marching In."

"Sometimes I think I'll scream if I hear that song one more time," Tory muttered to herself.

"Ah, but the tourists love it," said a voice at her shoulder.

With a little half scream, Tory whirled around to find Slade grinning at her. "What are you—how did you—"

"You weren't hard to find," he said. "All I had to do was follow the trail of bowled-over bodies left in your wake."

"I didn't knock anyone down," she said crossly. "And I'll thank you not to sneak up behind me like that."

"You're just mad because I caught you talking to yourself."

"No, that's *not* why I'm so mad." She lowered her voice when a strolling couple stared at her. "I'm mad at myself for even considering the possibility that you might be a nice guy after all." She backed away from him. "You certainly set me straight on that score." She turned and strode off rapidly in the direction of the river. She was passing the statue of Andrew Jackson in the middle of the square before Slade caught up with her again.

He must have been practicing an apology, because he still sounded a bit rusty. "Look, I'm sorry for that crack I made back in the restaurant," he said. "It was completely uncalled for, especially after you were polite enough to listen to my morbid reminiscing."

"I told you, I didn't mind listening to you talk about your past." She slowed to a more leisurely pace. "I thought it was . . . well, *nice* that you felt you could confide in me."

"Yeah, well, I'm glad you feel that way. Now if you'd only return the favor."

Tory halted. "What are you talking about?"

"I'm talking about the reason for our having dinner together." At her blank stare, he snapped his fingers as if trying to bring her out of a trance. "Fontaine, remember? We were going to talk about your business partner and why he emptied out your bank account last week."

"Oh. That."

"Yes, *that.*"

Before Tory had a chance to gather her scattered wits and formulate a response, they reached the wooden boardwalk cresting the levee along the Mississippi. Her sigh was lost in the gentle splash of waves rippling against the embankment. "I suppose I should start at the beginning."

"Usually a sensible idea." Slade drew her to a bench facing the water. "Let's sit down and watch the ships go by for a while."

Tory eyed him with suspicion. "I thought you wanted to talk about Gideon."

"We can do both. And you don't have to cower at the far end of the bench like that. I promise I won't bite."

That wasn't what Tory was afraid of, but she inched a little closer to him, anyway.

He leaned his head back and expanded his broad chest, filling his lungs with the moist tropical air. Tory drew a deep breath, too. The night was rich with the mingled aromas of honeysuckle and ship fuel and coffee from a nearby café. "Mmm, smell that," Slade said with an appreciative sigh. "Nothing else like it in the whole wide world."

The expanse of bench between them was gradually shrinking. Faint strains of jazz drifted over from a nightclub on Decatur Street. The plaintive wail of a saxophone solo soared up to pierce the starry sky. Its mournful, bittersweet lament stirred a poignant yearning inside Tory's soul. She shivered.

"Don't tell me you're still cold." Somehow Slade was sitting right beside her, his breath ruffling wisps of hair at her temple. He eased his arm around her shoulders and began to rub vigorously up and down. "It's gotta be at least eighty degrees out still."

"I'm...fine," she replied, her words vibrating as Slade jostled her with his helpful attentions. Of course, her voice would have quivered anyway, considering how her heart was pounding. Slade's sensual aura of raw masculinity enveloped her, making her thankful that at least she was sitting down. She doubted her knees would have supported her at that moment.

"So tell me," she began, casting about for some neutral topic of conversation that would take her mind off the swooping butterflies in her stomach, "how did a Yankee from Chicago wind up in New Orleans?"

Slade gave her shoulder one last squeeze. "A few years ago I went through some major changes in my life." He trailed a finger down Tory's spine. The jackhammer in her chest shifted into a higher speed. "I needed a change of scenery—someplace to make a fresh start."

"But why New Orleans?"

"Because it's completely different from Chicago, I suppose." His eyes shone like burnished emeralds in the golden glow from a street lamp across the boardwalk. "I visited here once a long time ago. The place made quite an impression on me."

"It does on most people," Tory said. For some reason she was pleased that Slade had fallen in love with her city.

"Let me guess—I'll bet you a million dollars you came here for Mardi Gras."

Slade paused a beat. "You lose," he said. "I came here on my honeymoon."

Tory flew to the far end of the bench so fast she nearly toppled off. Her heart stuttered painfully, as if a *real* jackhammer had buried itself in her chest. "I should have known," she exclaimed, trying to choke back her dismay and indignation. "You're married!"

The butterflies collapsed in a heap at the pit of her stomach.

Chapter Six

"*Was* married," Slade corrected her. "Past tense." He stretched over and chucked Tory under the chin. "But you got a little upset there, didn't you, thinking I might be unavailable?"

She swatted his hand away. "I've no doubt you wouldn't hesitate to make yourself *available*, as you put it, even if you *were* married."

"Ah, Tory, that's where you're wrong." He clasped his hands behind his head and leaned back. "I was a completely faithful husband."

She hesitated. Curiosity got the best of her. "So...what happened?"

The effect of his shrug was to raise one elbow in the air. "The usual. Same old story. Divorce."

"How long have you been—"

"Four years. Look, could we get on with this?" He bounded to his feet as if unable to sit still one second longer.

Well, she didn't need to be hit over the head with a sledgehammer to take the hint. Obviously Slade's marriage was one chapter in his life he didn't want to talk about. Considering his willingness to reveal other unhappy chapters, his divorce must have been extremely traumatic.

Tory wondered if he were still in love with his wife. *Ex*-wife, she reminded herself. Not that it made any difference to her *whom* Slade Marshall was in love with.

He propped himself against the lamppost, arms folded and one foot crossed over the other. "You say you met Fontaine a year ago?" he asked.

The halo of light didn't quite reach his face. Tory couldn't see his eyes, but she heard the businesslike, almost stern tone, in his voice. Apparently they were back to being investigator and chief suspect.

She shifted her thoughts, trying to figure out how much she could tell Slade without throwing suspicion on people she cared about. Then his earlier words came back to her. Slade was right: she was a fool for trying to protect someone who'd betrayed her. Tory was through trying to cover up for Gideon.

"As I said, I met him a year ago," she began. "He'd moved to New Orleans shortly before from one of the parishes in southwest Louisiana. His ancestry is Cajun, and he'd recently inherited a share of some land where his family had trapped and fished for generations."

"Where did you meet him?"

Tory frowned. "Truthfully I don't remember the first time I laid eyes on him. Sooner or later, you just get to know everyone who lives in or hangs around the Quarter." She rubbed her forehead. "I think the first time I actually spoke to him was while watching a parade about a year ago. Must have been for the Fourth of July." She flipped up her palms. "Who knows? New Orleanians love parades. There must be one down Bourbon Street practically every week."

"So you became friends with Gideon."

"Well, not exactly..."

"It was more than that?" Tory detected a sudden alertness in Slade's posture. He was certainly curious about whether or not she and Gideon had been lovers.

"It was less than that," she corrected him.

Slade cocked his head to one side. "You'll have to elaborate on that remark."

"What I mean is, you couldn't exactly call Gideon and me friends. Friends have to trust each other, for one thing, and I never quite trusted Gideon."

Slade scratched the back of his neck. "Yet you went into business with him."

"I was desperate," Tory said simply.

"Hmm, yeah. Desperate."

No doubt he was wondering if she were desperate enough to burn down the Creole Courtyard for the insurance money.

"Why didn't you trust him?" Slade asked.

"It's hard to say exactly." Tory's gaze followed an oil tanker's slow progress upriver. "Gideon has this footloose, devil-may-care quality about him. He's only a kid—well, that's not quite true. He's in his mid-twenties, I suppose. But he *acts* like a kid—reckless, impulsive, always trying to see how much he can get away with."

"Hardly the ideal business partner." Slade refolded his arms and shifted his weight from one leg to the other. "If that's all he was."

Tory looked up sharply. "I told you, there wasn't anything personal between us."

"Okay, okay." He tucked his hands into his pockets. "I'm only trying to figure out how someone as responsible and down-to-earth as you are got tangled up with such an unreliable character."

"I told you, I was desperate." Tory focused her sights on the twinkling lights of the twin-span highway bridge a mile up the river. "You see, Gideon had all this money he'd gotten from selling the land he inherited to an oil company. I think he had dreams of investing it and living off the proceeds so he'd never have to work another day in his life." She laughed ruefully. "Not that he ever worked too hard, anyway, unless playing poker qualifies as work."

She twisted her hands in her lap. "I tried to be honest with him, to explain that it might take years before the guest house turned into a money-maker, but Gideon insisted he wanted to invest." She shook her head regretfully. "I think he was enamored with the idea of becoming a fancy French Quarter hotelier or something."

"How did your partnership work out?"

Boy, Slade sure didn't need his trusty clipboard to come up with some touchy questions. Tory rose to her feet and stepped to the opposite edge of the boardwalk, a few yards from Slade's lamppost.

"Things worked out fine for a while," she said. "I used Gideon's money to pay for the most urgently needed repairs. At first I was worried he might insist on helping me run the business, but I should have known his aversion to work would keep him out of my hair." She smiled, pushing the hair in question back over her shoulders. "The only times Gideon ever showed up at the guest house were when he had a bunch of visiting relatives in tow or was trying to impress some new girlfriend."

"That must have thrilled LuAnne."

Tory's eyes widened in surprise. "How do you know about LuAnne's crush on Gideon?"

"I got her address from the university and interviewed her this afternoon." Slade nudged himself away from the lamppost. "Every other word out of her mouth was 'Gideon.' Doesn't take a rocket scientist to figure out your former maid has a major case of the hots for that guy."

Tory didn't even want to ask how he'd managed to con LuAnne's address out of the school. "What did LuAnne say about last night?" she asked, trying to sound casual.

Slade bent forward, peering cautiously from side to side before whispering confidentially, "She didn't do it."

Tory jerked back abruptly. "Of course she didn't. What I meant was—"

"—Did her story jibe with yours." He reached out and twirled a lock of Tory's hair around his finger. "Don't worry, LuAnne told me the same story you did—she left early when you gave her the night off, et cetera."

Tory tugged her hair free. "Ouch!" Really, for a hotshot investigator, Slade was incredibly unprofessional. "Does she have a—a—an alibi?"

"What's the matter, are you suspicious of LuAnne all of a sudden?" His mouth twitched at the edges.

"No, of course not," Tory said indignantly. "But according to you, *someone* must have set the fire. *I* didn't do it, and I know darn good and well Robby didn't do it, so I'm only trying to think of *someone*—"

"Let's get back to Gideon."

Tory shook her head emphatically. "It couldn't have been him. He—well, he's out of town."

"Tory, Tory." Slade stroked his thumb along his jaw. "I thought you were going to come clean with me."

"I *am*—oh, all right," she said, resigning herself to the inevitable. She stared unhappily at the shimmering reflections cast by lights along the river. "It's my own stupid fault," she said finally.

"What is?" Slade's voice was a low rumble that set her nerves thrumming.

"This whole mess with Gideon." Tory threw her hands in the air. "I should have listened to my instincts and known he couldn't be trusted. I should have known he wasn't the type who could patiently wait years for a return on his investment. I shouldn't have taken his money, but I was so—so—"

"Desperate," Slade finished for her. "And quit pacing. You're making me seasick."

"I guess everyone else saw what I was too stubborn to admit—that the Creole Courtyard was a losing proposition. I couldn't find any other investors." She bowed her head in despair. "I don't know—maybe I took advantage of Gideon."

"Seems like the other way around to me." Slade tipped her chin up with his finger, forcing her to meet his eyes. "Gideon's the one who left you high and dry, remember."

Tory looked away, embarrassed for Slade to see the tears in her eyes. What a mess she'd made of everything, what a beautiful job of botching up!

Swallowing, she forced down the lump in her throat. With her back to Slade she went on, "You know the rest of the story, it seems. Two days ago I got a call from the bank, telling me my checks were bouncing all over the place." She wiped the moisture from her eyes. "That's when I discovered that Gideon had cleaned out our account last week."

Slade rested his hands on her shoulders. "Where is he now?" he asked gently.

Tory dropped her head back and looked up at the sky. "I only wish I knew." Without thinking, she leaned back against Slade. "I tried to find him, of course. I checked the apartment he rents on Royal Street, along with all his usual hangouts. No one had seen him for days. He's simply dropped out of sight."

A paddle-wheeled riverboat brimming with tourists splashed by, heading for its berth. From the sounds of music and loud laughter bubbling across the water, everyone was having a marvelous time. Their carefree merriment only increased the bleakness of Tory's mood.

"I suppose Gideon's hiding out with his relatives," she said with a sigh, "although he has nothing to worry about. Legally he's entitled to that money, even if it bankrupts me." She buried her face in her hands, muffling her voice. "Not that it matters anymore. Not with the Creole Courtyard gone."

"Hey, hey, what's this?" Slade turned her around to face him. "This can't be the same sunny, optimistic Tory Clayton who told me only this morning how lucky she was."

"Did I say that? I must have been in shock."

"Come on, now. No one was hurt in the fire, you still have your memories..." He ducked his head to peer into her lowered face. "Any of this sound familiar?"

A reluctant smile tugged at the corners of Tory's mouth. Amazing how nice Slade could be when he really tried.

"There, that's more like it," he said, giving her a little shake. "You had me worried for a second. I mean, when Tory Clayton gets down in the dumps, the rest of us are *really* in trouble."

To Slade's relief, Tory had stopped looking as if she were about to fling herself into the river in front of a speeding boat. He could hardly blame her for feeling depressed. Despite his little pep talk, her life really *was* kind of a mess. But he shouldn't let himself feel sorry for her, or wonder where she would live and how she was going to support herself and her family.

He *sure* as hell shouldn't be worrying about what was wrong with Grandma Clayton and whether or not Robby would manage to stay out of serious trouble long enough to grow up. Slade had learned from bitter experience that it didn't pay to care too much about other people.

It was one thing to care about humanity in the abstract. After all, that was why he'd become a firefighter and then an arson investigator. But it was another matter entirely to get intimately entangled with people on a one-to-one basis.

He'd finally managed to detach himself emotionally from his own family. He certainly didn't need to shackle himself to a new one.

So why did the sight of Tory fighting bravely to hold back tears practically drive a stake through his heart?

He tried again. "Look at the bright side. At least you don't have to—oh, hell, come here, sweetheart." With that he pulled Tory roughly against him, furious at the fates for the hand they'd dealt her, furious with himself for caring.

But all Slade wanted to do at that moment was banish Tory's unhappiness and lighten the heavy burden on her fragile shoulders any way he could.

He stroked her hair, marveling at its silken texture and the glossy black sheen imparted by the street lamp. She smelled of jasmine, and her cheeks felt like dew-laden magnolia petals when he clumsily tried to brush the tears away.

When she lifted her head from his shoulder her deep blue eyes shone like the starry midnight sky with an expression so innocent, so trusting, that it nearly broke his heart. He had no business getting involved with her like this.

Because where Slade was concerned there was only one possible outcome to a romantic relationship. And he thought Tory had endured enough disaster lately.

But some unnameable, overwhelming force seemed to draw them together as surely as two ships on a collision course. He was unable to steer his gaze away from hers, or to heed the warning sirens blaring inside his head. He saw Tory's slender throat constrict as she swallowed, saw the tip of her tongue as she moistened her trembling lips.

They drifted closer together, breaths mingling and drawn with anticipation, until their lips met in the inevitable collision.

A surge of desire swept over Slade like the crash of breakers when he felt Tory's mouth warm and eager beneath his, eagerly welcoming and responding to his kiss. He circled his arms around her, loving the sweet, soft sensation of her breasts pressed against his chest. Her cascading hair tickled the backs of his hands, and her fingers made delicious whispering sounds as she made tentative, experimental forays across his unshaven jaw.

Even more shocking to Slade than the explosion of heat in his loins was the rush of tenderness that flooded him, threatening to drown his determined, well-practiced detachment. His emotional core, the secret, well-protected compartment he had so successfully sealed off for years from any genuine human contact, was being battered from all directions by wave after wave of rediscovered feelings.

Not to mention the torrent of feelings totally new to Slade's experience.

A tiny moan of pleasure escaped from Tory's parted lips, loosening Slade from his precarious ledge of restraint. He eased his tongue inside her mouth, finding her even more intoxicating than he'd imagined.

That was it: he was drunk. With his senses swimming, it was the only explanation Slade could conjure up for this reckless plunge into oblivion. But deep inside he knew he wasn't drunk, that if he succumbed to this foolhardy temptation he would find himself trapped by an even more dangerous addiction.

Fear was like a life preserver tossed out to rescue him from treacherous emotional currents. Unable to resist one final taste of Tory's sweet, velvety mouth, Slade finally dragged his lips from hers. He held her at arm's length, panting, forcing himself to meet her eyes without flinching.

The hurt bewilderment scrawled on her lovely pale face was like a dozen lashes with a whip. Slade did his best to steel himself against the pain—both his own and Tory's. Not an easy task while her lips glistened in the moonlight with the moisture of his kiss.

"We have to stop this," he said, the ache in his soul making his voice come out more harshly than he'd intended. "It isn't . . . proper . . . for us to get involved like this."

At any other time the notion of Slade Marshall caring about propriety would have entertained Tory immensely. But not now—not when she could still feel the lingering pressure of his insistent mouth on hers and the heart-stopping thrill of his hands caressing her, comforting her, assuring her that everything would turn out all right, as long as Slade Marshall was in her life.

Ha. What a joke. From the look on his face he didn't even want to share the same *state* with her, much less share her life.

A sob rose in her chest, threatening to burst from her lips and totally humiliate her in front of Slade. Not that she wasn't about ninety-nine percent humiliated already, the way he'd thrust her aside after she'd so eagerly thrown herself into his arms.

Well, that's what she got for letting self-pity get the best of her. She'd let Slade catch her off guard in a moment of weakness. Next time she wouldn't be seduced by his phony words of comfort and his treacherous pats on the shoulder.

Not that there was going to *be* a next time, of course.

At least they both agreed on *that* issue. "If anyone found out I got involved with a suspect during an investigation, it would mean professional suicide." Slade's lips moved stiffly while he spoke. Probably he felt contaminated by her kiss.

"You needn't worry," Tory replied with a sniff. "I haven't spotted any watchdogs from the state insurance commission lurking behind the lampposts. Of course, they might be out on that freight barge spying on us through a pair of binoculars."

"Look, it's not that I'm paranoid about being seen with you." He jammed his fingers through his hair so viciously he gave the impression of tearing it out. He set his jaw at a belligerent angle and cursed under his breath. At least Tory *assumed* any words muttered in that tone must be curses.

"Then what is it?" she asked, irritated with herself for prolonging this obvious brush-off. But somehow she couldn't quite believe that Slade would let some vague threat to his job squelch the undeniable chemistry between them.

"Getting involved with you would be...unprofessional."

So Tory was mistaken. Both about Slade's priorities and about the mutuality of their feelings. Apparently, he was quite willing to sacrifice a potentially rewarding relationship for his precious career.

Well, why should that surprise her? Slade had made it perfectly plain that superficial relationships were the only ones that interested him. And whatever kind of strange current had passed between them a moment ago, it was anything but superficial.

At least for Tory.

"Heaven forbid I should tarnish your professional reputation," she said. "It won't happen again, I promise."

The rigid set of his features shifted slightly. "I didn't mean—"

"You made it quite clear what you meant. Are you through interviewing me?"

"Tory—"

She dodged beyond reach of his outstretched hand. "Because it's awfully late, and I've got to get home. I mean, back to Don's place." A lump in her throat pinched off the end of her sentence.

The silence between them grew as oppressive as the humidity.

"Yeah," Slade said finally. "I guess I'm through interviewing you."

"Okay. Well. Goodbye, then."

"Hey, hold it," he called. His feet pounded on the boardwalk as he jogged after her. "Let me walk you back to your car."

She kept moving as fast as she could in those stupid high heels. "My car's parked in the garage where I rent space. I'm walking back to Don's."

"Not at this hour you're not. Not by yourself, anyway."

"Don't be ridiculous. I've lived here all my life—"

"I'm sure that'll impress the average purse snatcher. But just to be on the safe side, I'll walk you home."

At the edge of Jackson Square she was forced to wait for a mule-drawn carriage full of tourists to pass, the driver informing his passengers in a loud monotone, "And here on the left is the Presbytère, part of the Louisiana State Museum...."

"I'll be perfectly safe," Tory insisted as Slade dogged her steps across St. Ann Street. "Look at all the people still on the streets."

"I'll bet some of them have more on their minds than seeing the sights and browsing through T-shirt shops," Slade said.

She stopped in front of a closed-up antique store. "Look," she said, annoyance joining her anxiety to get away from him, "cut the Sir Galahad act. I'm perfectly capable of walking a few blocks without a bodyguard. I don't *need* you to escort me, I don't *want* you to escort me, and I wish you'd leave me alone!"

Without waiting for a reply, Tory strode briskly down the street, past darkened apartments and shops barricaded with iron gates. Her heels wobbled on the uneven stone sidewalk, and she nearly sprained an ankle stepping off the curb.

But at least she'd gotten rid of Slade.

Damn him, anyway. Who did he think he was, barging into her life with his sly accusations and then luring her into his arms with his smooth-talking charm, just so he could have the pleasure of crumpling her up and tossing her aside like a used hot dog wrapper?

Well, to be honest, Slade hadn't *looked* exactly pleased while he was so cold-bloodedly disposing of her. Maybe he wasn't as hard-hearted and calculating as he acted. But actions and words spoke louder than unreadable facial expressions. Tory was sick and tired of trying to figure Slade out. Why should she bother, anyway? All she wanted from him was the damn insurance money. And if he used that kiss as a pretext to delay or deny her that check, she would report him to the insurance company and see that he never—

A looming hulk stepped from a dark doorway and blocked Tory's path. Fear rose in her throat, choking off her gasp of surprise. She hesitated for only an instant before trying to step around him.

It was like trying to sidestep a Sherman tank. The man maneuvered in front of her without even appearing to move. Adrenaline pumped through Tory's bloodstream. She stepped off the curb, intending to dart across the street, or maybe attract the attention of a cruising taxicab driver.

"Hey, what's your hurry?" The man's sausage-sized fingers were suddenly wrapped around Tory's wrist.

If only she'd had time to take that self-defense class LuAnne had wanted them both to sign up for last winter! "Let go of me!" she yelled, hoping the anger she was trying to inject into her voice would conceal her chattering teeth.

"I only want to—"

"You heard the lady."

Tory nearly swooned with relief at the sound of Slade's voice.

"Is there a problem?" he continued pleasantly, although his voice carried an undertone that was decidedly *un*pleasant.

The Sherman tank must have noticed it, too. He dropped Tory's hand like a live grenade. "No problem," he said in a voice laced with the Brooklyn-type accent common in New Orleans. "I only wanted to ask the lady a couple of questions, is all."

Today seemed to be Tory's day for being interrogated. Now that Slade was standing next to her, balancing his weight on the balls of his feet as if preparing to spring to her defense, her terror evaporated.

Squinting in the poor light to get a better look at the man who'd accosted her, Tory realized he was vaguely familiar. Not too many characters of his height and breadth lurking around the French Quarter unnoticed.

"Haven't I seen you somewhere before?" she asked.

"'S possible." He chewed on a wad of something Tory doubted was bubble gum. "I'm lookin' for a friend of yours."

Tory sincerely doubted they had any friends in common. "Who?"

"Gideon Fontaine."

She snorted. "Join the club," she said. "I'm looking for him, this gentleman here is looking for him, and probably a sizable portion of the New Orleans female population is looking for him, too."

"What do you want with Fontaine?" Slade asked.

"And how did you know where to find me?" Tory chimed in. It was a relief not to be on the receiving end of a question for a change, she decided.

The man chewed some more before replying, then spat into the gutter. Definitely not bubble gum. "I heard you was staying at the Bayou Bed and Breakfast after your place burned down. Figured you'd show up sooner or later if I waited long enough."

The French Quarter grapevine was operating with its usual speed and efficiency, Tory noted. If only she could remember where she knew this guy from . . .

"What do you want with Fontaine?" Slade repeated, this time enunciating his words loudly and clearly as if addressing someone who wasn't too swift.

The man eyed Slade suspiciously. "That's my business," he said. To Tory he growled, "You see Fontaine, you tell him Jake's lookin' for him, got that?"

"Sure, since you asked so nicely and all." Her sarcasm was wasted on the human tank, who gave one curt, satisfied nod before turning and lumbering down the street, probably off to lay waste to some small country.

"*That's* who he is," Tory exclaimed, snapping her fingers.

"Who?"

"That guy works for Jake Ireland."

"Who?"

"You sound like an owl. Jake Ireland. He owns one of those tacky souvenir shops down on Decatur. Our friend there is one of his hired hands."

"I bet *he's* good for business."

"The store's just a front. Ireland runs some kind of high-stakes poker game in the back late at night after the store closes." Slade fell in beside Tory as she started slowly down the sidewalk. She pressed one finger to her chin. "Now what could Jake Ireland want with Gideon?"

"Come on, it's pretty obvious, isn't it?"

"Well, I don't suppose Ireland sent one of his goons after Gideon because he's anxious to sell him some postcards, if that's what you mean." She frowned. "Maybe it has something to do with that poker game?"

"Uh-huh."

"Maybe the time or location's been changed?"

"And Ireland sent his messenger boy to inform all the regulars personally? Uh-uh. It doesn't work that way. Your pal Gideon must owe Ireland a sizable chunk of change."

"Quit calling him my pal. And why are you so sure Gideon owes him money?"

"It's the only explanation that makes sense. Why else would Ireland be so anxious to find him? Besides, it fits, doesn't it?" Slade poked her arm. "That's probably why Gideon cleared out your bank account."

Tory clapped her hands over her face and groaned. "I had a hunch it might have something to do with gambling debts."

"You might have mentioned your hunch to me a little sooner."

Tory uncovered her face. "What for? It has nothing to do with the fire."

"Doesn't it?"

They arrived at the entrance to the Bayou Bed and Breakfast. "Here we are, safe and sound," Slade said, holding the gate open for Tory. "Good thing I can't take no for an answer, huh?"

She rang the after-hours bell. "What are you talking about?"

"I mean, if I hadn't ignored your protests and decided to follow you anyway, you might not have made it back here."

"For heaven's sake, the man only wanted to ask me a simple question." She heard approaching footsteps inside. "I hardly needed you to come to my rescue."

The door was opened by a gray-haired, fiftyish man in his bathrobe. "Hi, Don." Tory stepped quickly inside the foyer.

"Fine," Slade said, cramming his hands into his pockets and rocking back on his heels. "Next time you can fend for yourself."

"There isn't going to *be* a next time," Tory informed him, shutting the door in his face. "Not if I have anything to say about it," she added in an undertone.

"Tory? Who was that?"

"Him? Nobody." Her host's appearance registered for the first time. "Oh, no—did I wake you up, Don? I didn't realize it was so late."

"No problem." He yawned and tightened the sash of his bathrobe. "I had to get up to answer the door, anyway."

She smiled feebly at his joke. Then she remembered something. "Is Robby—have you seen my brother tonight?"

"Sure." Don waved sleepily at the stairs. "He came in a couple hours ago. I gave him the room next to yours."

Relief accompanied Tory up the narrow, curving staircase—relief mixed with guilty gratitude. She knew darn good and well that the only reason Robby had shown up here tonight was because of Slade's influence.

Slade, whose kiss had stirred Tory to such a fever pitch of desire.

Slade, whom Tory had vowed to avoid like the plague from now on.

Slade, in whose face Tory had just slammed the door.

Chapter Seven

Slade tossed aside his pen and leaned back in his chair, propping his feet on top of the report he'd been working on. His eyes felt gritty when he rubbed them. Small wonder, considering over the last two nights he'd gotten a grand total of maybe four hours of sleep.

You're just stressed out from working too hard lately, he told himself. His insomnia had absolutely nothing to do with a certain alluring guest house owner.

He shoved back from his desk and switched off the ceiling fan he'd installed while converting his above-ground basement into an office. Not for the first time he reflected how lucky it was—for him, anyway—that the land around New Orleans was too swampy for normal underground basements. The ground floor of his house had not only protected the main living quarters from the floods that ravaged the city back in the old days, it also provided a perfect place for Slade's office.

When he'd bought the nineteenth-century raised cottage three years ago, Slade had chuckled at its architectural designation. Some cottage. With its twelve-foot ceilings and broad colonnaded gallery, both designed to cool the house in the days before air-conditioning, it was a far cry from what Slade considered a cottage. Back in the section of Chicago he came from, this would practically be called a mansion.

It certainly hadn't looked too impressive when Slade had first bought it, though. It had looked downright seedy, in fact. But the Lower Garden District was a neighborhood in transition, with hordes of young professionals buying up and restoring the historic, rundown homes to their former glory.

Slade had rolled up his sleeves and done most of the renovations himself, and by the time he was finished had fallen in love with the sound craftsmanship underlying the frayed electrical wires and outdated plumbing. The house's practical yet exotic design was reminiscent of West Indian architecture, and was about as far removed from your basic Chicago row house as you could get.

Which was just fine with Slade.

As he trudged upstairs and got a beer from the refrigerator, he thought of how much he loved this city, this funky neighborhood, this solid, comfortable house.

So what the hell had been eating him the last couple of days, anyway?

He popped open the beer and swallowed a mouthful of foam as he stepped outside. He shut the door quickly behind him to keep the sultry air from invading the air-conditioned coolness inside, then crossed the front gallery. Lounging against the cypress railing, he stared morosely at the Mississippi River, visible about half a mile away between a couple of sprawling warehouses.

"Maybe you need a vacation," he said.

In the street below, a couple of kids on skateboards gave him mystified looks, then burst into loud guffaws as they continued down the block.

Great. Now the whole neighborhood would think he'd gone loony.

Know that crazy Yankee up the street? He talks to himself. Slade could hear the gossip already.

Well, since when had he cared what other people thought? If social pressure to conform had ever been a factor in Slade's behavior, he'd probably be in prison by now.

Maybe he was still struggling too hard to escape his miserable legacy. At the moment he had three full-time investigations for three different insurance companies going at once. What was he trying to prove, anyway? And to whom?

Maybe it was time he found another line of work. The stress of dealing with lowlife arsonists and distraught fire victims had to take its toll after a while.

But as always, whenever Slade considered changing careers, he remembered that awful night in Chicago thirteen years ago, when he was still a firefighter.

He'd been one of the first at the scene of a blazing South Side tenement, and realized immediately that the building would be a total loss. What concerned him, however, was not the destruction of property but the hysterical woman out front on the sidewalk. "My babies, my babies!" she screamed over and over. "They're still inside!"

She was too distraught with terror to respond to Slade's questioning, but one of the other residents huddled outside in pajamas and blankets told him the woman lived in the back apartment on the top floor.

Without hesitation Slade dashed into the inferno and up three flights of stairs. He had to feel his way down the narrow, smoke-filled corridor. Once inside the apartment he flung open cupboards and closet doors, straining to hear a sound—any human sound—over the crackle of flames.

He found a child about three years old cowering under the bed. He or she—it was impossible to determine through the smoke and soot if it were a boy or girl—made faint whimpering sounds in Slade's ear as he carried it from room to room, frantically searching for any others. The woman *had* said babies, hadn't she? So there must be at least one more trapped inside this apartment, right? Doomed to die unless Slade found him or her or them.

Despite his protective mask, the smoke was starting to make him woozy. When the child in his arms went limp, Slade knew with a sinking heart he had to get out of the building. Maybe he hadn't heard correctly; maybe there *were* no more babies.

But when he deposited the unconscious child in the arms of the paramedics, the mother screamed even more hysterically than before. "Where's Lucy? Where's my baby? Oh, God, she's still inside...."

Instantly Slade headed back into the inferno, but another firefighter blocked his path. "It's too late! You'll never make it back out! It's suicide!"

Slade shoved him aside and tried to dodge up the front steps, but other firefighters physically restrained him. It took four of them to hold him back.

Little Lucy died in that fire, but something was born inside Slade. As he stood in front of a cheering audience three weeks later to receive a medal for heroism, all he could hear was the roar of flames and the screams of a heartbroken mother. That morning he'd found out that the fire had been set by the landlord, who'd been unable to obtain a permit to tear down the building and put up something more profitable.

A white heat had burned inside Slade from that day forward, a flame stoked by rage against those who could ruthlessly commit such a crime, regardless of who got hurt or lost their homes. Or died.

From the ashes of that fire rose Slade's determination to do everything in his power to track down the people responsible for such atrocities and see that they were punished.

He'd enrolled in college courses at night and after six long years earned a degree in criminology. He'd worked as an investigator for the Chicago Fire Department and then for various insurance companies before striking out on his own.

Every step of the way he was plagued by the memory of that fire, by the searing heat on his face and the burning smoke in his lungs and the tormented cries in his ears.

Each time he wondered if he shouldn't slow down a little, maybe cut back his hours or try teaching for a change, Slade remembered that blaze and felt the white heat rise up inside him. Something drove him to do this work, the same way something had driven him to yank himself up by his bootstraps and drag himself out of the wretchedness of his upbringing.

The same way something drove him now to pour the dregs of his beer down the sink, hop in his car and head for St. Charles Avenue.

He knew he should stay away, shouldn't even *think* about paying her a visit.

But he kept driving, anyway.

"Nana, I'm not going to listen to any more of this. I mean it!" Tory clamped her hands over her ears and began to sing loudly. "Oh, when the saints . . . go marching in . . ."

Marie Clayton sighed with disgust and pressed her hands over her own ears. "Land sakes, child, quit that awful caterwauling! You're setting my recovery back."

Tory's hands hovered an inch from her ears. "So you won't mention going into a nursing home anymore?"

"If that's what it takes to keep a little peace and quiet around this hospital, then I guess I owe it to the other patients." She smoothed an invisible wrinkle from her pink nightgown. "Honestly, Victoria, I don't know what comes over you sometimes."

"There's a full moon tonight, Nana."

"You know I don't put stock in such foolishness. Voodoo and vampires and the like—ha!" She wagged a crooked finger at her granddaughter. "I'll wager your peculiar behavior lately has a lot more to do with a certain handsome fire investigator than it has to do with any such superstitious folderol."

"If I've been acting strange lately, maybe it's because my home and business went up in smoke three days ago." Tory fluffed her grandmother's pillow. "Or maybe I'm worried about *you*."

"All the more reason why I should—"

"Ah-ah-ah," Tory warned. "You promised. No more talk about nursing homes. You're coming home with me when the doctor checks you out of this place tomorrow, and that's final."

"But Victoria, dear, we don't even *have* a home." The old woman's eyes filmed over, and Tory realized with a stab of grief that the loss of the Creole Courtyard had upset her grandmother far more than she let on. It was so like her to put up a brave front for Tory's sake. And it made Tory even more determined to rebuild the guest house.

"Nana, I've been checking some figures and talking to some contractors, and it looks like we'll be able to rebuild." *If* the insurance check comes through, she added to herself. An unwanted vision of Slade Marshall forced its way into her mind. Tory shoved it firmly out again. She was getting lots of practice at that lately.

Marie arched a skeptical eyebrow. "But how is that possible? From what you've told me, the Creole Courtyard is in ruins. That scoundrel Gideon has absconded with all our money—"

"Mostly *his* money, Nana. And there wasn't that much of it left in the account, anyway." Tory perched on the edge of the hospital bed. "You may have been right, Nana. Maybe this fire *was* a blessing in disguise. The insurance money will pay for new plumbing, new furnishings...."

A spark of hope began to gleam in her grandmother's eyes, making Tory feel slightly guilty for raising her hopes prematurely. That insurance check was still a big question mark, and without it they were sunk. The Creole Courtyard would vanish forever.

Marie's face lit up suddenly, and Tory turned to discover the source of her grandmother's pleasure. It took a minute to identify behind the enormous bouquet of flowers and the giant box of chocolates.

Slade.

Damn him.

"Why, Mr. Marshall, how lovely to see you! Please do come in." Marie extended her hand as if bestowing a favor on one of her subjects. "Victoria, dear, look who's come to call! It's Mr. Marshall."

"So I see," Tory replied, grinding her molars together.

"Now don't just sit there—help Mr. Marshall with those lovely flowers. I'm sure there's an empty vase or pitcher around here someplace." She patted her braided coil of white hair. "Such a delightful surprise, isn't it, Victoria?"

"Delightful," she muttered.

"Dear, just toss out that bouquet over there. It's starting to wilt, anyway."

"Nana, those are the flowers *I* gave you—"

"Please do sit down, Mr. Marshall. Oh, I do so love yellow roses. And how on earth did you know that chocolate-covered cherries are my favorite?"

"They're on sale in the hospital gift shop this week," Tory mumbled, stuffing the roses into the newly emptied vase.

Her grandmother shot her a poisoned look. But the smile she turned on Slade was pure sugar and sunshine. She patted his hand. "We're so delighted to see you, Mr. Marshall—aren't we, Victoria? But surely a handsome, vital man like yourself has better things to do than visit a sick old lady?" She batted her lashes meaningfully in Tory's direction.

"I can't think of a more pleasant way to spend the afternoon," he replied. "And I took the liberty of checking with the head nurse, who tells me you're being released tomorrow, so you can't tell me you're sick." He winked at her. "I heard a few other things, too. Anyone frisky enough to keep those nurses hopping sure can't call herself old, either."

At least Nana had the good grace to blush. "Have you been harassing those poor overworked nurses again?" Tory asked. Forgetting her intention to ignore Slade, she threw her hands up in exasperation and told him, "She buzzes the nurse every time she wants the TV channel changed."

"Is it my fault I can't figure out the buttons on this contraption?" Marie asked with a dignified sniff.

"Here, let me show you." Within moments Slade had Marie zapping through the channels like a regular couch potato.

"Why, how simple it is once you show me how it works!"

Tory rolled her eyes at her grandmother's transparent gushing. Picking up a magazine, she plopped herself down in the other guest chair and pretended to read. But her gaze strayed from the page and she found herself studying Slade while he chatted with her grandmother.

Amazing how he always looked so cool and collected even when he'd just stepped out of the heat. His tan chinos didn't have a wrinkle in them, and the collar of his short-sleeved cotton shirt looked as fresh and crisp as it must have when he first pulled it out of the package. She couldn't help noticing how the blue-and-green checked pattern brought out the vivid green in Slade's eyes.

There was something different about him, something she couldn't quite put her finger on. Whatever it was, it made him look even sexier than she remembered. It wasn't his hair, which still had that same tousled look as if he'd just ridden in a convertible. His mouth still looked as she remembered—sensual and satisfied, with a recurring quirk at the corners as if he were constantly on the verge of breaking into a grin.

Her gaze clung to his lips as she relived in exquisite detail the searing pressure of his mouth, the heat of his breath mingling with hers, the knee-melting thrill of—

"Robert!" her grandmother exclaimed in delight.

Tory wrenched herself from her fevered reverie to find her brother hovering in the hallway, shifting awkwardly from foot to foot, hands jammed in his jeans pockets.

"Robert dear, come in!"

Tory hastily rose and pushed her chair toward him. "Come on in, Robby. It's okay."

"I, uh, just came by for a second." His Adam's apple bobbed up and down as he swallowed. Cautiously he stepped into the room, as if he expected a booby trap of some kind.

Slade stood and extended his hand. "Hey, Gator."

Robby brightened. "Hey, Mr. Marshall." He hesitated, then shook Slade's hand in a short, abrupt gesture. "Didn't think I'd run into you here."

"I could say the same thing." As Robby's look of discomfort returned, he added hastily, "And call me Slade, by the way."

"Sure ... Slade." Robby stuck his hand back into his pocket. "How you doin', Nan—uh, Grandma?" He glanced quickly at Slade, who pretended to be engrossed reading the ingredients of chocolate-covered cherries.

"I'm fine, Robert, just fine. The doctors can't find a thing wrong with me." Marie took his hand and patted it vigorously. "And I feel even better, now that my grandson has come to see me."

"Yeah, well, sorry about that, Grandma." He shrugged sheepishly. "You know how it is."

Marie motioned at the chair Slade had recently vacated. "Sit down, dear. I want to hear all about everything you've been doing while I've been in the hospital." She clicked her tongue and sadly shook her head. "I know about the terrible fire, of course, but why don't you tell me about your summer classes? We have lots and lots to catch up on...."

So much for the fascinating Slade Marshall, Tory thought with amusement. Indeed, her grandmother seemed to have forgotten both Tory and Slade's presence.

She might not have seen her grandson for years, the way she was chattering with him.

And Robby was actually making what was, for him, an effort to be sociable. Responding verbally, nodding in the right places...

Tory bit her lower lip in wonder. Would miracles never cease? Robby had been uncharacteristically cooperative the last couple of days, attending his classes... coming home by his curfew time. And now, without Tory even having to nag him, he'd come on his own to visit Nana!

Tory didn't kid herself about the cause of this sudden transformation. Whatever his faults, no matter how much he'd hurt and humiliated her, she had Slade to thank for the change in her brother. Robby hadn't come right out and asked about Slade, but his too-casual questions about how the investigation was proceeding gave him away.

And Robby's pleased reaction when he'd bumped into Slade just now confirmed Tory's theory.

Her feelings were mixed. On one hand she was tickled pink that Robby had finally found a positive male role model—one who didn't wear a grubby leather jacket or call himself Snake.

But in a city full of decent, respectable men, why did Robby have to pick *Slade* to idolize? What would happen when the investigation was over and Slade was out of all their lives for good?

Worse, what would happen if Slade and Robby actually became friends, so that Tory had to keep running into him? As far as she knew Slade's only family was in Chicago, and he wasn't exactly attached to them. She could envision Robby bringing Slade home for Thanksgiving dinner, Christmas Day, Super Bowl Sunday....

"Tory? You all right?" Slade's forehead was furrowed with concern. "You went kind of pale all of a sudden."

"I'm fine," she said, pressing a hand to her brow.

"Good. Because we need to talk."

Her hand jerked away from her face in alarm.

"About the investigation," he said, clarifying.

"Oh. That. The investigation. Right." She glanced at the one-sided gabfest continuing between the room's other occupants. "I guess those two won't miss us if we step out into the hallway for a minute."

Robby gave Tory a silent look of mock horror as she passed, but his eyes twinkled. She ruffled his hair, and a wave of love engulfed her. No matter how badly he'd treated her, she would always be grateful to Slade for giving her her little brother back again.

For a while, anyway. She sighed and crossed her arms as they meandered slowly down the hall. "What is it you want to talk to me about?"

Slade rubbed his jaw. *That* was what was different about him! She'd never seen him clean-shaven before. He actually looked almost... respectable. Not that his appearance mattered in the slightest to her.

"I did some poking around after our encounter with that big gorilla the other night," he said. "Turns out this Jake Ireland guy has the reputation of being a pretty nasty character. I also found out—" Slade made a slashing motion across the top of his head "—that Fontaine is in debt up to here with him."

Tory's heart sank to her stomach. "So you were right."

"The amount Fontaine swiped from your account is a drop in the bucket compared to what he owes Ireland."

They walked in silence, shoes clicking on the polished linoleum. "So... what does this mean?" Tory asked finally.

Slade shrugged. "Maybe Fontaine panicked. Maybe he set the fire for the insurance money, so he could pay off Ireland. Or else—"

"Ms. Clayton? Tory Clayton?" Turning, she saw an orderly miming a receiver to his ear. "There's a phone call for you at the nurses' station. They say it's urgent."

Heart hammering, Tory sped down the hall. It couldn't have anything to do with Nana...she was fine only a minute ago, and besides, why would the doctor call her on the hospital phone?

Her hand was shaking when she picked up the phone. "Hello? I don't hear anything!"

"Push the flashing button," said the nurse behind the desk.

Slade reached over Tory's shoulder and punched the button for her.

"Hello?"

"Tory? Tory, is that you? Oh, thank heaven I finally found you! You've got to come, quick!"

"What? Who is this? LuAnne?"

"Tory, I'm so scared, I don't know what to do! They've got him!"

"Got *who?* LuAnne, slow down. I don't know what you're talking about."

The high-pitched voice shrieking over the phone line was laced with hysteria. "Gideon! They've got Gideon!"

Bewildered, Tory stared at the mouthpiece before replying. "Gideon? What are you talking about, LuAnne? Gideon's off in the bayou somewhere."

"No, he's not." LuAnne gulped. "He's here. In New Orleans."

Questions and possibilities whirled through Tory's brain in a dizzying blur. "But how...when...?"

LuAnne's words poured forth in a flood of panic. "He came by my apartment last night, okay? He—he didn't have anyone else to turn to...no one else would help him...." Her voice choked up. "I—I went to his place in the Quarter this morning, to get him some clothes, but they—they must have followed me home! They showed up here a little while ago and practically broke down my door, and then they hauled him away in a car! Oh, my God, Tory—what if they kill him?"

"What if *who* kill him? LuAnne, you're still not making any sense, I still don't understand—"

Slade covered the mouthpiece. "Ask her where they took him."

Tory tilted the receiver so he could hear. "LuAnne, where did they take him?" she repeated, not having the foggiest idea who the "they" was that she was referring to.

"I don't know! They said something about going to see Jack or Joe or somebody, but—"

"Ask her if they said Jake," Slade whispered.

"Ask her yourself," Tory whispered back in exasperation, handing him the phone.

He made negative fanning motions with his hands. Tory groaned. "LuAnne, is it possible they said they were taking him to see *Jake?*"

"What? Jake? Yes, yes, that's what they said. Tory, what are we going to do? You've got to help me!"

"LuAnne, listen to me." Tory took a deep breath. "As soon as I hang up the phone, you call the police. Then—"

LuAnne wailed in dismay. "We can't call the police, Tory. When they were dragging him out the door one of them said if I ever wanted to see Gideon alive, then no police! Gideon made me promise not to call them!"

"Well, then..." Helplessness overwhelmed Tory. What on earth did LuAnne expect her to do when—

"Hey, wait a second! Where are you going?" she hollered after Slade.

"To save your friend Gideon's neck," he replied as he sprinted down the hallway dodging gurneys and supply carts.

"Not without me, you're not! LuAnne, help is on the way." Tory slammed down the phone and took off after Slade, ignoring the nasty looks and shushing sounds from the hospital staff.

Like Slade, she bypassed the elevator and went flying down the stairwell and outside into the parking lot. She caught up with him just before he pulled out.

He rolled down the window with a frantic cranking motion. "What the hell do you think you're doing?" he growled, jamming the transmission into reverse.

"Coming with you, of course."

"Don't be ridiculous. This is no place for—"

"Spare me the chivalry, all right? If you don't let me come with you I'll follow you in my car, anyway. I know where Jake's place is, remember?"

His teeth gnashed like the car's grinding gears. "Stubborn, pigheaded, crazy—" He lunged across the front seat to unlock the passenger door. "All right, get in. But don't say I didn't warn you."

She'd barely flung herself into the front seat when Slade jerked the car backward and took off with a screech of rubber.

As they raced toward the Quarter, Tory prudently kept quiet and hung on to the edge of her seat for dear life. Slade's jaw was fixed in a steely, determined slant. His knuckles formed two white ridges gripping the steering wheel. His eyes never left the road as he dodged expertly through the downtown traffic and into the crowded, narrow streets of the Quarter. He must have done a thorough job of research, because he never once paused to ask Tory where to find Jake's combination souvenir emporium and poker palace.

Miraculously a car drew away from the curb as they pulled up in front of the shop. Slade pounced on the parking space like a hawk nabbing a mouse. Tory was halfway out of the car when he seized her by the wrist. "Where do you think you're going?"

She tried in vain to wrench herself free. "I'm going after Gideon, of course. Isn't that why we're here?"

"That's why *I'm* here. *You're* here to wait in the car and call the cops if I'm not out in ten minutes."

"I'm not going to sit out here in the car while you're inside getting yourself killed. Gideon's not your responsibility, anyway."

"He isn't yours, either. But he's an important witness in one of my cases, which makes him my business."

"You might as well face the fact that I'm not letting you go in there alone."

"Oh, for cryin' out loud..." Slade dropped her wrist in disgust. "I don't have time to argue."

"Good. Then let's—"

"Hold on there, Wonder Woman. What exactly do you have in mind? A frontal assault? I doubt Ireland will turn over Fontaine just because we stroll in the front door and say pretty please. We're not exactly asking to buy one of his souvenir T-shirts, you know."

"Well, what brilliant strategy do *you* have planned, then?" Tory glanced nervously at the shop entrance. Someone had shooed out all the customers and hung a Closed sign in the window.

"You know this neighborhood better than I do. Where does the back entrance lead to?"

Tory gnawed her lip. "Let's see...I think Ireland's shop and the French restaurant next door used to be one big building, so they probably share a walled-in courtyard." She squinched her eyes shut, trying to remember if she'd ever been back there exploring when she was a kid. "I think they put up a wall to divide the courtyard, but I'm pretty sure there's a connecting door."

"I hope you're right. Come on."

Slade loped around to the curb and grabbed Tory by the hand, dragging her into the darkened restaurant next door. "What do you think you're—"

"I beg your pardon, Monsieur, but we will not be opening for dinner until five—"

"That's okay. We just want to look at your courtyard. We're writing a book. Write down your name for us, will you? We wouldn't want to spell it wrong in print."

Despite their desperate situation, Tory couldn't help giggling at the befuddled expression on the maître d's face. Slade towed her through the kitchen and back into the courtyard. Three-story brick walls surrounded them on all sides. Except for the way they'd come in, the only exit was through a connecting door in the newer brick wall bisecting the courtyard.

Which was locked, naturally.

Tory watched anxiously over her shoulder for any sign of pursuit from the restaurant, while Slade pulled some kind of metal pick from his pocket and fiddled with the lock.

"How do you happen to have *that* thing?" she whispered.

"Haven't you ever heard the Boy Scout motto?"

"Yes, but I'm surprised *you* have."

"Tory, I'm hurt." He jiggled the pick. "I may not have been a Boy Scout, but I still believe in being prepared."

A bead of sweat crawled down Slade's temple while he worked. Tory stifled the impulse to brush it away.

Then the lock clicked and the door fell open a crack.

At least Slade's youthful escapades had taught him *something* useful.

Slade peeked through the opening, then stuck his head through and looked around. He raised a finger to his lips and beckoned Tory to follow him.

Hugging the wall, Slade carefully picked his way through a clutter of empty shipping cartons, old newspapers and crumpled beer cans. Jake Ireland certainly wasn't going to win any civic beautification awards if the selection committee ever got a load of this place, Tory thought as she stepped over a discarded pizza box.

The building's back windows were boarded up except for a rickety air conditioner that rattled and stuttered and dripped water onto the ground. Obviously Jake wanted to protect his midnight poker games from prying eyes.

Unfortunately the boarded-up windows also prevented Slade and Tory from seeing what was going on inside. And the clattering air conditioner made eavesdropping impossible.

Slade jiggled the knob of the back door, then bent to examine the deadbolt lock. Tory chewed on a knuckle when he pulled out his trusty pick again, but the noisy air conditioner covered the sounds of their breaking and entering.

At least, she *hoped* it did.

She had to restrain herself from hopping from foot to foot with impatience and fear. She still couldn't believe Gideon was back in New Orleans. The big question mark now was whether or not he'd been in town the night of the fire. And if he had been, did that prove he was somehow involved?

Much as Tory hated to believe she'd so completely mis-judged her former business partner, she had to admit she'd much prefer that Gideon turn out to be the arsonist than Robby. Of course, if Gideon had set the fire, Tory would probably never see a penny of the insurance money. For some reason insurance companies were usually reluctant to pay off claims when one of the owners had torched the property. Tory gulped, imagining her dreams of rebuild-ing the Creole Courtyard quickly evaporating.

"What are you waiting for, a bus?" Slade snatched Tory's wrist and tugged her after him. She'd been so wrapped up in the possible consequences of Gideon's guilt, she hadn't even noticed that Slade had conquered the deadbolt. "You're the one who insisted on tagging along," he growled in her ear, "so stick close."

She yanked her wrist free of his grip, but nodded in si-lent assent as they crept slowly into the building. Ahead of them a long corridor led to the front of the store. Peering around Slade's shoulder, Tory saw a door about halfway up the right side of the hallway.

Following Slade's lead, she flattened herself against the wall and edged down the corridor. As they neared the doorway and the clatter of the air conditioner receded, a loud angry voice filtered from the room beyond.

"—Never seen such a dim-witted, boneheaded move in my life! What are you, crazy? Nabbing him in broad day-light, in front of witnesses? What are you usin' for brains, anyhow?"

Mumble mumble.

"What do you mean, you *thought* I wanted him as soon as possible? I don't pay you guys to think. Do I pay you to think? *I* do the thinking. *You* do as I tell you."

Tory perched on tiptoe and whispered, "That's Jake Ireland," in Slade's ear. He gave a curt nod in response.

"I don't want neither of you geniuses *thinking*. I suppose you were *thinking* the other night when you torched Fontaine's building, huh, Vinnie?"

Tory whipped her hand over her mouth to smother a gasp.

"If I'd wanted you to burn the place down, I'd have *told* you to burn the place down."

Tory clutched Slade's arm. When he turned slightly to squeeze her hand, he could see even in the dim corridor how pale she was. Her eyes looked like dark, bottomless pools.

"Now some damn arson investigator's been nosin' around, askin' questions. If you could *think,* Vinnie, you'd have known it wouldn't take long for any *idiot* to figure out that Fontaine here owes me big."

Slade resented that remark, but he wasn't about to speak up in his own defense right then.

"Now the cops are gonna figure *I* torched that place to teach Fontaine a lesson." Ireland's voice was getting hoarse from shouting. "See what happens when you two clowns try to *think?* You do as I tell you. And I'm tellin' you, *don't think!*"

When Slade looked over his shoulder at Tory again, he saw that anger had replaced her shock and fear. Cheeks flaming, eyes shooting off sparks, fists clenched with outraged indignation... Slade was glad *he* wasn't on the receiving end of her fury for once. Gently he extricated her dug-in nails from his arm.

Motioning her to stay where she was, he dropped to the floor and peered through the doorway. The room was stacked with a jumble of crates and boxes that partially concealed his view of the room's occupants.

Which was fine with Slade, since it partially concealed him, too. He slithered quickly across the floor to the other side of the door, but he got enough of a glimpse to confirm his head count. Besides Jake Ireland, there were three other men in the room. Slade couldn't be sure, but he thought one of the two goons was the man who'd accosted Tory on the street the other night.

His hasty reconnaissance showed the room's fourth occupant tied to a chair. At least, Slade was pretty *sure* no one would willingly sit with his arms and legs splayed in such an uncomfortable position.

It had to be Gideon Fontaine. And what worried Slade more than the ropes tying him to the chair or the gag stuffed in his mouth was the fact that Jake Ireland was so casually tossing around talk of arson in front of him. A hood like Ireland would never be so indiscreet...unless he had absolutely no intention of letting Fontaine leave this place alive.

Across the doorway, Tory had gone pale again. Apparently the same realization had dawned on her.

They didn't have much time. Slade might have been willing to take chances where Fontaine's worthless hide was concerned, but not when Tory's safety was involved. Any second now Ireland might conclude this dressing-down session and come out into the hall.

Slade looked around for a weapon, an escape route, something he could use to distract the bad guys long enough to spirit Tory and Fontaine to safety. Maybe there was an overhead crawl space or heating duct they could hide in.

His gaze fell on the narrow metal pipe running along the center of the hall ceiling. A fire sprinkler system, and an old one by the looks of it. He'd be willing to bet it hadn't been inspected or maintained for years. He craned his neck to get a better view of the nearest smoke detector. When installed, the alarm system had probably been rigged to notify automatically the fire department in case of fire. Was it still connected? Did the damn thing even work at all?

Only one way to find out. Slade winked at Tory while he patted his pockets. Aha! There they were.

He stretched up on tiptoe and positioned his hands right under the smoke detector.

Then he lit a match.

Chapter Eight

Slade held his breath. The match burned slowly down toward his fingers. Damn it, this ancient sprinkler system didn't work, after all. Not even so much as a peep came from the fire alarm. The sensors must be rusted over or clogged with grime....

Ow! He bit back a curse as he dropped the match stub to the floor.

Then all hell broke loose.

An earsplitting cacophony pierced the air—an urgent, echoing series of blasts like the *dive!* signal in a submarine movie. The resemblance grew even more striking when the overhead sprinkler system erupted, sending geysers of water cascading in all directions, as if the submarine had sprung a leak under torpedo attack.

Slade had time for a brief rush of satisfaction. *There, that ought to flush them out!*

Slicking his waterlogged hair from his face, he motioned Tory to flatten herself against the wall. For once she obeyed, dashing water from her eyes and flashing Slade what he could have sworn was a grin.

He gave her a thumbs-up signal, then crouched beside the door. He'd have to pick them off one at a time as they came through, so he'd have only seconds to put each one out of commission. Over the gush of water he heard Jake Ireland's angry bellow. "Get back here, you clowns!"

A lumpish figure barreled through the door. Slade tackled him with a loud *"Oof!"* It figured the big one would come out first. It was like tackling one of the sides of beef in the Chicago slaughterhouse where Slade had worked one summer.

The guy's fists were the size of rump roasts, but Slade had surprise and agility on his side. As momentum slammed them both into the wall, Slade felled him with a right cross.

But he'd taken too long. He could see the other goon coming straight for him, an eager, violent gleam in his slitted eyes, ready to launch himself into the hallway and tear Slade to pieces before he could struggle upright.

Then Tory stuck out her foot.

The goon tripped and flew through the air, crashing headfirst into the wall next to his fallen *compadre*. Slade took advantage of the man's temporary daze to pummel him in the stomach. When he doubled over, Slade knocked him out with a quick, hard uppercut to the chin. Well, Marquis of Queensberry rules didn't count for much growing up in the streets of Chicago.

He patted the man down quickly and found what he was looking for tucked into his belt. Checking the safety, he leaped to the doorway. He felt like yanking Tory into his arms and kissing her silly, but instead he punched her lightly on the shoulder. "Good work," he said. She smiled shakily in return.

Then he lunged into the room. Jake Ireland was cursing and kicking the chair as he tried to drag his trussed-up prisoner toward the door. Shouting to be heard over the din, Slade braced one fist with the other and aimed the gun. "Hands up, Ireland!"

As Ireland's head snapped up and worry joined the anger and frustration in his face, the fire alarm grew erratic...weaker...and finally choked into silence. Ireland's hands climbed slowly toward the ceiling. Water dripped onto his sodden business suit.

Slade felt moisture seeping into his shoes.

In the distance he heard sirens.

When Tory recalled those next few minutes, they came back to her as a series of disjointed images and corresponding emotions. Relief at the sound of feet pounding down the hall to their rescue. Shock and horror at her first glimpse of Gideon's battered face. Satisfaction when the police hauled off Jake Ireland and his thugs, including Vinnie, who had burned down the Creole Courtyard.

And a disturbingly poignant, powerful emotion when Slade grabbed her in a sweet, sodden embrace and kissed her with a warm ardor that took Tory's breath away and made her forget she was standing in six inches of water. He pulled back his head and framed her face with his hands. "You're the greatest," he said in a fierce whisper.

Water dripped from his hair into her eyes. Tory blinked rapidly. She couldn't recall ever being quite this happy in her entire life.

Now, watching LuAnne fuss over Gideon in his hospital bed, Tory slipped furtive glances at Slade and wondered if she would ever have a chance to fuss over *him* that way. She sighed. Not likely. She had a feeling Slade was probably the world's crabbiest patient.

Gideon, on the other hand, was positively basking under LuAnne's tender ministrations. "Ah, that's it, *cher*... just a little to the left... ahh..."

LuAnne beamed down at his bandaged face while she kneaded his shoulders. "Is there anything else I can get you, Gideon honey? Another pillow? More juice?"

Slade, propped against the windowsill, rolled his eyes at Tory. He unfolded his arms so he could stick a finger down his throat. Tory giggled.

"Well, now, since you mention it, *cher,* some fine Kentucky whiskey would go down awful good right now."

"Don't you dare smuggle him any liquor, LuAnne," Tory warned. "We wouldn't want to hinder Gideon's recovery in any way." With sinister glee she rubbed her hands together. "I can't wait until you're fully recovered... so I can wring your rotten neck!"

"Ah, my poor Tory." Gideon clicked his tongue and shook his head sadly. "What a lot of trouble I've caused you, eh?"

"Trouble? *Trouble?*" Tory had trouble keeping herself from leaning over the bed and strangling him. She ticked off points on her fingers. "First you bankrupted me. Then, because of you, everything I own went up in smoke." She poked a finger in Slade's direction. "Today we almost got killed trying to save your sorry skin, and to top it all off my new dry-clean-only blouse is ruined!"

The contrite look on Gideon's bruised face would have melted Tory's heart... if she'd believed for one second it was genuine. Instead, she burst out laughing. She reached over and tugged a lock of his black hair.

"Ow!"

"Be glad someone else got to you first, or I'd beat the stuffing out of you myself, you good-for-nothing scoundrel!"

"Tory, stop that!" LuAnne looked poised to fling herself across Gideon's body and take his punishment herself. Her bee-stung lips pursed into a pout. "Hasn't Gideon been through enough today without you threatening him?"

Personally Tory thought Gideon had emerged far more unscathed than he deserved. Beneath white swatches of gauze and red smears of iodine, his skin glowed with a healthy tan, and his mischievous black eyes snapped at Tory like firecrackers. Still as handsome, as charming, as incorrigible as ever. No doubt the minute LuAnne's strawberry-blond head was turned he'd be pinching the nurses and setting up romantic trysts with them.

Slade cleared his throat and pushed himself off the windowsill. "Well, at least you won't have to worry about Jake Ireland for a while. Turns out some of those containers in his back storeroom were packed with more than T-shirts and souvenir coffee mugs."

Gideon's eyes widened. "Drugs?"

"Counterfeit currency. When you toss in the kidnapping and assault charges, it looks like your friend Ireland's going to be behind bars for quite a while."

"What about that horrible Vinnie person?" Tory asked. "The creep who started the fire?"

"Hey, easy," Slade said. "You're going to break the arm off that chair if you clutch it any harder."

She forced her fingers to uncurl. "If only I'd known the other night when he stopped me that he was the culprit, I'd have—I'd have—"

"I think we get the picture," Slade told her. His eyes twinkled. "Vinnie will get what's coming to him, don't worry. The other thug is cutting a deal with the DA right now. I'm sure the prosecution will agree to reduce some of the charges against him in exchange for his testimony against Vinnie."

He turned to Gideon. "I guess Jake wasn't satisfied with the down payment you offered him on your gambling debt."

"You can say that again." He took Tory's hand. "*Cher,* can you ever forgive me for taking that money out of the account?"

"Well..."

"You must understand—I was desperate! Jake threatened to kill me if I didn't pay up. I thought the money from the account would satisfy him for a while, but..." He sighed theatrically. "I didn't realize how unreasonable he could be until it was too late."

Tory squeezed his hand. "I just hope you've learned your lesson."

Gideon crossed his heart with a melodramatic sweep. "No more gambling—I swear it!"

"Uh-huh," she said. "I'll believe *that* when I see it."

Slade looked as skeptical as Tory, but all he said was, "Anyway, it seems Jake sent Vinnie out to find you the night of the fire. Vinnie came by the guest house looking for you, and when he found the place deserted, decided to scare you with a warning message. That's why the proof of arson was so obvious. Vinnie didn't even try to hide the evidence." Slade flipped idly through Gideon's chart at the foot of the bed. "He figured that by acting on his own initiative he could score points with Ireland or something."

"As they say, all's well that ends well, eh?" If Gideon was bothered by the slightest guilt for all the trouble he'd caused, he hid it well.

"Hmm. No thanks to you." Slade set down the chart.

LuAnne pushed her glasses onto the bridge of her pert nose. "I think it's time for Gideon to get some rest, don't you?" she chirped brightly.

Gideon took her hand in his. "Ah, what would I do without my precious LuAnne?"

"Yes, well, I guess we'll be leaving now." Slade swept Tory into the hall, their departure unnoticed by the two lovebirds billing and cooing like long-lost sweethearts. "I was going to suggest we get something to eat," he said, pressing the elevator button, "but after that nauseating display I don't think I have much appetite left."

Tory laughed. "LuAnne's in heaven. She's been after Gideon for a year, and now she's finally got her big chance."

As they stepped into the elevator, Slade said, "I just hope he doesn't hurt her too badly."

Tory glanced up in astonishment, but Slade was staring straight ahead with approved elevator-riding etiquette. Who'd have thought old Love-'Em-and-Leave-'Em Slade Marshall would worry about LuAnne's feelings?

Once again, he'd demonstrated that Tory might be wrong about him. *Careful, kiddo,* she warned herself. Revising her opinion of Slade might destroy her emotional safety net. And without that last defense, she could very well end up falling for Slade Marshall. Hard.

"There are two things I can't figure out," Slade said, holding open the door to the parking lot.

"What?"

"First of all, why did Gideon come back to New Orleans once he'd safely skipped town?"

"As a matter of fact, he told me the whole story while they were patching him up in the emergency room."

"Care to share it with me?"

Tory scanned the parking lot, then headed toward her car. "It turns out Gideon's kind of persona non grata with his relatives these days. They think the way he sold his share of the inheritance to that oil company was like selling out his birthright and betraying the family." She fished her keys from her purse. "When Gideon showed up on the bayou, begging them to hide him . . ."

" . . . They slammed the door in his face."

"Basically. With a few sentiments like 'good riddance' thrown in." Tory unlocked her door. "He had nowhere else to go, and eventually wound up on LuAnne's doorstep."

"Knowing *she* would never slam the door in his face."

There it was again, that undisguised concern for Lu-Anne's emotional well-being. This new side of Slade touched an unsettling chord inside Tory. All of a sudden there didn't seem to be any good reason why she shouldn't fall head over heels in—

She cut off the thought. Okay, so maybe Slade was a nice guy after all under that brash exterior. All the more reason he must attract scores of women.

The idea made Tory's heart take a swan dive. She wasn't the kind of woman who could share a man—especially a man like Slade.

"What's the other thing you can't figure out?" she asked abruptly.

He rested his forearms along the top of her car door. "Where you were the night of the fire."

"Oh, that." Tory ducked her head, then gave a sheepish shrug. "I was sitting in a bar on Bourbon Street."

Slade gawked at her. "You lied to an arson investigator just to protect your precious reputation? Good grief, half the people in New Orleans are sitting in a bar at any given moment."

"Not in *this* bar." Tory grimaced. "I knew if you ever found out what kind of place it was, you'd know instantly that I wasn't there just to while away a pleasant evening."

Dawning suspicion crossed his face. "It wasn't by any chance a dive called the Purple—"

"—Doubloon," she finished, shaking her head. "Let me guess—it's your favorite watering hole."

"Hardly." He scratched his head. "You constantly amaze me, Ms. Clayton. What the hell were you doing in a dump like that?"

She fiddled with her keys. "Waiting for Robby."

"Robby?"

"He was on the verge of flunking out of summer school," Tory said helplessly. "He refused to talk to me till I threatened to kick him out of the house, and then the only place he'd agree to meet me was that awful bar."

Slade nodded. "Suddenly it all fits." His brows knit together. "Well? Were you able to talk some sense into him?"

"That's just it—Robby never showed up." Tory took a deep breath. "Then the Creole Courtyard burned down and I thought—I mean, I didn't seriously *believe*—but I couldn't take the chance that *you* might suspect—"

"—That Robby set the fire."

"Yes, if you'd found out that he didn't show up, right about the time someone was setting the fire. It might have looked like he tricked me into leaving the guest house deserted that evening."

Slade shook his head as if he'd recently received a blow. "So you thought *Robby* . . ."

"No, of course not, but—well . . . we'd had an argument the day before, about money and helping out around the guest house. Robby got mad and yelled that he wished the whole place would burn down."

"And then it did."

Tory nodded. "You can see why I thought... well, let's say I thought things might look suspicious to—to an outsider."

"Like me." Slade barely pulled back, but the effect was of a turtle retreating into its shell.

"You're not an outsider—I mean, maybe you were at *first,* but now..." Tory swallowed. "Gosh, it's obvious how much Robby looks up to you, and Nana thinks you're the greatest thing to come from up north since my grandfather..."

"And what about you?" Slade fixed her with a penetrating gaze that made her decidedly uncomfortable. "How do *you* feel about me?"

Tory's eyes darted back and forth as she scanned his face. What kind of confession was he hoping to wring from her, anyway? And why did he want to hear it?

"I—I like you," she said hesitantly. "Of course I like you." *Way too much for my own good,* she amended silently. "After all, I wouldn't chase after bad guys and get drenched by overhead sprinklers with just *anyone.*"

The pinched lines of tension around his mouth turned to creases of amusement. "I should hope not," he said, tugging on a stray lock of her hair. "By the way, in case I forgot to mention it, you were terrific back there." Chuckling, he rubbed the back of his neck. "The way you stuck out your foot and tripped that guy..." His eyes were sparkling with what Tory could have sworn was genuine admiration. "Your timing was perfect. And our rescue mission would probably have turned into disaster if you hadn't... stepped in."

Their mingled laughter was as refreshing to Tory's ears as the splash of water in a courtyard fountain. Resolutely she pushed aside the forlorn image of her beloved stone cherub, gracing the silenced fountain amid the blackened walls of the Creole Courtyard.

After all, she could rebuild the guest house now! "How soon will I be getting the insurance check?" she asked. Immediately she realized how the words must have sounded to Slade. His green eyes narrowed as a wary gleam stole into them. "Don't worry," he replied stiffly. "You should have it by the end of the week."

Tory's hand flew to his sleeve. "Slade, that didn't come out the right way." His expression remained stony. "I'm so happy and excited that I'll really be able to rebuild the guest house, I—I didn't think before I spoke." She fumbled for the right words this time. "I don't want you to think I've been buttering you up or something just so I'll get the check faster."

His granite mask began to crumble. "I keep forgetting how lousy you are at deception." A smile erased the remaining brittle traces from his face. "I should have remembered that if you actually *were* trying to butter me up, I'd have seen right through your act from the very beginning."

"Gee, thanks . . . I think."

He seemed to find her confusion highly entertaining. "Tell you what," he went on. "Why don't you come back to my office right now and you can sign on the necessary dotted lines? I still need to wrap up my report, but your signature would speed things up."

As he ushered Tory into the front seat of her car, he added almost as an afterthought, "Then afterward I'll take you to dinner. My treat, this time." Before Tory could utter one peep of protest he pointed out, "It's the least I can do, after you saved our necks today."

Unconsciously Tory's hand strayed to her now-dry but still uncombed hair. "I don't know, Slade—I must look a mess. My clothes..."

"I know the perfect place. Your clothes won't matter a bit. Not that there's anything wrong with the way you look, actually. New outfit?"

"It was before it got doused by the sprinklers."

"At least come back to my office and sign the papers. It's on your way back to the Quarter, anyway."

How could she refuse when he was being so reasonable? And she *was* eager to expedite the insurance check....

"Okay," she agreed. "I guess I could stop by your office for a minute."

"Great." He slapped the hood of her car. "Follow me."

That, Tory thought, watching Slade saunter back to his car, was exactly what she *shouldn't* do.

Slade grinned at Tory's puzzled expression in his rearview mirror. He could practically read her mind as he led her down the shady street he lived on. She was wondering what kind of office building could possibly be located around here.

He felt a twinge of guilt for deceiving her. On the other hand, he hadn't said his office *wasn't* in the basement of his home, had he?

He cranked up the car stereo to drown out the voice clamoring inside his head—the one warning him that he was playing with fire by bringing Tory home. But it was like watching himself ride a roller coaster, careening recklessly around the curves, unable to veer from his predestined track.

He had no idea how this evening was going to end, or even how he *wanted* it to end. All he knew was that his investigation was complete and he was about to run out of excuses for seeing Tory.

Slade wasn't ready to watch her sashay out of his life. Not yet, at least. Not until he'd had a chance to convince himself that she was no different from any other woman, that she was nothing special ... certainly not worth risking his peace of mind for.

Aw, hell. His internal debating match was probably academic, anyway. He'd lay odds that Tory would refuse to set one foot inside his house once she realized how he'd tricked her. He sensed that she was as leery of the chemistry between them as he was.

Ironically, that only intrigued him further.

Damn it, this was ridiculous! He was letting his glands get the best of him. Why not simply get this over with? He could hop out of his car, apologize to Tory for misleading her, send the paperwork over to Coliseum Insurance, and let her sign the papers there. She would get her check in the mail and Slade would never have to see her again.

Unless they happened to bump into each other at the Purple Doubloon or something.

Logic told Slade this was the smartest move he could make. Well, for once logic could take a flying leap.

He coasted to the curb in front of his house, half wondering whether Tory would gun the accelerator and run him over as he approached her car.

When she rolled down the driver's window, air-conditioned coolness drifted out to meet him. "Where's—your office?" she asked, craning her neck to scan their immediate vicinity.

"In the raised cottage over there." Slade snapped his fingers. "Didn't I mention my office is the first floor of my house?"

"No, you did *not* mention it." She pulled her sunglasses down to the tip of her nose and glared at him over the bridge. "As you are perfectly well aware."

"Tory, you wound me deeply." He clapped his hand over his heart. He couldn't help it; his flippant response was as instinctive, as natural, as holding his breath under water. "Are you implying that I lured you here under false pretenses?"

Even as he watched the indignant retort form on Tory's lips, Slade found himself wondering why he couldn't be honest with her. What prevented him from simply telling her he wanted more time to get to know her better? Why was a man who dashed into burning buildings and tackled two-ton criminals so scared of a little personal rejection?

Tory surprised him. Again.

She stepped out of the car, locked the door and slung her purse over her shoulder. "Okay," she said. "Let's go sign those papers."

Drat, he hated it when she acted so unpredictably. But he had to admit—he also enjoyed it. Maybe the reason he liked her so much was because she kept him on his toes.

He swept back his arm. "This way, *cher,*" he said, imitating Gideon.

Tory snickered as they walked up the front sidewalk. "That sounds pretty funny with a Yankee accent."

He lapsed into his best southern drawl. "Why, sugah, Ah'm sure Ah don't know *what* y'all mean!"

Tory groaned. "I think you've seen *Gone With the Wind* a few too many times."

"What are you talking about?" He unlocked the door and ushered her inside his office. "That's exactly what you sound like."

"It is not!" she scoffed.

"Is too!"

"Is not!" Her eyes twinkled merrily as she clamped her hands on her hips and screwed up her face in mock indignation.

Slade still thought it was the loveliest face he'd seen in a long time. Maybe the loveliest face he'd seen, period.

It took every scrap of his self-control not to seize that face in his hands and kiss it soundly.

He dug his nails into his palms until the pain restored some sanity. "Here are the papers," he said, more roughly than he'd intended. He dug through the clutter on his desk for a pen. "Sign here... and here... and one more place. Here."

He leaned over her shoulder and studied her careful, economical script as if her signature were John Hancock's. Damn. Despite all they'd been through today, that elusive, vaguely floral scent of hers still clung to her like morning mist.

Slade sniffed her hair. Maybe her body chemistry created that sexy, feminine fragrance on its own. How else could she smell so good after being drenched by sprinklers?

He sniffed again.

Tory set down the pen. "Do you have a cold?" she asked.

"Huh? What?"

"You sound like you've got the sniffles."

Slade scooped up the papers and patted them energetically into a neat stack. "Yeah, maybe I'm coming down with something." He coughed experimentally. "After getting soaked earlier, I mean."

Oh, he was coming down with something, all right. But it wasn't a cold.

Tory clasped her hands behind her back and wandered slowly through the office. She scanned the books on his shelves and inspected his computer setup. "I like what you've done with this place," she said, touching the frame of a surrealistic Mardi Gras scene he'd bought at a street fair in the Quarter.

"Would you like to see the upstairs?" Slade could have bitten off his tongue. He ought to shoo Tory out the door and out of his life. Instead, he led her up the staircase.

Slade's home wasn't at all what Tory had expected. On the more than one occasion when she hadn't been able to resist imagining where he lived, she'd pictured a typical bachelor pad—cheap rented furniture, fast-food wrappers strewn everywhere, posters of dogs playing poker taped to the walls.

Instead she found a definitely masculine yet tastefully decorated, comfortable home. It was sparsely furnished, but the pieces were of high quality and had obviously been carefully chosen. She recognized the native Louisiana style of several nice antiques. Lots of tan and peach and cream-colored fabric accented the rattan furniture, and touches of pale green here and there gave the room an airy, tropical feeling in keeping with the architecture.

"This place is wonderful," she said, noting the antique ceiling fan whirling lazily overhead. "Did you...hire a decorator?"

"Nope." He folded his arms and surveyed the room with obvious pride. "Did the whole thing myself. And let me tell you, this place was a dump when I bought it."

"How long did it take you to restore it?"

He straightened one of the bulky stuffed cushions on the couch. "I bought the house three years ago, and I'm still not finished with it." He scuffed the hardwood floor with the toe of his shoe. "I want to sand these down and refinish them, for example."

"I'm really impressed," she said. "You've done a fantastic job." Another side of Slade she'd never seen before. She was glad she'd come inside, although at first she'd felt a little like the fly entering the spider's parlor. But she'd had a queer premonition that if she drove away without signing the papers, she might never see Slade again.

It was that disturbing prospect that made her choose to overlook the sneaky way he'd lured her to his house.

If his current behavior was any indication, however, Tory had had nothing to worry about. For once Slade was behaving like a perfect gentleman.

So why did she feel vaguely disappointed?

Tory wavered. Common sense told her to smile politely, shake Slade's hand and bid him goodbye forever. But something else was shaking her by the shoulders, nudging her forward and urging her to—

Taking a deep breath, she settled herself onto the couch, crossed one leg over the other, and smiled expectantly at Slade. "So," she said, "you mentioned something about dinner?"

"Dinner?" From the look that skittered across his face, she'd caught him completely off guard. He recovered quickly, though. "Well, originally I thought we could eat here, but I just remembered my cupboards are bare, so…" He spread his hands helplessly.

"Oh, that's all right. I'm not fussy. We could just have an omelette or something."

A muscle fluttered at his temple. "No, I'm serious. All I have in the refrigerator is some leftover Chinese food and a moldy orange."

Tory bounced to her feet and headed for the kitchen. "Perfect," she said. "I love Chinese food."

"It's three weeks old!"

She opened the refrigerator and nabbed a white cardboard container. She pried it open, then wrinkled her nose. "At least."

Slade grabbed the box from her hands, shoved it back inside the refrigerator and firmly closed the door. When he gripped Tory by the shoulders, a strange, almost frantic gleam flickered in his eyes. "Look, I know what you're thinking." His fingers twitched. "You're thinking this is where I reveal one of my previously hidden talents and whip up a gourmet meal out of one tomato and a box of saltines." He clutched her more insistently. "But that ain't gonna happen, sweetheart, because the most complicated cooking I can manage is peeling the plastic cover off a microwave dinner!"

Tory absorbed the desperate light in his eyes, the resolute slant of his jaw. "You . . . you really can't cook?"

He shook her gently. "That's what I've been trying to tell you!"

Tory gnawed thoughtfully on her fingertip. Then she smiled. "Fine," she said. "We can call out for pizza."

"Tory . . ."

"Where's your phone?" She broke away from Slade and sped back to the living room. Part of her was appalled by her own behavior. Never in her wildest dreams could she have imagined acting so pushy, so determined, so dead set on heading straight for trouble.

But this might be her last chance with Slade, and Tory hung on to it as desperately as a mountain climber clinging to a ledge by her fingernails. She just couldn't let go.

Slade snatched the receiver from her hand and slammed it back into its cradle. They stood there glaring at each other, the only sound in the room the ragged rhythm of Slade's breathing.

Tentatively Tory raised her hand and touched the side of his face. Under her fingertips she felt his jaw muscle flex, and then something melted in his steely demeanor. He closed his eyes, then with a groan pulled her roughly against his chest.

The rapid thud of Slade's heart filled Tory's ears, creating a dizzy counterpoint to her own. A shudder racked his body, and as it subsided he tangled his fingers in her hair and tilted her head back. Cradling her face in his hands, he shook his head almost sadly. "Ah, Tory," he muttered in a low growl, "why didn't you run while you had the chance?"

Then he lowered his head and blotted out all awareness but the exquisite, heated bliss of his lips on hers.

Chapter Nine

Slade had kissed his fair share of women, but the sensations that rocked him while kissing Tory Clayton went far beyond anything in his experience. Tory was a magnitude ten on the Richter scale of kissing.

He'd halfway hoped that by tasting the forbidden fruit of her lips, he could cure himself of his hunger for her. But that hope was dashed the instant she melted against him and matched his kiss with an ardent response of her own. Now the more he sampled the sweet softness of her mouth, the more he craved her.

God, she felt wonderful in his arms! Somehow every curve and swell of her slim body nestled perfectly into a corresponding hollow of his hard, muscular frame. He could almost believe some cosmic overseer had magically designed them to fit together.

Romantic nonsense, of course. But knowing that didn't temper the devastating effect she had on Slade. His hands seemed to move of their own volition from her shoulders and down the gentle rise of her breasts, sliding around her narrow waist and pulling her even closer against him.

He glided his tongue between her parted lips, eliciting a purr of pleasure from deep in her throat. Before the vibrations faded he tore his mouth from hers and planted a tortured trail of kisses along the slender white column of her throat.

Her head fell back as he feasted on the tantalizing flesh. Encouraged by her response, he raised one hand to cup her breast ever so tenderly. Fire flared in his abdomen, and it took every ounce of his self-restraint to caress her breast slowly... gently....

Wave upon wave of desire radiated from the touch of Slade's hand. Tory felt as if her body were gradually turning molten as flames licked along her skin, setting her nerve endings aflame with ecstasy.

She molded herself more snugly into Slade's embrace, twining her arms around his neck for support as the strength in her limbs ebbed away. Her knees began to buckle.

They sank onto the couch. With an impatient flick of his wrist Slade tossed aside a cushion to make more room. "Comfy?" he asked gruffly, drawing her down beside him so they were lying face-to-face.

"Mmmm..." Tory nodded as she traced the rugged outline of his face, learning every bold slant, every irregular angle. He had a tiny scar near his hairline, a sunburst of faint crinkles at the corner of each eye.

When she slipped the tip of her little finger along the moist underside of his lower lip, he growled and nipped her finger playfully. When he bared his teeth she noted a tiny chip missing from the corner of one of his upper incisors. Souvenir of some long-ago street brawl, perhaps? Tory shivered, unable to bear the thought of Slade in pain or danger.

"It's getting mighty warm in here, don't you think?" he said in her ear.

"Mmm, must be a hundred degrees or so."

"Maybe there's something wrong with the air-conditioning." As his fingers tiptoed down the front of Tory's blouse, the buttons fell open like magic.

When the air hit her naked skin she gasped, because at that moment Slade propped his head up on one elbow and slid the other hand beneath her blouse and around her bare waist. He flattened his hand and skimmed his palm over the rise of her hips, back down the valley of her waist and up the gentle hill of her breast.

Tory closed her eyes, hoping Slade couldn't see the heart-stopping effect he was having on her. Once he discovered how completely under his spell she was, Slade would have her completely at his mercy.

And Tory wasn't quite ready to make herself that vulnerable to him. Not yet, anyway.

But her reserve was melting fast. Slade buried his face in her neck and began to assault her with kisses, using his mouth and tongue to arouse an incredible upwelling of pleasure inside her. He moved his hand over her lace-enclosed breast, teasing the sensitive crest with his thumb, cupping the straining mound in his big hand, kneading her gently.

When Tory opened her eyes, the room spun around one way while the ceiling fan whirred the other. Maybe that was the reason her stomach plunged into a sudden roller-coaster swoop that left her dizzy and panting for oxygen.

Or maybe it was the fierce, blazing desire etched on Slade's face when he leaned across her to fiddle with the fastening of her bra. When this barrier snapped open it was as if Tory's teetering emotional barricade toppled as well. With barely restrained impatience Slade peeled off her blouse and bra and flipped them over his shoulder.

Tory swallowed, shy under his admiring gaze yet reveling in the appreciative, lustful gleam in his narrow eyes. "You're even more beautiful than I'd imagined," he said with a note of wonder, skimming his hands over her quivering, heated flesh. "And believe me, I have quite an imagination."

"I...believe you." Goodness, but she was having trouble catching her breath. What a marvelously passionate mood it would create if she were to pass out from hyperventilating!

Tory made a conscious effort to slow her respiration rate. But then she completely forgot about minor details like breathing when Slade lowered his head and captured the rosy tip of her breast with his lips.

Rapture exploded in all directions, sending an electric current zapping from the top of her head to the tips of her toes. The hot, urgent core of her being contracted, and she arched against him, silently begging him for more...more tortured kisses, more intimate caresses, more of his bare skin pressed against hers.

Through her dazed fog the thought occurred to Tory that perhaps it was time for her to reciprocate, to initiate some intimate forays of her own. She'd practically forgotten how, it had been so long since she'd been this close to a man, so involved, so...in love?

Nonsense. Tory immediately dismissed the possibility. She'd never been in love in her entire life. Oh, she'd had high-school sweethearts, and one or two serious boyfriends in college. But she'd been so busy running the guest house, trying to raise Robby and take care of her grandmother—there simply hadn't been *time* for a mature, adult relationship to flower into love.

So what made her think she would recognize love when she saw it, anyway? These overwhelming, heart-wrenching feelings she had for Slade were no doubt simply a grown-up version of a schoolgirl crush, a powerful infatuation ignited by her gratitude toward him for all he'd done to help her family.

And let's face it, Tory admitted—Slade was the only man who'd shown this lively an interest in her since, well, since ever. Therefore, logic would indicate she was merely letting a combination of flattery, gratitude and chemistry get the best of her.

Well, she'd convinced her brain, anyway. Now if she could only convince her heart, soul and body.

Her brain was outvoted.

With trembling fingers Tory fumbled with the buttons of Slade's shirt. Approval rumbled in his chest, encouraging her to continue even though she felt as clumsy as a child trying to dress herself for the first time. Fortunately several of his buttons had been torn off, casualties of his earlier skirmish with the two thugs. At least she had fewer to worry about.

Then the last button was undone and she was tugging his shirt from his trousers. Slade shrugged himself loose and cast his shirt behind him to join Tory's blouse on the floor. Tentatively she reached out to weave her fingers through the glorious mat of nut-brown hair covering his chest. His pectoral muscles were as solid and well-developed as they'd looked through the contours of his shirt.

When she raised her heavy-lidded eyes, Slade was watching her with a fierce intensity that startled her. Her hand froze on his chest. He started to speak, had to clear his throat and begin again. "You want this, don't you?"

he asked in a voice that made the entire length of her body tingle.

"I—" Her throat was parched; her tongue felt swollen and thick. She licked her lips. "Yes," she whispered.

"Good." Slade's response was nearly smothered as he drew Tory abruptly against him and began to nuzzle her neck with increased enthusiasm. The tempo of his caresses accelerated a beat, stirring something wild and reckless inside her. As he edged his hand lower and lower down her curving, straining profile, a smoldering tension began to build inside her.

He spanned her waist, stroked the backs of her thighs... her bottom... her hips... all the while continuing his relentless barrage with mouth and tongue. When he eased his hand into the heated recess between her thighs, Tory thought she would explode.

She writhed against him, shocked by the wantonness of her own response, yet driven by a blinding passion unlike anything she'd ever known before. She was half-crazed with desire, desperate for Slade to unzip her slacks, to assuage the burning need building up inside her.

Yet maddeningly he seemed content to tease her, caressing her through her clothing, creating a delicious friction against her lower body that would drive her over the edge of sanity if he kept it up much longer. His lips moved onto hers, and he kissed her with a leisurely thoroughness that was a frustrating contrast to the frenzied longing raging inside her.

Tory's last thread of propriety and reserve snapped. With increasing boldness she inched her hand lower... lower... until it rested on the fly of his trousers. As she began to explore with her fingers, Slade raised himself up with a groan.

With one swift movement he shifted Tory beneath him and sheltered her with his body, partially resting his weight on his forearms so as not to crush her. She felt the hardness of his lower body bearing down against hers, spearing her with a primitive thrill of naked desire.

For the first time she felt almost calm, as she surrendered to the inevitable fate where Slade would lead her. Lifting her hand, she brushed aside a few damp, dark strands of her hair that clung to his flushed cheek.

Slade seized her hand and pressed a fevered kiss into her palm. He felt racked by a strange fever himself, swept by a delirium that alternately exhilarated and terrified him. What kind of sorceress was she, anyway? Somehow in the space of a few days she'd gotten into Slade's bloodstream so that with every beat of his heart her name echoed in his ears.

How could he resist her now, with her black hair spread in wild disarray over his couch, her lips shiny wet and swollen with his kiss, her soft, dewy breasts rosy with desire? She gazed up at him with those sparkling sapphire eyes...shining with such trust, such willingness...as honest and open as the sky.

In the back of Slade's mind he knew he should be on guard against her, that somehow she posed a threat to him. But at the moment, with Tory's sleek, warm, delightfully feminine flesh nestled beneath him, Slade couldn't for the life of him remember why.

He hoisted himself to his feet and knelt to scoop her up in his arms. "Sweetheart, let's go into the bedroom...."

Her wordless, wide-eyed nod was all the assent he needed. As he lifted her effortlessly to his chest, his glance fell upon the antique oak sideboard he used as a bar. A crystal decanter stood at one end where he'd forgotten to put it away after the last time he'd used it.

He stared transfixed at the decanter, as if it were a prism meant to hypnotize him. He broke out in a cold sweat, and for a moment was back in Chicago...back in time...back to his wedding day....

The decanter had been a wedding present. After he and Kathleen had split up, Slade had smashed, burned or torn into shreds most of his share of the wedding presents they'd haggled over so furiously when it came time to divide up the property. He hadn't cared as much about getting his share of the loot as he had about keeping it out of Kathleen's scheming little hands.

In retrospect he'd acted like a kid throwing a temper tantrum. Considering his lack of culinary skills, he could really have used that automatic egg poacher, for example.

But he hadn't shattered the decanter. Maybe because during that nightmarish period of Slade's life the decanter, frequently filled and frequently emptied, had come to seem more like a close personal friend than a symbol of betrayal.

And now it served as an all-too-vivid reminder of what Slade had suffered the last time he'd let himself fall for a woman, the last time he'd allowed his emotions to determine his actions.

Like a series of snapshots he saw the decanter emerging from its silvery wrapping paper, saw it perched inside the mahogany china cabinet Kathleen had splurged on during the first year of their marriage, saw it sticking forlornly out of one of the cardboard boxes he'd used to pack up his things on the day he moved out forever.

The sight of the decanter brought it all back—the foolish dreams, the gradual disillusionment, the dashed hopes, the shocking betrayal.

Slade had learned his lesson. He wasn't about to dive headfirst into disaster again.

He looked down at Tory, then glanced quickly away, unable to bear the tender, trusting glow in her face. His arms felt like wooden limbs, numb and detached from the rest of his body, as he lowered her awkwardly to the couch.

He felt like the world's biggest heel. But he'd hate himself even more if he went ahead and made love to her, knowing he could never give Tory the kind of commitment a woman like her would expect . . . and deserve.

Slade's surprising about-face left Tory bereft and confused. One minute he'd been ready to whisk her off to his bed, and the next minute he was depositing her against the cushions as if she'd become too heavy a load for him to bear.

Worst of all, he refused to meet her eyes, making it impossible for her to read even a glimmer of his thoughts. His body language was sending messages loud and clear, however. He jammed his hands into his pockets as if he couldn't stand to touch her. He paced impatiently back and forth as if he couldn't wait for her to leave. Finally he settled in a chair halfway across the room, folding his arms and crossing one leg over the other in a pose that could only be called protective.

Suddenly realizing she was still partially nude, Tory shielded her breasts with one arm while rummaging behind the couch for her bra and blouse. Face glowing a neon red, she managed to fasten the clasp behind her back and maneuver her arms through the sleeves of her blouse. This was definitely one of those moments when she wished the earth would open up and swallow her. In fact, this could very well be the single most embarrassing, humiliating, disappointing moment of her life.

Her fingers shook as she fumbled her buttons back into place. God, what a mess she'd gotten herself into! Once again she'd let her heart make decisions, and once again she looked like a fool. "When am I ever going to learn that this is just a game to you?" she asked in a low, husky voice she barely recognized as her own.

"It isn't like that," Slade said, slamming a fist on the arm of his chair.

It was only then Tory realized she'd spoken out loud. Well, this was probably the last time she would ever lay eyes on Slade Marshall—hopefully. She might as well go down swinging. "No?" She closed the last button. "What would you call it, then? A research project? You're investigating how far I'll let you go before I call a halt to your amorous adventuring?" She straightened her blouse with a defiant tug. "Guess I surprised you, huh?"

"Tory—"

"Because I didn't stop you, did I?" She shook her head in pretended sympathy. "So you had to draw the line yourself, poor guy."

He exploded out of his chair. "You've got it all wrong!"

"Do I?" She jumped to her feet to face him on a more equal level.

"Yes! I—I—oh, God." He dragged both his hands through his hair as if trying to tear it out by the roots. "Look, you don't understand why I—why I—stopped."

She propped her hands on her hips. "Care to enlighten me?"

"No! Yes...no." He rubbed his face with both hands, stared at the ceiling for a long moment, then slumped his shoulders as if defeated. "It isn't something I care to discuss."

Her heart gave a sickening lurch. So this was it: the end of the road. Slade was shutting her out for good, and she would never even learn the reason why. Damn it, it wasn't fair!

For heaven's sake, listen to yourself! she scolded silently. *Whining about fairness, when over the years you've learned the hard way that life isn't fair.*

Better finish this farewell scene before her emotions disintegrated completely. Next thing she knew, she'd be throwing herself at Slade's feet and begging him not to leave her. Considering the fact that this was *his* house and Tory would be the one to leave, clinging to his ankles would definitely be inappropriate, not to mention the final indignity.

She wished she could think of some stinging verbal barb to fling at him on her way out the door. On the other hand, it was probably just as well she couldn't, since she could feel tears prickling behind her eyelids and her control over her vocal cords was likely to be precarious at best. The last thing she wanted was to give Slade the satisfaction of seeing her break down and cry.

"I'll be going now," she informed him, backing toward the front door. "I hope you and your moldy Chinese food will be very happy together." *Oh, brilliant, Tory,* she thought. *He'll be reeling from* that *caustic comment for weeks.*

He was standing beside the antique sideboard, holding a glass decanter in his hands and studying it as if it were a crystal ball. Suddenly he set it down with a clatter that made Tory wince with the anticipation of breaking glass.

But her composure remained the only thing shattered.

She couldn't bear for their relationship to end this way, but what choice did she have when Slade refused to talk to her, to explain his sudden turnaround?

Her hand was grasping the doorknob when he finally spoke. "Wait."

Tory kept her fingers wrapped around the knob, but didn't open the door.

"The kindest thing I could do would be to let you walk out that door thinking I'm a complete cad," he said. She could hear the rueful grimace in his voice. "But then, no one ever accused me of being overly kind."

She heard his voice grow louder as he crossed the room. When he touched her shoulder, her head lolled to one side and she pressed her cheek against the back of his hand. She couldn't help it.

Still with her back to him, she whispered, "Talk to me, Slade. Tell me what's going on."

His grip on her shoulder tightened briefly. "There's a part of my past I don't talk about—with anyone."

Her quick blossom of hope withered and died.

"All I can say is that my... reluctance to get further involved with you has nothing to do with you personally. That is—oh, hell." He dropped his arm and took several steps backward. "Look, it has a *lot* to do with you personally. Because you're a terrific woman, Tory Clayton. You're smart, you're courageous, you're funny and warm and beautiful...and frankly, you scare the hell out of me."

She turned slowly in amazement. "I? Scare you? For heaven's sake, why?"

He shook his head, and the volumes of honesty and self-revelation squeezed into that one confession went back into hiding. His face was as unrevealing as a closed book. "Let's just say I was burned once before," he said, "and I've learned not to play with fire."

Now his cryptic, veiled remarks were beginning to annoy Tory. Why couldn't he take the honorable, straightforward route for once and simply explain his bewildering actions?

"How very witty," she said, taking refuge behind a wall of uncharacteristic sarcasm. "I suppose that next you'll be telling me we're like fire and water, or that we don't make a good *match*."

"Well," he said, trying unsuccessfully to smother a grin, "you have to admit, sparks do fly when we're together."

"That's it—I'm outta here." She flung open the door and would have swept down the front steps in a tide of fury and disgust if Slade hadn't grabbed her by the elbow.

"Hey, hold on a second. Don't go away mad."

"I was mad ever to get involved with you in the first place."

"See? That's what I love about you. Your sense of humor doesn't desert you even in the most trying of situations."

Considering the circumstances, his casual use of the word *love* particularly rankled. Clamping her lips together, Tory yanked herself free and fled across the gallery and down the front steps. Right now she would have given anything to be someplace else—next to an erupting volcano, in the eye of a hurricane, in the middle of a war zone. *Anyplace* would be better than this peaceful, shady New Orleans street in the middle of summer with Slade Marshall dogging her heels.

She half expected him to clobber her over the head and drag her back inside by the hair or something. That seemed to be his usual solution whenever he couldn't get his way. At the very least he would try to wrest her car keys away. But Tory flung herself into the driver's seat unmolested.

It was only when she cranked on the ignition that Slade leaped up and stretched himself across the hood of her car.

"Get off there!" she cried angrily, horrified to find herself on the verge of tears again. She rolled down the window and stuck out her head. "I mean it! Get off, or you're going to find yourself bouncing down the fast lane of the Pontchartrain Expressway!"

He waggled his finger at her. "I know you better than that, Tory. You couldn't hurt a fly."

"But I have no problem whatsoever with big obnoxious jerks who think they can get away with manipulating people!"

With that, she threw the car into first gear, released the emergency brake and stepped on the accelerator. Hard.

The car screeched away from the curb, narrowly missing the rear bumper of Slade's Corvette. Through the windshield Tory saw his jaw drop and his eyebrows fly up in surprise. She barely had time to register the grudging admiration mixed with his shock before he vanished.

"Oh, my God!" She slammed on the brakes, then cringed when she noticed the delivery van bearing down on her in the rearview mirror. The driver swerved, honking angrily and shaking his fist at her as he roared past.

Tory whipped open her door and hurled herself into the street. Speeding around the back of her car, she spotted Slade sprawled next to the curb. "Oh, no...oh, no..." she mumbled over and over like a magical incantation that would make him be all right.

One arm was thrown across his face, and pathetic groans drifted into the air to tug at her heartstrings. With his bare feet and bare chest he looked so vulnerable, so victimized.

And she, Victoria Marie Clayton, had done this to him. Oh, God, if she'd killed him she would hate herself for as long as she lived.

She flung herself next to him. "Slade, Slade, are you all right? Where does it hurt? Oh, Lord, I'm so sorry...I didn't mean to—"

His chest was heaving now with what looked like death spasms. Not that Tory had ever seen any before, but these tortured convulsions and the harsh, rhythmic barks erupting from his throat could only be...

Laughter?

Tory delicately pinched Slade's wrist between two fingers and raised his arm off his face. She peered at him suspiciously. He peeled open one eyelid and peered back at her. Then he winked.

She tossed his arm aside as if disposing of an especially repulsive piece of garbage. "I should have known." She jumped to her feet and glared down at him. "Is there no depth to which you won't stoop to make a fool out of me?"

"Aw, Tory, come on." He extended his arm so she could help pull him to his feet. "You're the one who tried to use me to fill in that pothole over there."

She batted his outstretched hand away. "You're lucky I didn't go ahead and finish the job. I should have backed over you while you were lying there pretending to be hurt."

He studied her thoughtfully for a moment before bounding easily to his feet. "I wouldn't blame you if you had."

Sharp pain made Tory realize she'd been digging her nails into her palms. She forced herself to unclench her fists. "You think that makes everything all right, don't you?"

Slade scratched his head. "What?"

"You think that admitting you're a rat makes it okay to be a rat. You're like a little kid who says he's sorry for pulling the cat's tail, then goes right ahead and does it again. He doesn't understand that saying he's sorry every time doesn't mean he can keep doing it over and over again."

Damn it, now she had a rock digging into the bottom of her foot. She bent her knee so she could reach behind her and slip off her shoe. Hopping up and down on one foot, she continued, "You've got this idea that confessing your sins somehow exonerates you. Well, it doesn't." She captured her shoe and probed inside it for the offending pebble. "Admitting your sins only means something if you intend to change your ways." She brandished her shoe at him. "And I know you, Slade Marshall. You *love* being an arrogant louse. You *like* using people. You'll never change." She wobbled on one leg as she slipped her shoe back on. "And being proud of it doesn't let you off the hook."

"You've got it all figured out, haven't you?" During her tirade Slade had completed a thorough inspection of his fingernails. Now he crossed his arms and leaned his face close to hers. "So tell me one thing, Tory Clayton." His teeth flashed like a hungry wolf's. "Why the hell is a nice woman like you getting mixed up with such a rotten scoundrel like me in the first place?"

She opened her mouth to utter a devastating retort, then closed it so hard her teeth clacked. In his usual blunt, no-holds-barred style, Slade had hit the nail right on the head. What the hell *was* she doing mixed up with him?

She shook her head sadly. "I haven't the faintest idea," she said in a barely audible voice.

His triumphant expression dissolved into a mixture of sympathy, understanding and regret. "Ah, Tory." He reached out to toy with a lock of her hair. "Don't you see how bad we are for each other?"

Tears clogged her throat, and she could only manage one curt nod.

Slade feathered his fingers down her temple, over her cheekbone, along her jaw. "I make you crazy, and you—well, like I said before...you scare the living daylights out of me."

"But why?" Tory formed the words with her lips, but no sound came out.

One edge of Slade's mouth twisted into a bitter half smile. "Because you're so good. Because we could be so good together."

"But you said—"

"Shh." He placed a finger across her lips. "Because I can't shrug you off like other women. You've already become far too important to me."

Tory's eyes flicked back and forth as she searched desperately for some flaw in his reasoning.

"I don't want to need you, Tory. Because I've learned through harsh experience that you can't count on the people you need." He cupped her face in his hands. "The only person you can count on is yourself."

"Oh, Slade . . ."

He bent his head so their foreheads bumped. "I have a feeling that losing you could make my past misfortunes seem like a picnic in comparison." He drew back and probed her with his gaze. "I can't risk that, Tory. Call me a coward, but I have to get out now, before it's too late. Before I fall in—before I . . . come to care for you too much."

Tory ached to assure him that he didn't have to fear losing her; she longed to promise that she would never, ever leave him. But how could she? Right now her feelings toward Slade were confused, to say the least. She wasn't sure how she felt about him right this minute, much less how she might feel about him weeks or months or years from now.

Besides, that stern, unyielding look on his face left no room for argument. For better or worse, Slade had made up his mind. Pleading with him now would only destroy whatever self-respect Tory had left and tarnish whatever few precious memories she could salvage from this relationship.

And when you got right down to it, hadn't they both said all there was to say?

Except one thing.

Tory kissed her fingertips, then pressed them to Slade's lips. She grazed his cheeks with one knuckle, remembering how rough and unshaven he'd looked the first time she saw him.

Now this was the last time she would see him.

"Goodbye, Slade," she whispered, hoping she'd turned away before he could see the tears shining in her eyes.

This time he let her go.

She stumbled back to her car and groped for the ignition. Choking back a sob, she put the car in gear and pulled away. But she couldn't resist one last glance in the rearview mirror.

Slade was standing in the middle of the street, feet planted apart and one hand shading his eyes as he watched her drive away.

Blindly Tory fumbled for the windshield wiper switch. Then she realized it wasn't rain that blurred her vision.

Chapter Ten

Tory paused in front of Robby's room, shifting her armload of packages so she could press her ear against the door. Strange. Robby must have left the TV on when he left for school this morning.

As the bundles began to ooze from her grasp, she sidled down the hallway to the next door, then remembered the room key was still in her purse.

Damn. Add one more item to her list of things gone wrong lately. She juggled the parcels while groping for her purse, but as first one and then another slid to the floor, Tory finally sighed and dropped the entire load in disgust.

Stepping over the mess into the room she was sharing with Nana, she had to admit it was pretty ridiculous to buy out the French Market while Don Gerard was providing them with three square meals a day.

But Nana was so fond of fresh Creole tomatoes, and that sweet-potato pie she loved was sold exclusively at the little bakeshop at one end of the marketplace....

Well, it wouldn't hurt to keep spoiling her for a while, Tory decided as she rounded up her uncooperative packages. Her grandmother had suffered more than her share of bad luck lately. First her stay in the hospital...then the loss of the Creole Courtyard...and now the dislocation of living under someone else's roof.

Although Nana had appeared to be in seventh heaven when Tory had passed through the lobby just now. Ensconced behind the front desk with her old pal Don Gerard, Marie Clayton was having the time of her life swapping French Quarter anecdotes and comparing notes on the trials and tribulations of being a guest house proprietor.

Tory opened the door of the small refrigerator Don had thoughtfully provided and plucked out a root beer. At least *Nana* was enjoying their enforced sojourn here. Despite Don's protests to the contrary, Tory couldn't help feeling guilty that the three Claytons were occupying rent-free two rooms that could have gone to paying guests.

At least it was the slow tourist season, so Don probably wasn't turning away business because of them. Tory leaned back in her chair and sipped her root beer, reflecting that good old Generous Gerard would no doubt have put them up even at the height of Mardi Gras.

Friends like him were hard to come by. But as soon as the insurance check arrived, Tory intended to rent an apartment until the Creole Courtyard was inhabitable again.

The insurance check. That little reminder opened the gates for another invasion of the depression Tory had been trying to stave off for a week now.

One week. Seven days since she'd seen Slade. Let's see, seven times twenty-four would be how many hours?

"Cut it out," she said aloud, hoisting herself out of the chair and walking to the window. "It's over and done with. You should thank your lucky stars you escaped before you got *really* attached to him."

But if these feelings she couldn't seem to shake weren't *real* attachment, Tory didn't know what was.

She gazed down at Royal Street, watching shoppers and tourists and residents stroll by, disgusted with herself for the way her heart leaped whenever she caught sight of a tall man with wavy brown hair and a cocky stride.

A kid with an enormous tape deck grafted to his shoulder whizzed by on a skateboard. The raucous noise blaring from its oversized speakers reminded Tory that Robby's television was still on.

She set down her can of root beer and headed downstairs to ask Don for an extra key to Robby's room. No sense wasting electricity by waiting for Robby to get back from school. It wasn't even noon yet, and like as not Robby wouldn't come straight home, anyway. During the past few days he'd reverted to his old habits and spent most of his time hanging out with his ruffian friends.

On the off chance he'd forgotten to lock his door this morning, Tory tested the knob as she passed by. To her surprise, the room was unlocked. Well, maybe not so surprising. Carelessness wasn't much of a crime compared to some of Robby's other recent behavior.

She was halfway across the room to the TV set when she realized she wasn't alone. With a gasp she pulled up short. "Robby!"

He was lying on the bed, scruffy sneakers on the hand-made quilt, nose buried in a magazine Tory was willing to bet he wasn't reading for the informative articles. He lowered the magazine half an inch, gave her a "Hi, Tor," and retreated behind the pages again.

Fuming, Tory marched across the room and switched off the inane game show babbling away.

"Hey!"

At least she'd found *one* way to gain his attention. "What are you doing here, Robby? As if I didn't know." She snatched the magazine and flung it into the wastebasket. "You're skipping summer school again, aren't you?"

"No." His dark brows gathered into an angry V.

"Don't lie to me, Robby."

"Then don't call me by that stupid name." He swung his legs over the side of the bed and dragged himself into a slouch that vaguely resembled a normal sitting position.

"Robby is a perfectly good name. *Gator* is a stupid name."

"What would you know?" he mumbled, peering longingly at the discarded magazine.

"I'll tell you one thing I know, Robert Randolph Clayton, and that's—oh, for Pete's sake." As usual she'd allowed him to sidetrack her from the main issue. Amazing how good Robby was at manipulating her. Maybe it was a little trick he'd picked up from his short acquaintance with Slade.

"Robby, I'm warning you, if you keep skipping class like this—"

"I told ya, I ain't skipping school."

"And I told *you* not to lie to me."

"I ain't lying!"

"Then what are you doing home from school? Let me guess. You've got a sore throat. Tummy ache? Fever?" She tapped her foot. "Hangover, more likely. Robby, what am I going to do with you? I try so hard, but—"

"I got suspended."

"You *what?*"

At least he had the good grace to look uncomfortable. "You heard me," he mumbled.

"You're suspended from school? What on earth for?"

He gave a half-hearted shrug. "Fighting."

"Fighting?" Tory felt like he'd clobbered her with a two-by-four. She breathed in deeply, trying to recapture the wind he'd knocked out of her. "Well, I can see *you're* all right. What about the other kid?"

"Black eye, that's all." Robby seemed almost pleased with himself.

"How long are you suspended for?" she asked, wondering who she should call first, the school principal or the other kid's mother.

He yawned. "A week."

"You're suspended for a *week?*" Tory stared at him with dismay and disbelief. "Robby, how will you ever catch up with your classes? Did your teachers give you any assignments to work on during your—" she gulped "—suspension?"

"Who cares? I ain't gonna do 'em, anyway."

"You're not going to—what do you mean, you're not going to do them?" She shook her finger in front of his nose. "You most certainly *are* going to do your assignments, Robby. Otherwise you'll fall even further behind and you'll never catch up and then you won't graduate next spring!"

He climbed to his feet. "So what?"

They'd had this argument a hundred times before. Tory felt like an actress performing a memorized script from a bad play. "If you don't graduate from high school, you'll never get a decent job. And don't say *'so what?'*" she warned as he opened his mouth.

He knotted his fists. "Who died and made you queen, anyway?" he shouted. "It's my life and I'll do what I want!"

Tory reached out a hand to stop him, but he knocked it aside as he stormed out of the room. She followed him into the hall. "Robby!" she called after him, knowing it was useless.

She wasn't about to create a scene and disturb Don's paying guests by charging after her brother. She slumped against the wall and covered her face with her hands. "You handled that really well, Victoria," she muttered through her fingers. "Ever consider a career in diplomacy?"

This was even more of a disaster than the Creole Courtyard fire. The guest house could be rebuilt, but Robby was headed straight for self-destruction. And lives weren't as easily repaired as buildings.

If only I knew how to handle him . . . if only I'd been a better guardian . . . if only I knew someone who could talk some sense into him. . . .

The trouble was, Tory *did* know someone who could reach Robby in a way she couldn't. Someone Robby respected, someone who'd proved to be a good influence on him before.

Slade.

God, would she never be free of him? Somehow he'd managed to entangle himself not only in her own life, but in the lives of her family as well. Nana kept asking about him, wondering why he didn't drop by to visit anymore. And now Robby, whether he knew it or not, could definitely benefit from Slade's friendship.

Despite his rough edges, Slade would set such a good example for her brother. A couple of man-to-man talks might not turn Robby's life completely around, but they would certainly steer him in the right direction.

Impossible, of course. Tory had no intention of ever seeing Slade again, much less begging him to befriend her brother. She would willingly sacrifice her pride for Robby's sake, but even if she persuaded Slade to spend some time with her brother, what if Robby discovered the whole thing was Tory's idea? She would probably lose him forever.

Of course, that might happen anyway. Next March Robby would turn eighteen and become a legal adult. Tory's last remnants of control over him would evaporate. Even if he didn't get kicked out of school before then, nothing and no one could prevent Robby from dropping out when his birthday rolled around.

No one—except maybe Slade.

"So we're back to that again," Tory mused aloud. "I keep going around in circles and never seem to get anywhere."

A middle-aged woman coming down the hall gave her a strange look and a wide berth as she passed. "Great, now I'm scaring off Don's guests," Tory said to herself. She waggled her fingers at the woman. "Rehearsing a play," she said with a sheepish smile.

The woman ducked into her room and quickly slammed the door.

Tory sighed. She could hardly blame the poor woman for thinking her crazy. Maybe she *was* going crazy. Maybe that's why the corridor walls seemed to be closing in on her.

Maybe she needed to get out of this place for a while.

After making sure both rooms were locked, she headed downstairs. Her grandmother broke off her conversation with Don to direct a worried frown at Tory. "Victoria dear, is anything the matter?"

"I just need some fresh air, Nana. Thought I'd walk over to the river."

"But Robert came flying through here a few minutes ago like a crocodile was nipping at his heels."

"You didn't happen to see which direction he went, did you?"

Both Don and Marie shook their heads. "Victoria, what happened?"

Tory considered making up a story, then decided it was pointless. How could she possibly hide Robby's presence during school hours? Besides, her grandmother would kill her if she discovered Tory had lied to protect her. "Robby got suspended from school for fighting," she said.

"Oh, dear me." Marie slipped off her spectacles and tapped them against her chin. "Well, I can't say I'm surprised. That boy's been headed straight for trouble for quite some time."

"I feel so helpless, Nana! I wish I knew how to reach him, how to make him understand why school's so important."

Don shuffled some papers as if embarrassed to be witness to this family discussion. "Robby'll straighten out one of these days, Tory," he said. He nudged Marie. "After all, he comes from good stock, right?"

Marie tilted her chin up. "The best, of course."

"Even if he *is* part Yankee," Don continued with a mischievous wink.

"Oh, you..." Marie swatted him with her spectacles. "Don's right," she told Tory. "Robert will come around one of these days. Youthful hijinks, that's all it is. Why, I remember one time his father..."

As Marie plunged back into her reminiscing, Tory took the opportunity to slip out the door. Ordinarily she loved listening to Nana's stories, but right now she had too much on her mind.

Maybe the river breeze would blow away all the cares and problems cluttering her mind. When she reached the boardwalk that crowned the levee, Tory settled herself onto one of the few empty benches. The breeze wasn't exactly cool, but on a hot sticky day like today, any air movement was welcome.

Down the boardwalk a lone street musician played a rather screechy version of "Won't You Come Home, Bill Bailey?" on his saxophone. Occasionally someone dropped a handful of coins into the instrument case propped open on the ground in front of him. Tory watched a bunch of tourists crowd around him while one of their group snapped a picture. The saxophonist didn't miss a note—not that his performance would have suffered much if he had.

She leaned her head back against the bench and closed her eyes. If she could only lose herself in the sounds and smells of her surroundings, maybe she could blot out the more unpleasant matters clamoring for her attention.

Nearby, the calliope on the paddle-wheeled steamboat *Natchez* began to play, its out-of-tune, noisy tooting intended to lure passengers for its next sightseeing cruise. The saxophone player blew harder. It was a valiant effort, but after a few earsplitting minutes of clashing melodies, he surrendered. As the calliope finally drowned him out, Tory pried open one eyelid and saw him packing up his sax.

She closed both eyes again. The sun's heat baked into her pores. No, with this humidity it was more like being in a lobster steamer than an oven. Only a native Louisianan could appreciate a day like today, she decided.

Inhaling deeply, Tory sniffed the delicious aroma wafting upstream from the Café du Monde, the best people-watching spot in the Quarter. She could almost taste the mouth-watering *beignets,* those little fried doughnuts piled with powdered sugar and inevitably served with a steaming cup of café au lait. Incredibly messy to eat...but incredibly tasty.

Tory's stomach rumbled.

"Hungry?" someone asked.

Immediately her appetite fled. Reluctantly she opened her eyes. "What are you doing here?" she croaked.

"I brought you the insurance check," Slade replied, pulling an envelope from his shirt pocket as he sat down beside her.

She took it from him and stared at it stupidly. "I—thought this would come in the mail."

He adjusted his sunglasses and shrugged. "I had to go by Coliseum Insurance this morning, so I figured as long as I was there I'd speed things up and pick up the check." He removed his sunglasses and folded them into his pocket. "I know how anxious you are to get the money."

"Well...thank you. I *am* anxious to get started with the rebuilding." Now that he'd taken off his sunglasses, Tory was surprised to see dark circles rimming his eyes. When she looked more closely, she noticed a new set of creases bracketing the corners of his mouth, making him look tired or worried or both.

No doubt he was simply suffering the aftereffects of one too many nights of carousing.

"So...how soon will the Creole Courtyard be rising from the ashes?" he asked.

"The contractor's ready to start as soon as I have the money for his first installment payment." She fanned the check back and forth. "He estimates it'll take about three months."

"Which probably means it'll take six," Slade said.

Tory gave a wry smile. "Probably."

"You gonna stay at that bed-and-breakfast place till then?"

"Uh-uh." She shook her head. "Now that I've got money in the bank, I'm going to find the three of us an apartment. Just until we can move back into the guest house, of course."

"Of course." A warning blast erupted from the ferry pulling away from the terminal across the river. Slade followed its progress as he asked casually, "So how's your family? Your grandmother home from the hospital now?"

"Oh, yes." For a moment Tory wrestled with the nearly irresistible temptation to tell him all about Robby. Maybe if she dropped big enough hints, Slade would offer to talk to him.

Bad idea. Slade would see right through her, anyway. He always did.

The silence between them was becoming awkward. After everything they'd been through, did they really have nothing to talk about?

"Gideon wants me to keep the whole insurance check," Tory said finally. "Even though part of it legally belongs to him."

Slade snorted. "That's the least he could do, after all the trouble he caused you."

"I suppose. Still, he's also going to sign his share of the partnership over to me. He didn't have to do that."

"The guy's a regular prince." Drawing one knee onto the bench, Slade turned to face her. "So you're going to be the sole owner of the Creole Courtyard again, huh? That should make you happy."

It *should* make her happy. Why, then, did she feel so miserable?

The calliope ceased its cacophony, making the silences between them even more pointed. They both stood up at the same time.

"Well, I have to get back—"

"Let me buy you an ice cream cone," Slade said.

"An . . . ice-cream cone?"

"Yeah, you know." He mimed a licking motion. "One of those delicious cold things that melt all over your hand if you're not careful? They come in chocolate, vanilla, pistachio . . . any of this ring a bell?"

She pursed her lips. "Yes, of course, but—"

"Come on. It's the perfect antidote for this sweltering weather. Besides—" he feigned a jab at her midsection "—I have audible proof that you're hungry, remember?"

Tory clutched her stomach, more to soothe its excited churning than to shield it from Slade. What did this unexpected invitation signify? She found it hard to believe Slade would bother tracking her down just to deliver the insurance check or inquire about her family's health. Could there be even a remote possibility that he regretted breaking off their relationship?

She didn't dare allow herself to believe it. But as long as the slightest spark of hope remained, Tory knew she would never have the strength of will to turn her back on Slade and walk away.

"An ice cream cone would be nice," she said, hoping she'd be able to keep it down, what with all the butterflies practicing kamikaze raids in her stomach.

"Great." His pleased grin erased some of the tiredness from his face. "Let's go to that place across the square, shall we?"

As they cut through the park, Tory thought of something. "How did you find me, anyway?"

"I'm an investigator, remember?" He punched her good-naturedly on the shoulder. Apparently punches and jabs were the only forms of physical affection she was going to get from him. "Actually your grandma told me. I dropped by the Bayou Bed and Breakfast looking for you."

"So you already knew she was home from the hospital."

"Well...yeah." He scratched his ear. "Guess I was just trying to make small talk when I asked about her earlier." Good grief, was that a blush creeping up his neck? Highly unlikely. Probably just sunburn.

At the ice-cream parlor, Tory finally settled on the strawberry-cheesecake flavor. Slade, predictably, selected a decadent chocolate-chocolate chip. The next few minutes were consumed by an orgy of slurping as they meandered back through the park, hot sun melting their ice cream almost as fast as they could eat it.

Tory settled onto a wrought iron bench across from the statue of Andrew Jackson. "Napkin?" She offered one to Slade.

"Mmm, thanks." He wiped a dab of chocolate from the corner of his mouth, and Tory found herself licking her lips in unconscious response.

"How's work going?" she asked.

"Oh...fine. Just fine." He pushed the last chunk of his cone into his mouth and licked his fingers. "Hey, your ice cream's dripping," he said.

"Huh? Oh, yikes!" Hastily she lapped up the melting trails dribbling down her cone. If she'd planned to wow Slade with her poise, her grace, her dignity, she was failing spectacularly.

"Here, you look like you could use this." Slade offered her his slightly used napkin, fascinated by her frantic efforts to keep pace with her oozing ice cream. Something about the movement of her mouth, the swirl of her tongue, the curve of her lips, struck him as incredibly sensual. A coil of desire unfurled in his loins, and he shifted uncomfortably.

This was ridiculous. He hadn't reneged on his vow never to see Tory again just so he could pass on her insurance check or buy her an ice cream cone.

Get on with it, he urged himself. But Slade knew what he'd come to explain would be as hard for him to say as it would be for Tory to hear.

The St. Louis Cathedral began to chime the hour, and as the last stroke died away he said, "You must really despise me."

Tory was in the process of poking the last bite of her cone into her mouth. She nearly choked on it. "What— why do you say that?" she asked when she'd recovered.

"Because of the way I treated you last week. Leading you on, letting you think I was going to make love to you, then changing my mind for no apparent reason."

Amazing how adorable she was when her skin flushed the color of pink camellias. "Well, now that you mention it..."

Slade gripped the back of the bench as if it could give him the moral support to continue. "The fact is, Tory, I *did* plan to make love to you. I wanted you—more than you'll ever know." He had to look away from those beautiful, bewildered eyes. "It simply wouldn't work out between us, that's all. Not because of you. Because of me."

"Why are you telling me all this?" she asked. The faint quiver in her voice was reflected in the glitter of moisture filming her eyes. "Why couldn't you stay away? Why did you have to come here and raise my hopes?"

Slade sprang off the bench as if propelled by an explosion of self-loathing. "I came because I wanted you to know the truth—the *whole* truth, about why I can't let myself get too close to any woman."

Tory lifted her hand. "Slade, whatever it is . . ."

He shook his head violently. "Let me tell you, all right? So we can both get this over with."

She swallowed, nodded her head.

He'd rehearsed this scene a dozen times over the last few days, ever since he'd decided that he couldn't let things end the way they had, with Tory thinking him a complete jerk. He'd lain awake night after night, wanting desperately for her to understand.

Why, then, was he having such a tough time figuring out how to start?

He dragged his hand over his jaw. "Remember I mentioned once that I'd been married?"

Tory's eyes widened with horror.

"No, no, I'm not still married. That isn't it."

Caution blended with the relief in her face. "What, then?"

"It's sort of a long story." He sucked in a deep breath. "I met Kathleen, the woman I was married to, while I was taking night classes toward my college degree. She was in my sociology class."

Tory examined her fingernails. "How long ago was this?" she asked, not completely succeeding at sounding casual.

"About ten years ago." Slade leaned back against the wrought iron fence circling the statue. "We dated for a couple of months, and then one day she told me she was pregnant."

Tory glanced up sharply, dropping the pretense of studying her nails.

"I don't know if we would have gotten married eventually anyway. Probably not. I knew it would be a struggle at first—I had two more years of school left and was still working full-time as a firefighter. But after the rotten childhood I'd had, I wasn't about to let any kid of mine grow up without a decent home and both a mother *and* a father."

"Does your child live with Kathleen now?" Tory asked the question so softly Slade could barely hear her.

He bowed his head. "No. There isn't any child." He looked up in time to see Tory flinch. "About a month after we got married, in the middle of the night, I got called out of bed to the scene of a really bad fire. I didn't get home until late the next day." A young couple paused to snap a picture of the statue. Slade waited for them to leave before continuing. "When I walked in the door Kathleen told me she'd had a miscarriage, that she hadn't been able to get hold of me and finally had to call a cab to get to the hospital."

Tory clapped a hand over her mouth. "Oh, Slade...I'm *so* sorry."

He winced. "You can imagine how I felt, not being there when Kathleen needed me. I kept torturing myself, thinking that if only I'd been home where I belonged, maybe my child would still be alive." He clenched his fingers around one of the tall spikes forming the fence. "Do you know, that was the first time in my life I ever seriously considered quitting the fire department?"

"Slade, what happened wasn't your fault! You couldn't have known—"

He cut her off with a weary slash of his hand. "It doesn't matter now."

"No... of course not."

He could tell Tory was puzzled by his seeming apathy. "All of a sudden, the reason we'd gotten married had vanished. Still, we'd made a commitment to each other, and I wanted our marriage to work. Despite the tragedy, for the first time in my life I had stability... a real home... someone to share my life with."

Tory waited silently, expectantly, for him to go on. Slade stared past her shoulder, seeing the years of his marriage race by—the good intentions... the deception... the shocking revelation. "Time passed. After a while I thought we should try to have another baby. Kathleen agreed. She seemed to have recovered from the miscarriage. So we tried." He chortled, but it wasn't a happy sound. "After three years of trying, Kathleen still wasn't pregnant. So she went to her doctor. I kept calling her from work all that afternoon to find out what he'd said."

Anger welled up inside Slade, but after all these years it had lost some of its force. "I rushed home to find Kathleen sobbing at the kitchen table. She said the doctor had told her the miscarriage had left her unable to have any more children."

"Oh, no..." The blend of anguish and sympathy in Tory's expression struck a grateful chord in Slade's heart. He'd never told this story to anyone before, but he was glad he was telling it to Tory.

"According to the doctor, the delay in getting to the hospital during her miscarriage had caused some kind of complications. I tried to question Kathleen, to get more details about what actually happened the day of the miscarriage. But she was so upset I felt like a monster for interrogating her."

"I can't even imagine what you must have gone through," Tory murmured.

Slade rubbed his forehead. "I was stunned," he said. "Maybe I didn't want to believe it because that would have magnified the guilt I already felt about not being home when it happened. But I had to try to make some sense out of the nightmare." He backhanded the sweat off his brow. "So the next day I went to talk with Kathleen's doctor myself."

Tory waited for him to continue. She'd torn her napkin into shreds, which littered her lap like white confetti.

"I don't know what I hoped the doctor could tell me," Slade said. "Maybe he'd made a mistake, maybe it was *my* fault we couldn't have another baby. I wanted to ask him about other options. Surgery, fertility specialists . . . I just couldn't accept that because I hadn't been home to get Kathleen to the hospital, I'd destroyed her chance to have another child."

"And . . . what did the doctor say?"

"Several interesting things. First of all, Kathleen hadn't been to see him in several years."

"What?" The color drained from Tory's face.

"Wait, it gets better."

"Slade, I don't understand—"

"Neither did I at first." He snorted. "And the doctor seemed kind of confused, too. I guess he assumed I already knew Kathleen's medical history, or he wouldn't have let it slip."

"Let . . . what slip?"

"Turns out Kathleen had been in a serious car accident as a child. She broke both legs and an arm, suffered extensive internal injuries, and spent months in the hospital. But that wasn't the bombshell he dropped."

"Bombshell?"

"That's what it felt like, anyway, when the doctor shook his head sadly and commented how tragic it was that her childhood accident had also made it impossible for Kathleen ever to conceive a child."

Chapter Eleven

Bombshell, indeed.

Slade might as well have fired one of those old Civil War cannons guarding the museum at one side of Jackson Square. His words hit Tory with the force of a dynamite blast, and in the blinding glare she finally saw the reason for his cynicism, his suspicious nature, his reluctance to form attachments.

"Slade, I—I don't know what to say."

"Well, I had plenty to say, believe me, when I got home from seeing Kathleen's doctor."

"Did she try to explain what she'd done?"

Slade guffawed. "How could she explain tricking me into marriage, putting me through the nightmare of losing a baby that never existed, and then torturing me with guilt?"

"She must have said *something*."

"Let me tell you, we both said *plenty* that day. Kathleen accused me of being a terrible husband—that if I loved her, her inability to have children wouldn't matter."

"Which wasn't the point at all."

"Of course not!" Slade flung his hands in the air. "Kathleen couldn't seem to get it through her head that the reason I was leaving her was because of the monstrous lies she'd told me, the way she'd betrayed me—not because she couldn't give me children."

Tory rose slowly to her feet and walked over to stand next to Slade. She gripped the fence railing, hoping it would help her regain some emotional balance. She was starting to sift through the fallout of Slade's explosive revelation, and the prognosis didn't look good. After all these years, Kathleen's deception was about to claim another victim. Tory.

"End of story," Slade said. "I packed a suitcase that day and never came back, except to haggle over who got the silverware and who got the bath towels."

"She must have been a terribly troubled woman," Tory said softly.

"That's very generous of you, but you give Kathleen too much credit. She was a spoiled, self-centered brat who didn't hesitate to trample all over other people's feelings if it got her what she wanted." Slade ruefully massaged the nape of his neck. "I recognized her shortcomings before I married her, but I never dreamed she would go to the lengths she did."

Without thinking, Tory touched his arm and said, "But I'm not Kathleen."

Did she only imagine it, or did he actually recoil under her touch? "No," he said gently. "You're the exact opposite of Kathleen. But I'm still me."

"You can't go through life hating all women just because one of them hurt you!" Tory cried.

Slade's mouth twisted into a sad smile. "I don't hate women," he said. "Not at all. And especially not you." He drew in a deep breath and dropped back his head to stare up at the sky for a moment. "Kathleen destroyed something inside me," he told the gulls wheeling overhead. "For the first and only time in my life I let myself trust someone, I let someone become important to me." He met Tory's eyes. "I opened myself up to another human being and allowed myself to become vulnerable."

"So you're never going to let yourself get close to another person again," Tory said, fighting back tears.

"I can't," he said simply.

"You mean, you won't."

"No. I mean that the part of me capable of loving someone wholeheartedly, without reservation, is gone."

"But how do you know, if you won't give it a chance?" This time Tory failed to choke back the sob welling up in her throat.

Slade cradled her face between his hands, his expression nearly as miserable as the way she felt. "Tory, don't you see? It wouldn't be fair to *you* if I let our relationship continue." She felt his fingers tremble against her cheeks. "I know myself, Tory. I know the way my relationships with women invariably end." Now she saw him through a blurred veil of tears. "It isn't only myself I'm thinking of this time—it's you. I can't stand to hurt you any more than I already have, sweetheart."

Tory drew in a long, shuddering breath. People were already starting to stare at them curiously. She wasn't about to create even more of a public spectacle by bursting into a noisy fit of blubbering.

Slade swabbed the tears from her eyes with the pads of his thumbs. "For what it's worth, I'll never forgive myself for doing this to you. But it's the only way."

"Just go," she mouthed in silent despair.

He pressed his lips to her forehead for an instant that seemed as long as summer, as brief as a heartbeat. "I'll miss you, Tory," he whispered. Then he was gone.

She opened her eyes to see him striding rapidly toward the nearest park gate. "You blew it, Slade," she called.

He froze, turned slowly.

Tory brushed the wet stickiness from her cheeks and tossed back her head. "We had something special, you and I. We could have been great together."

His Adam's apple bobbed once. "I know," he said. "That's why we have to end it."

Then a tour group shuffled between them, and when they drifted past Tory's line of vision, Slade was gone.

She gave the water shutoff valve a mighty twist with her wrench, and once again the soothing splash of the fountain filled the courtyard.

Tory stepped back to gaze at her handiwork with satisfaction. To save money on the Creole Courtyard's restoration, she'd been rolling up her sleeves and tackling some of the repair work herself during the past month.

The less money she had to pay the contractor and his workmen, the more sound a financial footing the guest house would be on when it finally reopened. Tory wasn't about to risk losing the place again.

Besides, working from dawn till dusk kept her mind off other more painful matters she could do nothing about.

She splayed her hand against the base of her spine and arched backward. Bones creaked and muscles whined in protest, but her physical exhaustion was a good feeling nevertheless. Her aching soreness made Tory feel as if she'd really accomplished something today.

And rebuilding the Creole Courtyard was progressing even faster than she'd dared to hope. From the outside you could hardly tell there'd been a fire recently. Thank heavens for the uncharacteristic dry spell New Orleans had enjoyed for the last few weeks!

Although if the storm clouds gathering overhead were any indication, that dry spell was about to end. Tory gathered up her tools, checked her watch and realized she was going to be late for dinner again. Nana would no doubt serve her up a hearty portion of scolding along with her reheated casserole.

But pitching in to fix up the guest house gave Tory a goal, a purpose—something to occupy her time and energy. If she weren't sweeping up debris or scrubbing off scorch marks or repainting the woodwork, she would be sitting around all day watching game shows and stuffing her face and moping about things that could never be.

Instead, she arrived before the work crew showed up each morning and stayed until long after they left at five. She could tumble into bed exhausted at night, instead of lying awake staring at the ceiling or crying into her pillow so Nana wouldn't hear her.

With a clang, Tory pulled shut the iron gate across the guest house entrance and started the two-block journey to the apartment she'd rented temporarily for Nana, Robby and herself.

Not that you'd ever guess Robby lived there. A lance of despair shot through Tory at the thought of her brother. Robby had refused to return to summer school after his suspension ended, and she dreaded the uphill battle she would face when the fall semester started in a couple of weeks.

He put in an appearance at home less and less frequently these days, and Tory could only imagine the trouble he was getting into with those hooligans he hung around with. She was at her wit's end and didn't know where to turn. She'd considered and rejected every possible solution she could think of. Bribery? Threats? Locking him in his room?

Hmm ... if she boarded up Robby's bedroom window and fed him a steady diet of pancakes and other food that could be slipped under the door...

Nonsense, of course. But it was a sorry sign of how desperate Tory was that she could halfheartedly consider the crazy scheme even for a minute.

Last week she'd suggested they both go in for some kind of family counseling, but Robby had laughed it off. "You got a problem, *you* go see a shrink. Me, the only problem I got is *you*."

For the thousandth time, Tory asked herself how on earth she'd managed to fail Robby so miserably. Her parents would be so disappointed in her if they could see what an inadequate guardian she'd turned out to be.

Tory's bleak mood matched the ominous gray sky darkening overhead. The wind had picked up, and she had to dodge crumpled newspapers and discarded food wrappers that blew across her path. She clutched her portable radio tighter. All day long newscasters had been broadcasting hurricane warnings for the entire Gulf Coast, with the predicted landfall somewhere in eastern Texas.

But the outskirts of the storm system were expected to swish through New Orleans during the middle of the night, and Tory noticed a few people had crisscrossed masking tape over their windows just in case the hurricane veered unexpectedly in this direction.

One blessing from the approaching storm front: the temperature had subsided half-a-dozen degrees in the past hour. Still, it was a relief to step into the air-conditioned apartment. "I'm home, Nana! Sorry I'm late."

She heard voices coming from the kitchen. Strange...unless Robby had stopped by to change clothes or grab a free meal. Tory set down the radio by the front door and hurried through the living room.

"Tory!" LuAnne bounced up like a jack-in-the-box, nearly jostling her glasses off her nose. "Oh, goody, you're here! Now we can tell you our news."

"News? Hi, Gideon." Tory lowered herself into the fourth kitchen chair just as her grandmother pushed herself to her feet. "Sit down, Nana. I'll get my dinner in a minute."

"In a minute it won't be fit for human consumption. It's already dried out like a shrunken head, sitting in that oven all this time."

"Ick!" LuAnne made a face.

"Sorry, Nana. I know I promised not to be late for dinner anymore."

"Humph." Marie clunked down a plate of something that had indeed metamorphosed beyond recognition.

Tory poked it experimentally with her fork. "So, what's this news of yours?"

LuAnne's smile was positively dazzling as she linked hands with Gideon. "We're engaged!"

Tory's fork clattered to her plate. "You're *what?*" She stared at Gideon for confirmation.

He waved his free hand helplessly. "It's the truth, *cher*. The fair LuAnne has captured my heart."

"Ooh, you say just the sweetest things, honey lamb!" LuAnne pinched his cheek fondly.

Rubbing the red mark left by LuAnne's enthusiastic gesture of affection, Gideon sneaked Tory a sheepish glance.

She couldn't help chuckling. "Well, well," she said, spearing a bite of dinner into her mouth, "Who'd have thought old Footloose Fontaine would ever settle down? When's the wedding?"

"Oh, real soon—"

"Not for quite a while yet—"

The two lovebirds eyed each other with dismay.

Tory swallowed and reached for her water glass. "Better get your stories straight, guys."

LuAnne laughed nervously. "We haven't exactly set a date yet."

"I kind of guessed that."

Marie carried the coffeepot to the table. "Oh, fiddlesticks—what does the date matter? What's important is that you've both found someone to share your life with, and I simply couldn't be happier for you." As she reached to fill Tory's cup, she gave her granddaughter an accusing nudge with her sharp bony elbow.

Terrific. Even Nana was ganging up on her. As if Tory had purposely broken up with Slade just to spite her grandmother.

Whatever appetite she'd mustered for her desiccated dinner promptly fled.

"More coffee?" Marie poised the coffeepot over LuAnne's cup.

"No, thank you, Mrs. Clayton. Gideon and I really have to run. Isn't that right, honey lamb?"

Gideon did indeed remind Tory of a sheep as he obediently followed LuAnne out of the kitchen. Tory saw them to the front door. "We surely didn't mean to barge in on your supper," LuAnne prattled on, "but I just couldn't wait to tell you our exciting news! I mean, Gideon hasn't even bought me a ring yet or anything...."

Gideon ran a finger beneath his collar, which appeared to be strangling him all of a sudden.

"And I knew how happy you'd be for us—oh, dear!"

A ferocious gust of wind practically blew them backward when Tory opened the door. Gideon peered up at the purple sky. "I do believe we're about to get wet, *cher.*"

LuAnne clasped her hands together. "Oh, Tory, could you please, please, *please* give us a ride to the streetcar? I wouldn't *dream* of imposing, but this dress is brand new and I'd *hate* for it to get ruined...."

Tory smothered an exasperated sigh. Telling Nana she'd be right back, she snatched up her purse and herded her visitors out the door. Maybe if they hurried, she could be safely back inside before the deluge started.

The parking garage where she rented a space was one block over. The blustery wind made walking as well as conversation difficult, and it was a relief to reach the shelter of the garage.

Tory groped for her keys, then stopped dead in her tracks as if someone had rammed a fist into her solar plexus. Frantically she scanned the nearby parking spaces. "Where—where—"

"Tory, what's wrong?" LuAnne asked anxiously.

"You look pale as a ghost, *cher.*"

"My car," Tory choked out. "It's gone. My car. It's been s-stolen!"

Distant lightning ripped jagged tears in the sky as Tory dashed up the steps to the apartment. In addition to cooler temperatures the storm had another beneficial side effect: if LuAnne hadn't been so worried about her precious new dress getting soaked, Tory wouldn't have discovered her car missing until tomorrow at the earliest.

She'd left Gideon and his betrothed to find their own way back to the streetcar stop, then broken some kind of sprint record getting back to the apartment to call the police.

The phone started ringing just as she jabbed her key into the lock. "I'll get it, Nana!" she hollered as she flew through the front door. She practically tore the receiver from her grandmother's hand, but she was impatient to get rid of the caller so she could phone the police.

"Yes? Hello?"

Marie tsk-tsked indignantly.

Silence. No, not silence. In the background Tory could hear tinkling glass and some kind of pounding music.

"Hello? Is someone there? Look, I don't have time for pranks—"

"Tory?"

The voice was so quiet she had to plug one ear with her finger to hear. "What?"

"Tory, it's me."

"Robby?"

"Yeah."

She hesitated, taken aback by this unexpected call.

"I'm sort of in trouble."

The back of Tory's neck prickled. "Robby? Can you speak up? I can barely hear you."

"I *can't* speak up. I don't want them to overhear me." His volume increased slightly, anyway.

"Don't want *who* to overhear you? Robby, what's wrong? What kind of trouble are you in?"

Marie's hand flew to her heart, and she clutched the arm of the couch for support.

"I don't have time to explain. They're gonna make me, uh, help them—help them—" he coughed "—uh, rob a liquor store."

Blood rushed to Tory's head, making her dizzy. "Robby, for God's sake, where are you?"

The background noise drowned out his response, except for the last word, "—Doubloon."

"The Purple Doubloon? Is that where you are? Robby, for heaven's sake, get out of there right now!" Tory heard what sounded like a door swinging open, followed by a faint rush of water. He must be huddled by a pay phone next to the restroom.

"Robby? Robby, talk to me! I don't understand what you're saying."

His voice was a barely audible thread connecting them. "It's like an initiation, see? To be in their gang. If I chicken out now, they said they'll beat me up real bad. They said they'd hurt you and Nana, too, Tor." She heard panic rising in his voice. "I'm really sorry I took your car, Tor, but you've got to help me!"

"You—*you* stole my car?" She jammed her knuckles into her temple as if that would somehow staunch the growing fear hammering at her skull.

"They told me stealing a car was the initiation, so I figured if I took yours I could give it back right away. But now they want me to drive it during this holdup."

"They want you to be the getaway driver?" Her voice rose to a wail of horror. "Robby, listen to me! You're not talking about some childish prank. You could go to jail or get hurt or—" she gulped "—be killed!"

"They're making me do this, Tor! You gotta get me outta this." She heard scuffling in the background, muffled voices, and then the line went dead.

"Robby? Robby?" Frantically she jiggled the switch. "Oh, my God..." She banged down the receiver.

"Victoria, what in heaven's name—"

"Let me think, Nana—just let me think!" Tory's first instinct was to call the police. But it sounded like someone had discovered Robby talking on the phone. If the police showed up now, the other gang members would assume Robby had called them. What if the police hauled the whole bunch of them off to jail? It would be all too easy for those hoodlums to take revenge before Tory could rescue Robby from the police holding cell. The newspapers were always full of stories about prisoners getting knifed by other inmates....

Okay, no cops. She would have to go to the Purple Doubloon herself.

Only one problem. Even if she got there in time, how the hell was she going to snatch Robby away from the clutches of those ruthless thugs? Somehow she didn't think good old Snake and Scorpion were going to be very impressed by a scolding from Gator's big sister.

Tory had one last hope. Her fingers were skimming through the phone book before she had a chance to consider the consequences. "Please, please be home," she prayed while she listened to the phone ring once...twice...three times...

Relief flooded her veins when she heard a loud click. "Thank God you're—" she began, only to plunge back into despair when she recognized the brusque, artificial voice of an answering machine.

She was practically in tears by the time the message ended and the recording beep sounded. "Slade, it's Tory. You've got to come to the Purple Doubloon as quick as you can. I don't know when you'll get this message, but please, I'm begging you—"

"Tory?" She heard a muffled curse, then another click. "There, it's off. Tory?"

Her words tumbled over one another in a rush. Even while she spilled out her story, she wondered if it were already too late, if Robby had already been whisked away by those awful punks....

"Meet me there." Slade spoke only three words before he hung up.

"Victoria, you're not going to that horrid place yourself, are you?" The color had leached out of Marie's face while she listened to Tory's half of the phone conversation.

"I've got to help Robby, Nana. Lock the door behind me, and don't open it for anyone."

"The police—"

"No! Whatever you do, don't call the police." Tory yanked open the door. "I'll be back as soon as I can."

"Victoria, be careful—"

She slammed the door on the rest of her grandmother's words.

Raindrops the size of quarters began plopping to earth as Tory made her way quickly toward Bourbon Street. Most of the buildings she passed had a balcony or some kind of awning out front, so she was able to stay reasonably dry by darting from one overhang to the next.

Getting wet, however, was the least of her worries.

What if she didn't make it there on time? What if Slade didn't show up, after all? What if those hoodlums actually forced Robby to go through with this holdup, and he got caught and went to jail?

What if there was a shoot-out and Robby got hurt—or worse?

Tory barreled around the corner, arms windmilling as she skidded on the slick sidewalk. The streets were strangely deserted because of the approaching storm, and the eerie emptiness of the normally teeming streets only added to her ominous sense of foreboding.

Almost there now... just a little ways farther...

Tory raced past her car, screeched to a halt, then charged back to where it was parked near the corner. For once praying that Robby had been his usual careless self, she wrestled with the closest door handle. If by some miracle he'd left the keys in the ignition, she could drive off and prevent the gang from using it.

Locked.

She stumbled around to the driver's side. Even if the keys weren't inside, she could release the emergency brake and push the car far enough away so they couldn't find it. The Honda wasn't that big, after all.

But it *was* locked tight as a drum, with all the windows rolled up. Tory slammed her fist against the roof in frustration. Why hadn't she taken time to have another copy of the key made after her other one had perished in the fire?

This was no time for second-guessing. At least now she could be fairly certain Robby was still at the Purple Doubloon. Tory took off again, careering around the corner like a runaway locomotive. She knew Slade couldn't possibly have beat her here—not unless he happened to have a rescue helicopter stashed in his backyard.

Still, her heart sank and she had to swallow her disappointment when she detected no sign of Slade in front of the bar. She dodged into the deserted entrance of a closed shop next door and tried to figure out her next move.

Marching into the Purple Doubloon and demanding the return of her little brother didn't seem like such a good plan. Considering the unsavory nature of the bar's clientele, she was liable to find herself conked on the head, shanghaied and aboard a boat to China before she knew what hit her.

Well, she would risk it for her brother's sake, but only as a last resort. She didn't want those gang members to find out Robby had called her. Somehow she suspected they wouldn't exactly be good sports about it.

Damn it, where was Slade, anyhow? If only he got here before the gang left, everything would be all right. Slade knew how to deal with hoodlums; he'd been one himself, hadn't he?

But for the time being, all Tory could do was keep an eye on the bar entrance and cross her fingers there wasn't a back way out.

Minutes passed. At least Tory *thought* they must be minutes, even though they felt like hours. Each time someone came out of the Purple Doubloon, fear constricted her throat and her fists knotted at her sides. By God, she would teach those punks a lesson if Robby got hurt....

All of a sudden a pair of headlights blinded Tory as a car zoomed around the corner and skidded to a halt in front of her. The headlights died, the door whipped open and a figure bounded around the car to the sidewalk.

Tory had never been so glad to see anyone in her life.

"Slade!" she hissed. "Over here."

He did a quick double take, then an instant later she was in his arms. "Oh, thank God...thank God you're here..." she murmured over and over into his thin windbreaker. Slade's heart thumped in her ear, the most reassuring sound in the world.

He hugged her tight for a moment, then tangled his fingers in her damp hair and tilted her head back. "Tory, are you all right?" He scanned her face anxiously. "Tell me what's happening.'' He jerked his head in the bar's direction.

Tory couldn't seem to let go of him, as if she were clutching a lifeline instead of the folds of his jacket. "They're all still inside—at least, I *think* they are. My car's still parked around the corner, so I'm pretty sure they haven't left yet."

"Have you gone inside?"

She shook her head, spraying Slade's face with droplets of water. "I—I didn't know what to do, I was afraid of making things worse."

He kissed her forehead. "Good. You did the right thing by waiting out here for me." He released her and paced back and forth a couple of times like an impatient leopard. Finally he snapped his fingers. "Okay, let's go."

"But what are we—"

He towed Tory behind him by her wrist. "Just follow my lead."

"But—"

Then the smell of beer and cigarette smoke assaulted her senses as Slade pushed through the door. He dropped her wrist. "Do you see Robby anywhere?"

Tory smothered a cough and squinted into the noxious haze. "No...I don't see—wait! There he is! I think that's him in the back room." She hustled along in Slade's wake, past a gauntlet of curious glances. The Purple Doubloon was doing a booming business tonight. Either the place held charms that completely eluded Tory, or a lot of people had ducked inside to get out of the rain.

In the back room, the smoky, beery miasma was illuminated by a weird fluorescent glow from the banks of video games along the walls. Strange electronic bells and whistles competed with the clatter and *ding!* of pinball machines. Robby was slouched against a cigarette machine, effectively pinned in by a group of leather-jacketed figures surrounding him. His arms were folded defensively across his chest and his lower lip protruded in a familiar stubborn expression that twisted Tory's heart.

As Slade shoved a path closer toward the group, Tory could overhear snatches of the heated discussion underway.

"—Chicken, huh?"

"—Know what happens, don't you, to people who flunk the initiation—"

Then Robby's voice rising briefly above the clamor: "Look, I don't want to join your gang anymore."

"What's the matter with you, Gator? You think you can—"

Slade elbowed his way past Robby's tormentors. "Gator, thank God we found you before it was too late!"

Robby's furrowed eyebrows flew up in surprise. "Hey, Slade." Cautious relief crept over the edges of his expression, but didn't erase the anxiety. "Tory—you here, too?"

"Of course she's here," Slade said quickly. "You think your own sister would desert you at a terrible time like this?" He clucked his tongue, shaking his head sadly from side to side.

"Who're you?" The meanest-looking punk stepped between Slade and Robby and thrust out his chest. Beneath his leather jacket Tory recognized a popular obscene T-shirt.

She was surprised when Slade retreated instead of holding his ground. She was even more surprised when he replied, "Why, I'm Gator's doctor, of course."

The gang leader crossed his arms and drummed his fingers on his formidable biceps. "Doctor, huh? Whatta you want with Gator here?"

"Why...to take him back to the hospital, of course." Slade edged closer to Robby. "Gator, I don't know what was so important that you had to break out of the isolation ward, but believe me—nothing is more important than your health."

"We've been so worried about you, Rob—I mean, Gator," Tory piped up, clasping her hands below her chin. "We've been looking everywhere for you."

The circle of gang members seemed to expand a little.

But the leader—Snake or Scorpion or Skunk, whatever his name was—stood his ground and eyed Tory and Slade with suspicion. "Yeah? So how'd you find him here?"

"Gator often mentions the Purple Doubloon," Slade said. "When he's having one of his episodes, I mean."

"Episodes?"

"Delirium. It's common during the last stages of the disease. Poor kid doesn't even know what he's saying when it happens."

A dozen pairs of eyes shifted in Robby's direction. He raised a fist to his mouth, coughed, then smiled feebly and shrugged.

"We searched everywhere," Tory said. "Then Dr. Smith remembered hearing you mumble the name of this place, so we decided to check here as a last resort." She darted to Robby's side and curled her fingers around his forehead. "How are you feeling, hon?" Her eyes widened. "Dr. Smith, he's burning up! We've got to get him back to the hospital right away!"

Slade checked his watch. "You should have taken your medication hours ago, Gator. Come on."

The gang leader planted himself in Slade's path and blew a big pink bubble of gum. "So what's this disease he's got, anyway?" he demanded, chomping noisily.

"We don't have time for this," Tory cried, tugging on Robby's sleeve. "We've got to get him back to the hospital, before it's too late."

Slade scratched his jaw. "Before we go, I must say how impressed I am with you boys."

The "boys" glanced at each other in uncertain confusion. The biggest one spoke for them all. "Huh?"

"I mean, the way you all stick by Gator. He may not have much time left, but he's sure lucky to have friends like you guys. Most people wouldn't get within ten feet of someone in his condition."

Robby's so-called friends all stepped back a pace.

"Considering how contagious it is, I mean."

Miraculously an opening appeared as the barricade of hoodlums melted away.

"Ready to go, Gator?" Slade threw his arm around Robby's shoulder.

"Hey! How come you two ain't afraid of gettin' it?" asked the leader with one final suspicious scowl.

Slade cast Tory a look of sympathy. "Gator's poor sister already has it, I'm afraid. She's in the early stages." He herded his patients in front of him. "As for me, well, I'm bound by the Hippocratic oath to care for the sick—" he rolled his eyes toward the ceiling with great resignation "—no matter how enormous the personal danger."

As he pushed Tory and Robby toward the door, he called over his shoulder, "If I were you boys, I'd schedule a checkup with my physician. Immediately!"

All chatter in the bar ceased instantly.

Then the three of them were out on the sidewalk. "Dr. *Smith?*" Slade grumbled at Tory. "Couldn't you have come up with something a bit more original than that?"

"So sue me."

"We have to take your car."

"Why?"

Slade gestured at his Corvette. "No back seat."

"Okay, come on. It's right around the corner." Tory grabbed Robby's arm and yanked him along beside her.

Rain splattered down on their heads as they sped down the street. "Of course, you could always sit in my lap," Slade suggested quietly in Tory's ear.

A delicious thrill ricocheted through her body, despite their recent hair-raising escape. "Later," she whispered from the corner of her mouth.

Slade laughed. "Deal!" he agreed. "Gator, hand me the car key, will you?"

Chapter Twelve

"I'll do it, Nana. Sit down. You've done too much already."

Marie Clayton waved her granddaughter's offer aside as she struggled to her feet. "Fiddlesticks! The day I can't clear away a few cups is the day you can cart me off to the nursing home." She peered at her grandson over the tops of her spectacles. "Robert, *you* can help me."

"Sure thing, Nana." He leaped hastily to his feet and started to pick up the remains of their snack. Marie Clayton was a firm believer that while cookies and hot chocolate might not solve all the world's problems, they were practically essential at times of high emotional stress. When the drenched, breathless trio had burst in the door after their narrow escape an hour ago, she'd insisted on rustling up some cookies and cocoa, clanging pots and pans and alternately clicking her tongue and gasping while they took turns relating their adventure.

"Whoa, there—hold on a second!" Tory pinned her brother's wrist to the coffee table when he reached for her empty cup. "You and I are going to have a serious discussion first thing in the morning, got that?"

Robby's eyes darted guiltily away from hers. He nodded.

Tory wanted to shake him and scream at him and hug him, all at the same time. "Do you have any idea what you put all of us through this evening?"

Robby transferred his glance to the overstuffed easy chair where Slade was lazily steering another pecan cookie into his mouth. "I'm real sorry about all this, Mr. Marshall."

Slade paused with his mouth open. "I may be your doctor, but you can still call me Slade." He poked the cookie into his mouth.

One side of Robby's face curved into a half grin.

"But I think the people you should be apologizing to are your sister and your grandma." He chewed complacently.

Robby's grin faded. Silently he collected a stack of plates and silverware. At the kitchen door he turned. Every trace of sullenness and defiance had been wiped from his face by his recent ordeal.

He gulped, and his mouth worked soundlessly for a moment. "I'm sorry," he finally croaked. "Tory, Nana...not just for tonight. I'm sorry for—for everything!" His chin trembled and his face went crimson as he fled into the kitchen.

Marie dabbed at her eyes. "I do declare, I believe that boy's going to straighten out after this."

"I sure hope so, Nana." Tory sighed. "But I'm afraid I won't believe it until I see it."

"Maybe he's learned his lesson, at least." Slade pushed himself to his feet. "I would think after tonight he'll be giving his former low-life pals a wide berth."

"Not as wide a berth as they'll be giving *him*." Tory said it with a straight face, but after a moment's useless struggle, both she and Slade exploded with laughter.

Marie smiled benevolently while they clutched their sides and doubled over with merriment. "Well, it's long past my bedtime, so I'll leave the two of you alone...."

"Good night, Nana," Tory managed to gasp as her grandmother disappeared down the hall.

"Sweet dreams, Mrs. Clayton," Slade called, his face contorted with mirth.

At last the chuckles died away, and an awkward silence descended. Tory wiped the tears from her eyes, wondering if she'd been giggling from relief or amusement. Probably from hysteria.

Slade reached for his windbreaker, which Marie had draped over the back of a chair to dry. "Guess I better be—"

"I'll give you a lift back to your car," she said quickly.

"Sure. Thanks."

Tory had so much she wanted to say to Slade, she couldn't figure out where to begin. So she concentrated on driving, instead. Her windshield wipers were fighting a losing battle with the sheets of water hurling down from the sky. Wind pummeled the car mercilessly, and to keep the Honda from veering sideways she had to grip the steering wheel so hard her knuckles turned white.

"Nasty storm." They were the first words Slade had uttered since they got in the car.

"Mmm." Tory squinted, trying to see ahead through the gloomy, wet night. "We're almost to your car...." She frowned, switched her headlights to bright, then dimmed them again. "That's funny."

"What?" Slade craned his neck.

"Isn't that the Purple—didn't you park your car right in fr—oh, no."

"Damn." Slade banged his hand on the dashboard.

"Guess that's what happens when you park your car in a tow-away zone," Tory said, cruising slowly past the Purple Doubloon, past the spot where there should have been a red Corvette. "I'll drive you to the impound lot."

"In this storm? Forget it. I'll ransom the car in the morning. The lot's probably closed now, anyway."

"Slade, I feel terrible about all this!"

"Why? Did you sneak off and report me to the parking police when I wasn't looking?"

"No, but your car wouldn't have been towed if you hadn't had to come bail Robby and me out of trouble." She turned the corner. "Let me drive you home, at least."

"Well . . . all right. I wouldn't want your conscience to keep you awake all night."

It took forever to drive the several miles to the Lower Garden District. Poor visibility combined with flooded intersections slowed their progress to a crawl, even though the streets were practically deserted. Most people knew better than to venture out on a stormy night like this.

By the time Tory floated to a stop in front of Slade's house, she felt as if she'd driven halfway across the country.

"Pull into the driveway," Slade told her. "Up close to the back door so we don't get so wet."

"Okay. Wait a second. What's this 'we' business?"

"You don't think I'm going to let you drive any farther in this weather, do you?"

"Don't be silly, I can make it back to the Quarter. Robby and Nana are expecting me to come right back—"

"You can call them from inside." He craned his neck to study the sky. "If the phone lines aren't down, that is."

"Slade..."

He speared out his hand and switched off the ignition.

"Hey!" Tory snatched at the keys and missed.

Slade stuffed them into his jacket pocket. "For all we know, that hurricane could have changed course and be headed right in our direction. And even if it's not, this storm is still dangerous."

"We made it here in one piece, didn't we?" Tory drummed her fingers on top of the steering wheel.

"I wouldn't have let you drive me home if I'd known the weather was going to keep getting worse. This wind's bad enough to blow a tree down on top of you, or knock down power lines in your path."

She could hardly disagree with him, not when she'd seen lots of storms do exactly that. Still...

"Where would...I mean, what would...?"

"I've got extra bedrooms, if that's what's worrying that suspicious little mind of yours."

She examined her cuticles. "Well, I don't know...."

Slade rolled his eyes and smacked his forehead. "For Pete's sake, I suppose you think I conjured up this storm just to get you into bed."

"No, of course—"

He poked her in the chest. "*You're* the one who insisted on driving *me* home, remember? And I happen to be grateful enough not to want you going back out into that storm and possibly getting killed. Now, come on, I'm tired of sitting here in the car." He dangled her keys in front of her, just out of reach. "Of course, you're more than welcome to spend the night out *here* if you'd rather."

Then he hopped out of the car, slammed the door and made a dash for the back porch.

It didn't take Tory long to follow. What was she worried about, anyway? That Slade would sneak into her bed after she'd fallen asleep?

Or that he wouldn't . . .

Inside the back door they shook moisture off hair and clothing. Slade brought a couple of bath towels, and in no time at all they were sitting barefoot in the living room, drinking coffee while their shoes dried next to the back door.

Through the mist rising from his mug Slade observed Tory and wondered what the hell he was doing. He should have found a place to stay in the Quarter, he should have borrowed her car and driven home by himself.

What he *shouldn't* have done was let Tory drive him home, knowing the storm would probably maroon her here.

But seeing her tonight for the first time in nearly a month had shown Slade how wrong he'd been.

Wrong to think he was learning to forget her, wrong to tell himself the sharp ache of missing her was subsiding as the days passed.

When he'd heard Tory's voice on his answering machine this evening a joyful thrill had slammed through him, setting his pulse racing, palms sweating and hopes soaring. It never occurred to Slade to reject her desperate plea for help. If Tory was in trouble—no matter where, no matter when—Slade would be there for her. He could no more turn his back on her than he could refuse to rescue someone from a burning building.

Damn it, maybe he *had* lured her back here. Maybe he'd unconsciously parked in that tow-away zone on purpose. Maybe from the moment he'd picked up the phone tonight, it was inevitable that they would end up here together.

"More coffee?" Slade sprang to his feet, nearly sloshing his remaining half mug onto the couch.

"I've still got some left, but a warm-up would be nice."

He could feel Tory's eyes tracking him as he left the room—those bewitching blue eyes that gave her away every time, proclaiming her anger, her fear, her laughter, as boldly as a flashing neon sign.

The same bewitching blue eyes that had haunted Slade's dreams every night for the past month.

Damn it, why couldn't he forget her? And now that Tory was under his roof, Slade didn't know quite what to do with her. Plan A certainly appealed to him: sweeping her off her feet, carrying her to his bed and making wild, passionate love to her while the storm raged outside.

Yet part of him preferred Plan B: tucking her into her own bed in the guest room with a heating pad and a cup of hot chocolate.

Plan C was locking her in the basement and throwing away the key so he wouldn't be tempted to carry out Plan A.

Slade handed Tory her refilled mug, scrambling desperately to come up with Plan D.

Plan D turned out to be finishing their coffee in silence while listening to the howl of wind and the tattoo of rain on the roof.

Tory set down her mug with a *clink!* on the glass-topped coffee table. "Well, it's getting sort of late, and boy, am I exhausted!" She yawned behind her hand.

That was Slade's cue to initiate Plan Whatever. He carried their mugs to the kitchen as a delaying tactic. When he came back the living room was empty. He found Tory peering through the doorway to one of his extra bedrooms. "Is this where you want me to sleep?"

Hardly. Tory must have realized how her question sounded, because she blushed a fiery red. "I mean, is this the guest room?"

"Yeah." Slade switched on the overhead light. "At least, it's the only extra bedroom with clean sheets on the bed, so I guess that makes it the guest room."

Tory edged past him. "Oh. Well, thanks. The, uh, bathroom?"

"Down the hall." He pointed.

"Well, um, thanks again. Guess I'll see you in the morning." She was leaning against the edge of the door, gradually closing it.

"Morning. Right." He backed into the darkened hallway. "Pleasant dreams, then."

"You, too." Her voice disappeared as the door clicked shut.

Slade scratched his chin. Well, that wasn't so tough, was it? At least Tory didn't seem to have any trouble choosing between Plan A or Plan B or—

"Slade?"

He paused at the door to his bedroom. Tory stood in a golden triangle of light spilling from the guest room. Slade waited while she padded slowly down the hall.

"I—I just wanted to thank you. For everything."

He smiled faintly. "No need, sweetheart. I'm glad I could help."

"There's so much I want to say to you—" She took a deep breath, then plunged ahead. "You've been so nice, not only to me, but to my whole family."

"Nice?" He tugged gently on a strand of her hair. "That's the first time you've ever called me *that*."

"Well, you are. When you're not being arrogant and infuriating and rotten."

"That's more like it."

"I mean, you've been so nice to my grandmother, and Robby—well, he doesn't say so, but I know he looks up to you."

That made him feel good.

"You've done so much for all of us, figuring out who set the fire—"

"Hey, I can't take all the credit. Part of it belongs to you."

"Me? After the way I lied and tried to hide things from you?"

"You were only trying to protect people you care about." Slade grazed her delicate jaw with the back of his finger. "I really admire that kind of loyalty, even when it makes my job more difficult."

"I'm sorry."

"Don't apologize. Loyalty like that is a rare quality." He tipped up her chin. "Your family's very lucky to have you, Tory."

She swallowed. "I feel like I'm the lucky one. To have a friend like you who's willing to risk his neck for my family and me."

"Friend?" He traced her lower lip with his thumb. "Is that what we are? Friends?" His face was so close to hers he could see her pulse fluttering rapidly at her temple.

"No," she whispered breathlessly. "Yes...I mean, I don't know *what* we are exactly...."

Slade drew back the silky curtain of Tory's hair and nuzzled the side of her neck. "I don't know, either," he said in a muffled drawl. "But I have to admit...the way I feel right now...couldn't exactly be called...friendly...."

Tory's head fell back. "Slade," she moaned.

As she sagged against him he scooped her up in his arms and carried her into his darkened bedroom. He laid her gently on top of the covers, silently thanking his lucky stars that this had been one of the mornings he'd decided to make the bed.

He stretched himself alongside her, skimming his hand over her body to explore every lush curve, every sexy contour. He'd had enough soul-searching, enough debate about the wisdom of getting further involved with Tory. Slade wanted her the way he'd never wanted another woman. He was going to make love to her, damn it, and he was going to do it tonight!

Strangely enough, he found himself more concerned with Tory's pleasure than with satisfying his own lustful desire. He caressed her breasts, unbuttoning a couple of buttons so he could slip his hand inside and feel her bare skin. "Is this all right?" he asked, his voice strangely loud in the quiet room. Outside the storm seemed to be fading.

Tory nodded. Then she lifted her hand to his face and touched him with her fingertips, tracing the cleft in his chin as if she couldn't quite believe he was really there.

"I missed you," he said abruptly.

In the dim light from the hallway he could see tears rimming her eyes. "I missed you, too," she whispered. "Oh, Slade . . . make love to me."

Slade could only guess how much those words had cost her. He cursed himself for putting Tory through such torment. He knew all too well how painful the past month must have been for her. Add that to all the times he'd started to get close to her, only to pull back at the last minute like a damn coward.

He'd never meant to play games with her emotions, and the realization that Tory still wanted him after all he'd put her through amazed Slade. "I'm going to love you," he said gruffly, brushing her hair from her forehead. "I'll make this a night you'll never forget, sweetheart. I swear it." He lowered his mouth a fraction of an inch from hers. "I want to make up for everything, if you'll let me, Tory...."

He wasn't sure who moved first, but all of a sudden their lips were joined in frenzied union as if they were tasting each other for the first time...melding together, velvety tongues gliding through parted lips, whispering sweet endearments.

Slade made short work of the remaining buttons on Tory's blouse, and seconds later her filmy bra followed her blouse to the floor. When he touched the zipper of her slacks, he sensed her tense up.

"Easy," he crooned, "we'll take it nice and slow, okay? Do you want me to stop?"

Tory's hair rustled on the bedcovers as she shook her head. "Good, because, sweetheart, I have to tell you...I really don't want to stop."

He eased her slacks down over her hips and tossed them on the floor with the rest of her clothing. Good thing Tory wasn't a neat freak about her wardrobe, he thought fleetingly.

He squeezed her bare feet. "They're cold," he said. "Don't worry—I'll warm them up."

"That...that feels good."

From her trim ankles, Slade smoothed his hands up over her shapely calves to her thighs. When his fingers passed behind her knees, she giggled. "That tickles!"

"Oh, yeah?" He couldn't resist returning to the underside of those adorable knees for one more teasing caress. "That's good to know. Might come in handy sometime."

"You're learning all my secrets," she said. "No fair."

"After all the secrets I've told you? I'd say we're even."
Slade brought her hand to his chest so she could help him
with his shirt buttons. Shrugging off his shirt, he admired
her lovely nude body shimmering in the dim light. "I know
I've told you this before, sweetheart, but it bears repeat-
ing." He slid his hand along her body to mold one soft
breast into his palm. "You're absolutely beautiful."

Tory twisted her head away from him.

"Hey, you're not embarrassed, are you?"

"No one—no one's ever said those things to me before." She covered his hand with hers. "Not the way you
do, anyway."

"High time you heard the truth, then." He took her
hand and eased it down to his belt buckle.

She fumbled clumsily for a minute. Slade's loins felt
ready to explode. He didn't want to be impatient, but
damn it, if she didn't hurry...

He jerked open his buckle with a quick flick of his wrist.

Tory swallowed. "I'm—I'm afraid I'm not very good at
this."

"You're doing fine," Slade assured her. "Believe me.
That buckle's kind of tricky sometimes, that's all." He had
his pants nearly unzipped when her words registered. He
zipped them up quickly. "Oh, Lord," he said with a con-
vulsive swallow, "don't tell me you're a—"

"No," she said hastily. "But I haven't had all that
much...experience. And it's...been a long time."

Slade curved his hand around her cheek and felt the heat
rising to her face. "Don't worry, love," he chuckled. "It's
like riding a bicycle. You never forget."

Tory sighed. "You won't believe this," she said, "but I
never learned how to ride a bicycle, either."

Slade threw back his head and laughed. "Sweetheart,"
he said, "in that case I'm sure going to have fun teaching

you." He planted a kiss on the tip on her nose. "Don't worry," he said in a low voice. "We'll take it one step at a time."

He shucked off his pants and underwear. Then he cradled Tory in his arms and savored the wondrous, exciting feel of her naked body pressed close to his.

Tory couldn't believe what was happening to her. For so long she'd imagined being with Slade like this, hating herself for her weakness, yet unable to banish the tantalizing fantasies of a man she could never have.

Only now it seemed she *did* have him—for tonight, anyway. She shoved aside any concern for the future. No matter what heartbreak might lie ahead, at least she would always have this one night with Slade to treasure. Even though she'd learned in the past month that memories were cold comfort indeed when the man you loved could never be yours.

There, she'd actually admitted it! She loved Slade Marshall, had from the first moment she'd laid eyes on him.

Well, that wasn't quite true. At first she'd thought him a rude, arrogant jerk. And sometimes he still acted like one.

But beneath Slade's abrasive facade Tory had discovered the finer, nobler aspects of his character. She'd seen his compassion for others, his willingness to help those in need. She'd seen the caring, vulnerable core that Slade refused to acknowledge even to himself.

But Tory had witnessed that secret, hidden side of him. And she loved him thoroughly for it.

Which must be why she was so eager to fling herself into what would surely turn out to be emotional disaster. But how could she respond logically when Slade's hands were all over her, leaving a heavenly trail of burning desire in their wake?

Everywhere he touched her she could feel his handprint left behind, as if he were branding her his possession forever. And oh, how much she wanted to belong to him, and know that he belonged to her!

Her breast nestled snugly into his cupped hand, as if they were made to fit together. When he teased her nipple, stroking the rosy bud to pebbly hardness, Tory thought surely she would faint with ecstasy as circles of rippling delight radiated from his touch.

But that exquisite delight was nothing compared to the earthshaking thrill that seared through Tory when Slade lowered his head to tease her with his mouth, nipping tenderly, plucking her nipple with his lips and then laving the straining, moist peak with his tongue.

She gasped sharply, and when her breath caught up with her, Tory reached for him tentatively, knowing instinctively that to pleasure him would only enhance her own excitement.

Slade groaned when she wrapped her fingers around the throbbing evidence of his desire. She moved her hand experimentally, reveling in the satisfaction of learning what pleased him.

He tore his mouth from her breast. "Sweetheart," he panted, "you'd better slow down, or I won't be able to wait much longer."

"I don't want you to wait any longer," she whispered. "I want you, Slade—now!"

"Ah, God...I want you, too!" He levered himself above her, and Tory felt muscles straining like steel cables as she dragged her hands down his arms.

Something molten and quivering coiled itself in the depth of her being, waiting for Slade to ignite a passionate explosion. When he eased himself inside her, Tory felt as if she'd been waiting for this moment all her life—this fusion of heart, mind and body, this linking of souls in the most intimate way possible.

The brief stab of pain passed in an instant. Tory tangled her fingers in Slade's hair, drawing him closer, deeper inside her, as smoldering tension built up to a blazing crescendo.

He ground out her name through gritted teeth. "Tory—" His facial muscles were contorted with passion, his green eyes glowing like a wild animal's. "I can't... hold back... much longer...."

Slade's body rose and fell above hers, and Tory arched her back to match his thrusting movements with eager abandon. She couldn't tell if the rushing roar filling her ears came from the storm outside or the hurricane of whirling desire building inside her, whipping her into a frenzy, raising her higher and higher, up and up until...

"Slade!" she cried out in a strangled voice. "Oh, Slade..."

"Yes, sweetheart... yes..." Through the turbulent maelstrom Tory heard his groan as he soared upward, following her to the dizzying heights of rapture.

Together they coasted down from the heavens, spiraling slowly back to earth until they landed in a damp, tingling heap, wrapped securely in each other's arms.

As they lay side by side Slade took Tory's hand in his. "See? Just like riding a bicycle." He traced a languid circle on her palm.

"Well, not *exactly* like riding a bicycle," she pointed out. "At least I hope not. Or I'm going to kick myself for never learning to ride one all these years."

His hearty chuckle drifted lazily toward the ceiling. "Sweetheart," he said, "you're one of a kind."

Tory tickled his chest with a lock of her hair. "Was I really... all right? I mean, it's been an awful long time since... well, you know."

"Fishing for compliments, are we?" Slade captured her wrist.

"No, of course not," she replied in a mortified tone. "I only meant—"

"I know what you meant," he said. "Believe me, you were fantastic. Out of this world. Mind-boggling. Totally—"

"Okay, okay," she said, rolling onto her back so she could cover her ears. "I get the idea."

Slade perched his head on his hand and gazed down at her with a tender, wistful expression Tory had never seen before. "Sweetheart, making love with you was incredibly special. Remember that, okay?"

"Okay." She couldn't help wondering if this would be the one and only time she would have to remember. Is that what he meant?

Slade tugged and wrestled with the bedclothes until they were both tucked between the sheets. "Let's get some sleep, shall we?" He slid his arm behind Tory's shoulders and hauled her closer against him. "This has been a pretty exhausting evening, wouldn't you say?"

"Mmm, yes." Tory snuggled against him, deciding Slade's chest made a perfectly wonderful pillow. Her final thought before sleep stole over her was that she would gladly endure a million more exhausting evenings just like this one.

The next thing Tory knew, sunlight was seeping through her closed eyelids. She stretched contentedly, yawning, and her hand fell on Slade's pillow.

Her eyelids snapped open like windowshades.

Except for a note pinned to the pillow, Slade's side of the bed was empty.

Chapter Thirteen

All Slade could see in any direction was water, as he roared past the midpoint of the twenty-four-mile-long causeway across Lake Pontchartrain. Last night's storm had blown over, and sunlight sparkled off the rippling surface like a truckload of diamonds spilled onto the lake.

It was still morning rush hour, so most of the traffic was streaming south toward New Orleans, opposite the direction he was traveling.

Damn it, he should turn this car around and head south with everyone else! Only the highway patrol or other official vehicles were supposed to use the crossovers spanning the parallel bridges of the causeway, but what the hell. The next time he came to one he would ... zoom right by.

Slade watched his chance to turn around recede in his rearview mirror. Then he stomped on the accelerator and raced toward the North Shore as if he were a fugitive with the FBI hot on his trail.

He was running away all right, but not from the FBI. At least he was honest enough to admit that. But honesty hardly made up for the despicable way he'd deserted Tory this morning, sneaking out of bed, slinking noiselessly out of the house, then making a mad two-mile dash for the impound lot to bail out his car.

Slade checked his watch. Would she be awake yet? Would she have found his stupid note and read his patently phony excuse for running out on her?

Dear Tory,
Big fire over by Audubon Park...have to go...see you later...

                                                                Slade

If he hadn't been so rattled he'd have come up with a better story than that. There was a telephone right next to his bed, for God's sake! Tory would know no one had called to alert him about any fire. Where else would he have heard about it, the morning news? Even if she gave Slade the benefit of the doubt at first, by the end of the day Tory would know there hadn't been any big fire near Audubon Park.

Slade's goose was cooked, all right. Charred to a crisp. Tory would never speak to him again, and he couldn't blame her. He'd never acted like this before, sneaking out of a woman's bed as the first rays of dawn spilled through the window.

But waking up this morning, seeing Tory on the pillow next to his, her face all soft and sweetly angelic with sleep, Slade had made a terrifying discovery.

He loved her.

What disaster, what folly! He'd taken every precaution to avoid this fiasco, but he'd fallen in love with her, anyway. He didn't want to love anyone, didn't want to need anyone.

Because you couldn't count on anyone but yourself. It wasn't *safe* to need anyone.

But listening to the steady rise and fall of Tory's breathing, smelling that elusive jasmine scent rising from her hair, watching the way her long black lashes dusted her cheekbones while she slept, Slade had felt the first stirrings of a powerful need.

Maybe he'd needed her all along. Maybe that was why he'd turned into such a basket case during their month-long separation. But that thought only terrified him more, made him step on the accelerator a little harder.

If he needed her this much already, how much would he need her a month from now, a year from now? If he let Tory any further into his life, he would grow even more dependent on her. Then losing her might destroy him.

Slade had battled his way back from a lot of emotional setbacks in his life. Along the way he'd learned to erect walls to protect himself from any more of those devastating setbacks. Now along came Tory, knocking down those walls he'd so carefully constructed as effortlessly as blowing the seeds off a dandelion puff.

Tory was dangerous. She was an enormous threat to Slade's emotional security and well-being. And he was scared to death of her.

"Geez, look at me! I'm a mess!" he told the radio disc jockey. "My heart's pounding a mile a minute, I'm panting like I just ran a marathon." Making a face, he wiped each hand in turn on his thighs. "My damn *palms* are sweating, for Pete's sake!"

He was a mess, all right. And he would be even more of a mess if he didn't chase Tory out of his life, pronto.

Well, after his cowardly escape this morning he probably didn't have to worry about that. Tory would probably give up on him for good. If Slade tried to see her again she would give him the swift kick in the rear he so richly deserved.

A flock of sea gulls swooped out to meet him as the car neared the North Shore. Slade hadn't the foggiest idea where he was heading or when he would find the nerve to come back and face the music.

But he had a near-certain suspicion that he could drive to the ends of the earth and still not leave behind his love for Tory.

"Land sakes, child, you look like something the cat dragged in!"

"We don't have a cat, Nana," Tory replied wearily, hoisting her coffee cup to her lips.

Marie shuffled over to the kitchen counter and poured herself a cup of coffee. Tugging her bathrobe primly around her legs, she lowered herself into the chair next to Tory. "My, we had a lot of excitement last night, didn't we?"

Tory's cup jerked and she burned her tongue. "You mean Robby's little adventure? Or the storm?" Nana couldn't possibly know about last night's other exciting events, could she?

"Why, I meant everything, I suppose." Her dark eyes twinkled over the arc of her cup rim.

"Hmm, yes. Last night was certainly exciting." And Tory wanted to blot it out of her mind forever. "I'm sorry I didn't phone to let you know where I was. I mean, you must have been worried about me, what with the storm and all...." Her voice trailed off.

"Heavens, no, I wasn't worried. Would you like a slice of cinnamon toast?" Marie struggled to her feet.

Tory resisted the urge to jump up and fix her grandmother's toast herself. Nana hated it when people babied her. "Nothing for me, thanks."

"Breakfast is the most important meal of the day, you know."

"I know. But I'm not hungry." How could she explain to Nana that she might never eat again? That the idea of forcing down food made Tory sick to her stomach as well as heartsick? "Why weren't you worried about me?" she asked, crinkling her nose in puzzlement.

"Why, I knew you were with Mr. Marshall, of course." Marie spread butter on her toast. "I trust him to take good care of you."

Tory could have sworn Nana winked. No, that was ridiculous. She must have a speck of dust in her eye.

"Well, I still should have called. Disappearing like that is the kind of stunt I'd expect from Robby." She set down her cup. "Where *is* Robby, by the way?"

"Oh, he was up bright and early this morning. Today's the day he goes to register for his fall classes." She sprinkled cinnamon on her toast. "School starts in a week or two, you know."

Tory gaped at her. "Robby went to register for *school?* Without my having to nag, bribe or threaten him?"

Marie nodded.

Tory sipped her coffee. "Maybe he *is* turning over a new leaf," she mused. Now, if she could only turn over a new leaf herself, by forgetting about Slade once and for all.

Him and his transparent excuses. He'd no more rushed off to the scene of a fire than he'd rushed off to perform an emergency appendectomy.

Tory shuddered, reliving her horrible awakening. Slade gone without a trace, leaving nothing behind but that terse note and the lingering fragrance of spicy after-shave clinging to his pillow... her clothes lying in a crumpled heap on the floor... her newfound happiness torn to ribbons.

Slade *had* been only using her, after all. Last night Tory had sensed such tenderness, such powerful emotions, emanating from him. During her dreams she'd even halfway convinced herself it was love.

Ha! Old Love-'Em-and-Leave-'Em Marshall had struck again. *I suppose I should be honored he even left a note,* she thought mournfully.

Well, now that Slade had gotten what he wanted, maybe he would leave Tory alone from now on. Maybe she was finally rid of his pesky presence for good.

Wouldn't that be for the best? Wasn't banishing Slade from her life what Tory had wanted all along? Apparently she was going to get her wish.

She ought to be thanking her lucky stars.

She ought to do an Irish jig in the middle of the kitchen table.

Why, then, the minute Nana finished her toast and left the room, did she burst into tears instead?

By the time Slade's car sailed down the interstate past the gleaming white bulge of the Superdome that evening, he'd put two hundred miles on the odometer.

But he still hadn't put his anxiety behind him. Driving slowly up the block he spotted a figure sitting on his front gallery, partially concealed by the lengthening shadows.

A knot of panic clogged his chest until he discerned it wasn't a woman waiting for him. When he turned into the driveway the figure detached himself from one of the columns. Walking toward the gallery, Slade discovered to his surprise it was Robby.

"Gator," he said, sticking out his hand. "What brings you out this way?" Maybe he'd heard about the way Slade had run out on his sister and was here to work him over with his fists.

Robby pressed his hand briefly. "I, uh, I'm not goin' by that name anymore." He cleared his throat. "You can just call me Rob."

"Rob it is, then. What can I do for you, Rob?"

He scraped one toe along the arch of his opposite shoe. "Well, I was sort of in the neighborhood, see. . . ."

Slade aimed a skeptical look at him. "This is kind of far from your usual territory, isn't it?"

"Yeah, I guess so." He studied his sneakers. "I was wonderin' if I could talk to you about some stuff."

"Sure," Slade replied, wondering what the hell this was all about. "Why don't you come inside and have a cold drink? I think I can scrounge up a root beer or two."

"Hey, thanks." Rob followed him inside and roamed restlessly around the living room while Slade fetched their drinks.

"All I have is cola," he said, returning from the kitchen. "That okay with you?"

"Sure." Rob took the can, popped open the top and gulped eagerly. He must have gotten pretty hot and thirsty sitting on the front steps. How long had he been waiting outside, anyway?

Slade motioned Rob to a chair, and the two of them sat down. Slade rolled the icy can between his palms. "So. . . what did you want to talk to me about?"

He wasn't sure what he'd expected, maybe a chewing-out for mistreating Tory, but Robby's—oops!—*Rob's* answer caught Slade way off guard.

"I, um, I wanted to talk to you about being a fireman."

"A fireman?" He rasped his hand over his unshaven jaw. "You mean, you want to hear what it was like?"

"Yeah. I mean—" he took a quick gulp "—I thought maybe, you know, I might wanna *be* one someday."

Slade swallowed a mouthful of fizzy soda while considering this. "Well, that's great," he said finally. "Fire-fighting can be a very rewarding career."

Rob's face lit up. "I had to go register for school this morning," he said eagerly, "but then I thought, see, that since I'm no good at school, I could drop out and—"

"Hey, there—whoa! Hold on a second." Slade measured his next words carefully. A young man's future was at stake here. He didn't want to come off sounding like some lecturing parent and alienate the kid.

"I know you don't think school's important," he said. "I didn't think so either at your age. But you know what I found out?"

Rob shook his head uncertainly.

"I found out that if you want to be somebody in this life, if you want to make something of yourself, you have to finish high school."

"But I *stink* at school! I flunk half my classes, and I'm never going to graduate the end of this year like I'm supposed to." He snapped the aluminum tab off the top of his soda can. "How come I can't quit now and join the fire department?"

"For one thing, because you have to have a high-school diploma to become a firefighter."

"You do?" He crushed the empty can in his fist. "But why? How come you need to know math and history and all that junk to put out fires?"

Slade set his drink aside and leaned forward, clasping his hands between his knees. "Being a firefighter means more than pointing a hose at a burning building."

Rob frowned.

"It means you're a responsible citizen. It means you've got what it takes to keep going when the going gets tough." Slade hoped he didn't sound too preachy. But being asked for advice and sharing the benefit of his experience was a novel event.

He just hoped he wouldn't blow it. "The fire department doesn't want quitters, Rob. They want people who can follow through with commitment, who can see a job carried through to completion. And getting your diploma is one way of demonstrating you have those qualities."

"But I'm a rotten student! They're going to take one look at my grades and turn me down anyway."

"They'll consider more than your grade-point average, believe me. I was a rotten student myself."

Rob gawked at him. "You were?"

"Until I decided to go to college and really apply myself." Slade picked up his can and polished off the last swig. "Don't you see? If you want to become a firefighter, that's all the more reason to buckle down and really try hard in school this year.''

Rob's lower lip protruded so far it nearly dragged on the floor. Slade tried another tack. "I bet you're not such a bad student, anyway.''

"Ha! You oughta see my report card.''

"Have you ever really tried? Have you ever studied real hard and done the best you possibly could?''

"Well . . . no . . .''

"See?'' Slade punched him lightly on the shoulder. "You can do it if you want to, Rob. I have complete faith in you.''

"You sound like Tory,'' he grumbled.

A sharp javelin of pain speared Slade right in the gut. "You ought to give your sister a break,'' he said softly. "You don't appreciate how wonderful she is, how lucky you are to have her.''

"Yeah?'' Rob retreated into his sullen shell again. "She treats me like a little kid—like she's my mother or something.''

"What's wrong with that?'' Slade asked. "She's done the best she could to take care of you all these years. If she doesn't treat you like an adult, maybe there's a reason—''

"She isn't my mother!'' Rob shouted, leaping to his feet. "My mother's dead! So's my father! They went away one day and they never came back! I suppose someday Tory'll do that, too!'' His face was flushed crimson, his fists knotted at his sides.

And suddenly Slade saw the whole thing. "That's what all this is about, isn't it?'' he said slowly. "Failing school, fighting, stealing, getting into trouble . . . you're doing it deliberately, aren't you?''

Rob's furious expression faltered. "I don't know what you're talking about."

"Maybe you're not aware of it. But unconsciously you're trying to push Tory away, so you don't have to worry about losing her anymore. Like you want to get it over with." In the back of his mind Slade sensed this realization had some significance beyond explaining Rob's problems.

But he didn't have time to explore any hidden meanings right now. Rob's jaw worked silently back and forth; his agitated expression was a mixture of denial and despair. At last he collapsed back into his chair and buried his face in his hands.

Slade knelt next to the chair and draped an arm awkwardly around the kid's shoulders. "Rob, don't you know that you never, ever need to worry about losing Tory? Why, she's the most loyal, stubborn, determined person I've ever met! She'll stick with you like glue no matter what happens!" He gave Rob a nudge in the ribs. "Didn't she prove that last night when you called her for help? She was there when you needed her, wasn't she?"

"Well, yeah," he replied through his fingers.

"I mean, she must have been plenty mad about you stealing her car, but she didn't hesitate for a second, did she?"

"Guess not."

"You *guess?* Well, let me tell you something, pal. I'm the one she called, and I'm here to tell you, your sister was frantic with worry. She would have stormed into the Purple Doubloon herself, fists swinging, if she hadn't managed to reach me. She would have risked anything to save you."

Rob rubbed his eyes with the heel of his hand. "Yeah?"

"Yeah. Your sister loves you, kid. She's never going to give up on you or turn her back on you or walk out on you." He pushed himself upright and gave Tory's brother a stiff pat on the back. "You don't have to worry about losing her the way you lost your parents, Rob. Tory'll never let you down."

"Guess I should have figured that out by now, huh?" He mustered a wobbly smile. "After all the trouble I've caused her."

"It's never too late to start over," Slade said, clapping him on the shoulder. "Believe me, I know."

Rob rose to his feet and edged toward the front door. "Gee, Mr.—I mean, Slade...I don't know what to say." He stuffed his hands in his pockets, then jabbed one in Slade's direction "Thanks."

Slade shook his hand thoughtfully. "Thank *you*, Rob."

"Huh? For what?"

A faint smile skittered across Slade's face. "Oh...for making me see something I was too blind, pigheaded and stupid to see before."

"Huh?"

"Maybe someday I'll explain it to you." He opened the front door. "Look, you need a ride back to the Quarter or anything?"

"Nah, I'm gonna take the streetcar. Thanks, anyway."

"Don't mention it. Oh, and Rob?"

Tory's brother halted on the bottom step and looked back up at Slade, eyebrows arched into question marks.

"When you're ready to apply to the fire department, you come see me. I'll write a letter of recommendation that'll knock their socks off."

Rob's face cracked into a grin. "Hey, thanks, Slade. I'm gonna do that." Then he turned away and started down the sidewalk, whistling.

Slade slowly closed the door, feeling as if he'd been struck by lightning—stunned, illuminated and electrified all at once. What an idiot he'd been! What a cowardly, dishonest, self-absorbed—

He charged out of the house, hopped into his car and took off with a screech of rubber against asphalt.

It was high time he took some of his own advice.

If it wasn't too late.

Tory balanced precariously on the top step of the ladder—the one stamped with a warning not to stand there. But the Creole Courtyard had such lofty ceilings she could just barely stretch high enough to fasten the screws holding the dining room chandelier in place.

There! She backed down a step and examined her handiwork. She'd spent the last two hours cleaning soot out of the chandelier's clogged fixtures. Hopefully now it would work again so she wouldn't have to buy a new one.

She'd finished just in time; it was getting dark outside. She brought her watch three inches from her eyes and squinted at it. Darn it, she hadn't realized how late it was! The work crew had left hours ago, but Tory had kept plugging away at various projects. Losing herself in the rebuilding work was the only way she could temporarily shove aside the heartbreaking memory of how Slade had abandoned her that morning.

She could still hardly believe he would be so callous and uncaring after what they'd shared last night....

"Stop it!" she scolded aloud. "Nothing he does should surprise you anymore." She stabbed her screwdriver into her back pocket so fiercely she nearly poked a hole in her jeans. "Quit mooning over him, will you?"

She bent over to grasp the top of the ladder and steady herself. As she started her backward descent, a voice behind her said, "Is somebody in here?"

Tory whipped her head around, saw a shadowy figure standing in the doorway, and promptly lost her balance. Arms windmilling, she teetered frantically for a few seconds before toppling backward to land in a pair of strong, sturdy arms.

Slade's.

She scrambled out of them as speedily as possible. Backing away from him, she stammered, "Wh-what do *you* want?" Her heart felt like it was doing a flamenco dance on her ribs.

"Ouch!" Slade was studying his hand. "Are you carrying a switchblade or something?"

Tory reached behind her and flipped on the light switch. The chandelier blazed to life. A brief surge of satisfaction and triumph flowed through her. Then she turned to Slade. "A switchblade? What are you talking about?"

"Something jabbed me when I caught you."

She frowned, then her forehead smoothed. "Oh, must have been this." She yanked out her screwdriver.

Slade winced. "Nasty weapon."

"Not half as nasty as you deserve."

"Yeah, well, I guess you're right about that." He dropped his injured hand to his side. "Tory, you have every right to be upset—"

"Upset?" she echoed. "Why should I be upset? Just because you snuck out on me? Because you tricked me into your bed and made me think I was more than a one-night stand to you? Because—"

"You *are* more than a one-night stand to me! Much—"

"Oh, knock it off, all right?" She lobbed the screwdriver into the toolbox on the floor. "What are you doing here, Slade?"

He took a step toward her. "I came to ask you for one more chance."

She took a step backward. "One more chance to do what? Hurt me? Make a fool out of me?"

"Tory, I can explain—"

"I've heard enough of your explanations. Remember the first time we met? I wanted to kick you off my property, but I couldn't. Well, things have changed a lot since then." She flung out her arm and pointed toward the street. "Get the hell off my property!"

Slade spread his hands. "Tory, sweetheart, if you'll only listen—"

"Don't call me 'sweetheart,' and get off my property!"

"Look, I realized something—"

"Get out!"

"—When I was talking to Robby today—"

"Robby?" Tory's outstretched arm sagged a fraction of an inch. "You...talked to Robby today?"

"Yeah." Slade swallowed. "He, uh, he's decided to chuck the name Gator, by the way. Wants to be called Rob."

"Rob?" Tory tilted her head to one side, considering. "Well, I can certainly live with that, I guess."

Slade smiled. "Great. Anyway, while Rob and I were talking—"

"Out!" She pointed toward the door.

His smile faded. "Hey, come on."

"I mean it! I'll have you arrested for trespassing! I'll get a restraining order to keep you away from me! I'll—"

"Tory, I love you," he said quickly.

She froze with her hand in the air and stared at him.

He inched closer. "It's true," he said. "I've tried denying it to myself for so long, but I can't anymore, sweetheart, and the best part of it is—"

Only Tory's lips moved. "Don't you dare say those words to me," she intoned, "unless you mean them."

Slade closed the distance between them and grasped her by the shoulders. "Tory, love—I *do* mean them! I love you. And I'm not afraid to admit it anymore."

She shook her head, trying to clear it, trying to figure out what kind of new trick this was. Despite her determination not to fall for his smooth-talking charm again, a wild hope began to prickle up Tory's spine.

"Why the sudden . . . change of heart?" she asked cautiously.

Relief flared in his sea-green eyes. "It's because of Rob, actually."

"Robby? I mean, Rob?"

"We had sort of a heart-to-heart talk earlier. Not about you and me, but it made me realize some things about you. About me. About both of us."

Tory's eyes followed Slade while he paced back and forth, trying to gather his thoughts. "I was so afraid to love you," he said at last. "Because of my past, because of the things I've told you about." He raked his fingers through his hair. "Whenever I let myself get close to people before, they always hurt me. I was tired of getting hurt. And I knew if I let myself get close to you and then lost you somehow, the pain would make my past hurt seem like a—like a...splinter or something." He wiggled his finger.

"Then today I realized something. I realized the only way I was going to lose you was by driving you away myself." He rubbed his forehead anxiously. "I—I haven't done that already, have I?"

Tory didn't answer him right away. She didn't want to make another mistake by letting her heart overrule her better judgment. Each step of their relationship she'd allowed herself to trust Slade, and each time he'd let her down.

Then she remembered how quickly he'd raced to her side last night when she'd needed his help to rescue her brother.

Maybe she *could* find it in her heart to give him one more chance....

Slade must have taken her silence for rejection, because suddenly he seized both her hands in his and gripped them tightly, almost desperately. "Tory, you brought back to life a part of me I thought was dead and gone forever! The part of me capable of trusting someone...needing someone...loving someone." He lifted a hand to caress her face. "I'm not afraid anymore, sweetheart. I'll take the risk of losing you...because without you nothing matters, anyway."

Tory pressed her cheek into his hand. "You won't lose me," she whispered.

His fingers trembled. "Do you really mean that?" he asked in a thick voice.

Tears misting her eyes, she nodded.

Slade bundled her into his arms. Tory happily buried her face in his neck and savored the scratchy feel of his cheek against hers. No matter what rocky course lay ahead of them, surely the way she felt right at this moment was worth the risk.

Slade cradled her face in his hands and kissed her soundly. Tory murmured a faint protest when he withdrew his lips from hers and pulled back. Then she noticed the look of apprehension on his face. "Slade, what's the matter?"

He cleared his throat. A muscle twitched nervously along his jaw. "Tory, um, I was wondering—I mean, I know I have a lot of nerve asking this, after everything I've put you through, but—"

"Yes."

"Will you marry m—" He blinked. "Did you say...?"

"Yes!" she repeated, prodding him gently in the ribs. "What's the matter, you hard of hearing?"

Incredible, disbelieving joy spread across his handsome, rugged face. Tory knew exactly how he felt. She wanted to fling out her arms and spin around and around till she collapsed in a dizzy heap. She wanted to dash upstairs to the balcony and shout the news to everyone in the street below. She wanted to whoop and holler and swing from the chandelier, for heaven's sake!

Intoxicating happiness bubbled up inside her like champagne. "I love you, Slade. You're the most aggravating, troublesome man I've ever met—but by God, I love you!" She threw her arms around his neck.

"Tory...my sweet, precious Tory..." Slade's voice tickled her ear. "I'll make it all up to you, I swear. I'll make you the happiest woman on earth."

She squeezed him tighter. "You already have," she told him in a shaky voice.

Slade unwound her arms from around his neck so he could feather kisses across her forehead, her cheeks, her eyelids. "The two of us are going to be so happy together...."

Tory dodged his enthusiastic kisses. "Uh-oh."

Frowning, Slade tilted her chin up. "What's the matter?"

"Well...I come as sort of a package deal, you know."

His frown evaporated. "Are you worried about your family?"

Tory flattened her hands against his chest. "I can't stop taking care of Nana and looking after Robby, you know."

Slade chuckled. "Sweetheart, do you think you're the only Clayton I want? No way! I want your feisty, matchmaking grandmother and your crazy mixed-up kid brother, too."

He circled his arms around Tory's waist, picked her up and spun her around and around until she pleaded for mercy. "Slade, put me down!"

He lowered her to the floor and planted a kiss on the tip of her nose. "Either I get your whole family," he warned, "or the wedding deal's off!"

"Okay, okay," Tory agreed, laughing breathlessly. "You win! You get the whole bunch of us."

"Good! Now, I've been thinking about cutting back my workload, so I'll be able to keep an eye on Nana while you're here running the guest house. As for Rob, I think your brother's really going to get his act together and straighten out from now on. And—hey, what's so funny?"

Tory covered her mouth with her hand, trying to stem the tide of giggles. "*You* are! You've got it all figured out, haven't you?"

Slade arched his brows indignantly. "You think *I'm* funny, huh? Well, you should see your face."

"What's wrong with my face?"

"You've got a smudge of soot on your cheek, that's what. You look like a chimney sweep."

"Oh, yeah? Well, *you* look like you climbed out of bed in a hurry this morning. Don't you ever shave?"

Slade rubbed his jaw, then threw back his head and roared with laughter. He captured Tory's wrist and yanked her into his arms. "I'm going to get you for that one, sweetheart."

"Mmm." Closing her eyes, Tory snuggled into Slade's embrace. "My love," she said with a happy sigh of contentment, "I'm counting on it."

* * * * *

This is the season of giving, and Silhouette proudly offers you its sixth annual Christmas collection.

SILHOUETTE

Christmas Stories

1991

Experience the joys of a holiday romance and treasure these heart-warming stories by four award-winning Silhouette authors:

Phyllis Halldorson—"A Memorable Noel"
Peggy Webb—"I Heard the Rabbits Singing"
Naomi Horton—"Dreaming of Angels"
Heather Graham Pozzessere—"The Christmas Bride"

Discover this yuletide celebration—sit back and enjoy Silhouette's Christmas gift of love.

Silhouette Special Edition

COMING NEXT MONTH

#709 LURING A LADY—Nora Roberts
Barging into his landlord's office, angry carpenter Mikhail Stanislaski
got what he wanted. But, for the hot-blooded artist, luring
cool, reserved landlady Sydney Hayward to his SoHo lair was
another story....

#710 OVER EASY—Victoria Pade
Lee Horvat went undercover to trap Blythe Coopersmith by gaining
her trust. She gave it too freely, though, and both were
caught...struggling against love.

#711 PRODIGAL FATHER—Gina Ferris
It wasn't wealthy, stoic Cole Saxon's wish to reunite with his prodigal
father; it was A-1 wish-granter Kelsey Campbell's idea. And from the
start, Kelsey proved dangerously adept at directing Cole's desires....

#712 PRELUDE TO A WEDDING—Patricia McLinn
Paul Monroe was a top-notch appraiser. Sensing million-dollar
laughter behind Bette Wharton's workaholic ways, he betrayed his
spontaneous nature and planned...for a march down the aisle.

#713 JOSHUA AND THE COWGIRL—Sherryl Woods
Cowgirl Traci Garrett didn't want anything to do with big shots like
businessman Joshua Ames. But that was before this persistent
persuader decided to rope—and tie—this stubborn filly.

#714 EMBERS—Mary Kirk
Disaster summoned Anne Marquel home to face the ghosts of the
past. With tender Connor McLeod's help, could she overcome
tragedy and fan the embers of hope for tomorrow?

AVAILABLE THIS MONTH:

#703 SOMEONE TO TALK TO
Marie Ferrarella

#704 ABOVE THE CLOUDS
Bevlyn Marshall

#705 THE ICE PRINCESS
Lorraine Carroll

**#706 HOME COURT
ADVANTAGE**
Andrea Edwards

#707 REBEL TO THE RESCUE
Kayla Daniels

#708 BABY, IT'S YOU
Celeste Hamilton

Silhouette Special Edition

is pleased to announce

WEDDING DUET
by Patricia McLinn

Wedding fever! There are times when marriage must be catching. One couple decides to tie the knot, and suddenly everyone they know seems headed down the aisle. Patricia McLinn's WEDDING DUET lets you share the excitement of such a time.

December: PRELUDE TO A WEDDING (SE #712) Bette Wharton knew what she wanted—marriage, a home . . . and Paul Monroe. But was there any chance that a fun-loving free spirit like Paul would share her dreams of meeting at the altar?

January: WEDDING PARTY (SE #718) Paul and Bette's wedding was a terrific chance to renew old friendships. But walking down the aisle had bridesmaid Tris Donlin and best man Michael Dickinson rethinking what friendship really meant. . . .

SSEWD-1

Take 4 bestselling love stories FREE

Plus get a FREE surprise gift!

Special Limited-time Offer

Mail to
Silhouette Reader Service™
3010 Walden Avenue
P.O. Box 1867
Buffalo, N.Y. 14269-1867

YES! Please send me 4 free Silhouette Special Edition™ novels and my free surprise gift. Then send me 6 brand-new novels every month, which I will receive months before they appear in bookstores. Bill me at the low price of $2.92 each—a savings of 33¢ apiece off cover prices. There are no shipping, handling or other hidden costs. I understand that accepting the books and gift places me under no obligation ever to buy any books. I can always return a shipment and cancel at any time. Even if I never buy another book from Silhouette, the 4 free books and the surprise gift are mine to keep forever.

235 BPA AC7Q

Name	(PLEASE PRINT)	
Address		Apt. No.
City	State	Zip

This offer is limited to one order per household and not valid to present Silhouette Special Edition® subscribers. Terms and prices are subject to change. Sales tax applicable in N.Y.

SPED-BPA2DR   1990 Harlequin Enterprises Limited

SILHOUETTE®
OFFICIAL SWEEPSTAKES RULES

NO PURCHASE NECESSARY

1. To enter, complete an Official Entry Form or 3"× 5" index card by hand-printing, in plain block letters, your complete name, address, phone number and age, and mailing it to: Silhouette Fashion A Whole New You Sweepstakes, P.O. Box 9056, Buffalo, NY 14269-9056.

   No responsibility is assumed for lost, late or misdirected mail. Entries must be sent separately with first class postage affixed, and be received no later than December 31, 1991 for eligibility.

2. Winners will be selected by D.L. Blair, Inc., an independent judging organization whose decisions are final, in random drawings to be held on January 30, 1992 in Blair, NE at 10:00 a.m. from among all eligible entries received.

3. The prizes to be awarded and their approximate retail values are as follows: Grand Prize — A brand-new Ford Explorer 4×4 plus a trip for two (2) to Hawaii, including round-trip air transportation, six (6) nights hotel accommodation, a $1,400 meal/spending money stipend and $2,000 cash toward a new fashion wardrobe (approximate value: $28,000) or $15,000 cash; two (2) Second Prizes — A trip to Hawaii, including round-trip air transportation, six (6) nights hotel accommodation, a $1,400 meal/spending money stipend and $2,000 cash toward a new fashion wardrobe (approximate value: $11,000) or $5,000 cash; three (3) Third Prizes — $2,000 cash toward a new fashion wardrobe. All prizes are valued in U.S. currency. Travel award air transportation is from the commercial airport nearest winner's home. Travel is subject to space and accommodation availability, and must be completed by June 30, 1993. Sweepstakes offer is open to residents of the U.S. and Canada who are 21 years of age or older as of December 31, 1991, except residents of Puerto Rico, employees and immediate family members of Torstar Corp., its affiliates, subsidiaries, and all agencies, entities and persons connected with the use, marketing, or conduct of this sweepstakes. All federal, state, provincial, municipal and local laws apply. Offer void wherever prohibited by law. Taxes and/or duties, applicable registration and licensing fees, are the sole responsibility of the winners. Any litigation within the province of Quebec respecting the conduct and awarding of a prize may be submitted to the Régie des loteries et courses du Québec. All prizes will be awarded; winners will be notified by mail. No substitution of prizes is permitted.

4. Potential winners must sign and return any required Affidavit of Eligibility/Release of Liability within 30 days of notification. In the event of noncompliance within this time period, the prize may be awarded to an alternate winner. Any prize or prize notification returned as undeliverable may result in the awarding of that prize to an alternate winner. By acceptance of their prize, winners consent to use of their names, photographs or their likenesses for purposes of advertising, trade and promotion on behalf of Torstar Corp. without further compensation. Canadian winners must correctly answer a time-limited arithmetical question in order to be awarded a prize.

5. For a list of winners (available after 3/31/92), send a separate stamped, self-addressed envelope to: Silhouette Fashion A Whole New You Sweepstakes, P.O. Box 4665, Blair, NE 68009.

PREMIUM OFFER TERMS

To receive your gift, complete the Offer Certificate according to directions. Be certain to enclose the required number of "Fashion A Whole New You" proofs of product purchase (which are found on the last page of every specially marked "Fashion A Whole New You" Silhouette or Harlequin romance novel). Requests must be received no later than December 31, 1991. Limit: four (4) gifts per name, family, group, organization or address. Items depicted are for illustrative purposes only and may not be exactly as shown. Please allow 6 to 8 weeks for receipt of order. Offer good while quantities of gifts last. In the event an ordered gift is no longer available, you will receive a free, previously unpublished Silhouette or Harlequin book for every proof of purchase you have submitted with your request, plus a refund of the postage and handling charge you have included. Offer good in the U.S. and Canada only.

SLFW - SWPR

SILHOUETTE® OFFICIAL SWEEPSTAKES ENTRY FORM

4-FWSES-4

Complete and return this Entry Form immediately – the more entries you submit, the better your chances of winning!

- Entries must be received by **December 31, 1991.**
- A Random draw will take place on **January 30, 1992.**
- No purchase necessary.

Yes, I want to win a FASHION A WHOLE NEW YOU Sensuous and Adventurous prize from Silhouette:

Name _____ Telephone _____ Age _____

Address _____

City _____ State _____ Zip _____

Return Entries to: **Silhouette FASHION A WHOLE NEW YOU,**
P.O. Box 9056, Buffalo, NY 14269-9056 © 1991 Harlequin Enterprises Limited

PREMIUM OFFER

To receive your free gift, send us the required number of proofs-of-purchase from any specially marked FASHION A WHOLE NEW YOU Silhouette or Harlequin Book with the Offer Certificate properly completed, plus a check or money order (do not send cash) to cover postage and handling payable to Silhouette FASHION A WHOLE NEW YOU Offer. We will send you the specified gift.

OFFER CERTIFICATE

Item	A. SENSUAL DESIGNER VANITY BOX COLLECTION (set of 4) (Suggested Retail Price $60.00)	B. ADVENTUROUS TRAVEL COSMETIC CASE SET (set of 3) (Suggested Retail Price $25.00)
# of proofs-of-purchase	18	12
Postage and Handling	$3.50	$2.95
Check one	☐	☐

Name _____

Address _____

City _____ State _____ Zip _____

Mail this certificate, designated number of proofs-of-purchase and check or money order for postage and handling to: **Silhouette FASHION A WHOLE NEW YOU Gift Offer,** P.O. Box 9057, Buffalo, NY 14269-9057. Requests must be received by December 31, 1991.

ONE PROOF-OF-PURCHASE

4-FWSEP-4

To collect your fabulous free gift you must include the necessary number of proofs-of-purchase with a properly completed Offer Certificate.

© 1991 Harlequin Enterprises Limited

See previous page for details.